CLUTCHING

AT

STRAWS

ALSO BY J.L. ABRAMO

Catching Water in a Net

J. L. Abramo

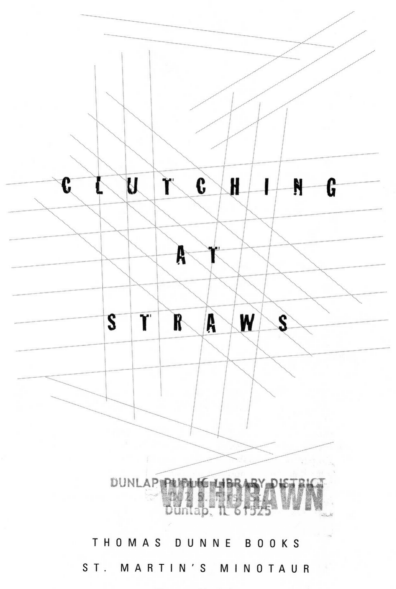

CLUTCHING

AT

STRAWS

THOMAS DUNNE BOOKS

ST. MARTIN'S MINOTAUR

New York

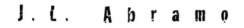

THOMAS DUNNE BOOKS.
An imprint of St. Martin's Press.

www.minotaurbooks.com

ISBN 0-312-30849-3

First Edition: April 2003

10   9   8   7   6   5   4   3   2   1

For my sister Linda

Acknowledgments

Thanks again to Ruth Cavin, Robert Randisi, St. Martin's Press, and the Private Eye Writers of America for giving Jake Diamond the opportunity to join the ranks of literary gumshoes.

Thanks to Steve Hamilton, Bob Truluck, S. J. Rozan, and Les Roberts for their advice and support.

Thanks to all of the Mystery Booksellers who graciously opened their doors and introduced a rookie to their loyal patrons, with a special word of appreciation to Ed Kaufman. And to the friends who put me up and put up with me while I signed books.

Thanks to Linda Michaels for her tireless dedication and hard work and her great success in publicity and promotion.

Thanks to all of the readers who found *Catching Water in a Net*, with a special word of thanks to all of those who asked for more.

And thanks to Janis McWayne for pouring on the encouragement and pouring the coffee.

Cast of Characters

LEFTY "AL" WRIGHT ....a well-spoken burglar

JAKE DIAMOND ....a San Francisco private investigator

DARLENE ROMAN ....Diamond's more than able assistant

ANGELO VERDI..............................a talkative specialty foods grocer

J. ANDREW CHANCELLOR ....a deceased judge

VINNIE "STRINGS" STRADIVARIUS ....a compulsive gambler
and nuisance

VIC "VIGS" VIGODA ....a small-time hood

LIEUTENANT LAURA LOPEZ ....a homicide detective

SALLY FRENCH ....Diamond's ex-wife
and current lady friend

JEREMY CASH..a bestselling author

FREDDIE CASH ....Cash's son, a kidnap victim

JOEY RUSSO...............................an Italian American businessman

SONNY THE CHIN ....Russo's right-hand son-in-law

BUZZ STANLEY ....a college gridiron legend

JOHN "JOHNNY BOY" CARLUCCI ....a San Quentin inmate

TONY CARLUCCI..Carlucci's brother,
a restaurant operator

KAY TURNER ....a public defender

LOWELL RYDER ....an assistant district attorney

HANK STRODE ....a security guard

SERGEANT JOHNSON..a homicide detective

BOB GENTRY ....an attentive neighbor

THOMAS KATT ....a police officer

PHIL MOSS ....a police officer, Katt's partner

BRENDA BIONDA..a person in hiding

TUG MCGRAW ....an adopted domestic pet

BOBO BIGELOW ....a person worth avoiding

CHANCE FOLSOM ....a movie actor

WILLIAM GUNDERSON ....a small-town chief of police

CHARLES KRUPP ....a governor of California

TROY WASINGER ....a theater artist

CHARLIE "BONES" MANCUSO ....a born suspect

DAVEY KING...a ghost

JENNY SOLOMON ....a dilemma

THE KITCHEN WINDOW

Sir, he made a chimney in my father's house,
and the bricks are alive at this day to testify it.

—WILLIAM SHAKESPEARE,

KING HENRY VI, PART 2

One

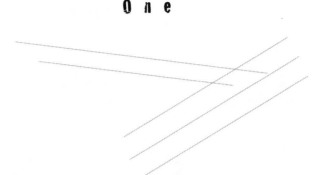

LEFTY WRIGHT SLIPPED THE RUSTY blade of his trusty paint scraper between the frame and sill of the kitchen window and finessed the latch open. He slowly raised the window, squeezed through, and shimmied like an alligator across the sink. When his palms reached the linoleum he went into a perfect handstand, which he would have held longer if not for the sore rib. He gracefully and silently tumbled into an upright position. Once inside the house he stood motionless for a full minute, infinitely patient, listening.

Lefty had found the two bundles of cash exactly where he had been promised they would be. Five thousand dollars in twenties and fifties under a flat stone on the ground below the window. A down payment. He had stuffed the cash into his inside coat pockets before entering the house.

Known as a top-notch second-story man by his peers, and a two-time loser by the courts, Lefty had been relegated to ground-floor entries since falling from a dry-rotted cedar balcony a few weeks earlier. He favored his right side as he moved quietly through the kitchen and into the dining area. Always the pragmatist, he decided to go directly up to the bedroom, knowing that was where he would find what he'd come for. He could quickly inventory the street-level rooms on his way out.

Lefty had been watching the place on and off since Saturday morning, noting the stuffed mailbox and the newspapers on the lawn. He hadn't seen a light come on or go off in the residence, and nothing seemed changed when he arrived now, just before ten on Sunday night. He had planned to arrive earlier but consoled himself with the fact that the tree-lined street was deserted at this hour. He had been assured that the sole occupant of the large home was not due back until late Monday evening. Lefty Wright was not one to be overconfident, but he couldn't help feeling that the odds that he was alone in the house were very good.

He pulled out his penlight, slid the tiny beam toward his feet, and moved slowly toward the carpeted staircase. Halfway up the stairs, he stopped and stood motionless again, listening.

After a silent count to sixty he continued up, a broad smile occupying the entire lower half of his face.

For the next thirty minutes, the house would belong to Lefty Wright.

At the landing, Lefty slipped off his Doc Martens and introduced his thick wool socks to the plush wool carpet. The bedroom door was open and he slipped into the room. The painting was directly ahead of him on the wall above the chest of drawers, where he had been told it would be.

The painting, an original by one of the lesser French impressionists, was fairly valuable itself. But artwork was nearly impossible to fence, and Lefty Wright was more interested in what he expected to find behind the painting.

He removed the painting, leaned it against the foot of the dresser, and looked at the safe. There was nothing safe about it. He had cracked tougher boxes when he was eighteen. He placed his ear close to the tumbler and began rotating the dial.

Twenty seconds later he was in.

The safe was unusually bare. A pair of diamond-studded monogrammed cuff links and a small collection of coins, neither of which interested Lefty. A heavy, nondescript gold chain and a Smith and Wesson chrome-plated .38-caliber snub-nose revolver,

4

which he couldn't resist. They went into the right front pocket of his coat. And the gray metal document box.

He removed the metal box and placed it lightly on the top of the chest of drawers. It was legal sized and approximately nine inches deep. He pushed the small latch and the box popped open. He quickly went through the papers and found the nine-by-twelve-inch envelope he had been told to look for. He laid the envelope on the dresser top, closed the metal box, and returned it to the safe.

Lefty had been instructed to leave the envelope on top of the dresser, for which he would earn himself an additional ten thousand dollars. As he reached down to his feet to pick up the painting, he made up his mind to improvise, in the event that he would be compelled to bargain for the balance of his payment.

He pushed the safe door closed, but did not spin the dial to lock it.

Lefty pulled out his Swiss Army knife and removed two of the staples that held the paper backing to the wooden picture frame. He lifted the envelope off the dresser and slid it between the backing of the painting and the canvas. Then he rehung the painting.

As he was about to leave the room he caught sight of the Rolex lying on the floor at the opposite side of the bed.

Lefty had a weakness for fine timepieces.

He crossed to the far side of the bed, and his foot struck an object on the floor. He glanced down to his feet and gasped.

Suddenly there were beacons of light streaming into the room from the street, accompanied by a harsh siren. Lefty had stumbled upon the head of a man whose contiguous anatomy lay under the large bed, and the instantaneous commotion from below had Lefty believing for a wild moment that the head had been rigged to some bizarre sort of silent burglar alarm.

Twenty minutes later Lefty Wright was handcuffed in the backseat of a San Francisco Police Department cruiser on his way to the Vallejo Street Police Station.

Two hours later Lefty Wright was booked for murder and locked behind bars.

He had been stripped of his most prized article of outer clothing, a tan knee-length London Fog slicker, along with its contents, five thousand dollars in legal tender, a chrome-plated pistol, a gold chain, a dime store penlight, a Swiss Army knife, and a rusty paint scraper.

His shoes had been left at the scene.

Lefty's adamant demands for a telephone call and a Pedro's Burrito Supreme went unheeded. He eventually assumed as comfortable a body position on the jail cell mattress as possible. When he woke to discover that he had actually slept through the night, it was his sole pleasant surprise.

After which he was rudely subjected to another interview session with two detectives, who differed only in theory from two detectives who had grilled him the night before and paid even less attention to his pleas of innocence. Then Lefty was at last allowed to make his constitutionally guaranteed phone call.

He called me.

TWO

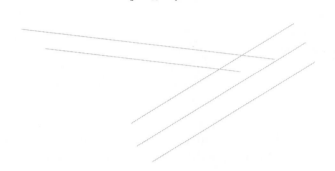

AUTUMN IN SAN FRANCISCO.

Late September, early October is my favorite time of the year in San Francisco. In terms of weather, September is the mildest month. Most of the tourists are gone and that is a great blessing. In July and August they're as thick as Buddy Holly's eyeglasses. The kids are back where they belong, the nine-week challenge of trying to find a single square inch of ground not infested by swarms of loud and reckless adolescents is finally over. Unless you're insane enough to venture anywhere near a school. I can hardly imagine a better place to be in early fall.

Though I admit, I'll take Paris in the springtime.

I had recently made it past my fortieth birthday fairly intact and I was possibly involved in a budding romance with my ex-wife. As I headed to the office on the first Monday in October, I was feeling pretty cozy.

I remembered in the nick of time that Darlene wouldn't be back at her post until the following morning.

Darlene Roman is my right hand; I can barely tie my shoes without her. She runs the office. Her boyfriend is L. L. Bruno, a defensive lineman for the 49ers. Darlene had taken off to Colorado for the weekend to watch San Francisco lose to the Denver Broncos. She had decided to stay the extra night to help pump

7

up Lawrence Lionel for the upcoming game against Oakland.

I was fairly certain I could squeak through one day without her, but I wasn't about to venture into an empty office with no coffee waiting. I stopped at Molinari's Deli on Columbus Avenue for a couple of large cups to carry up. My office sat two flights above the deli, and on a warm day when the wind was just right I could identify the daily lunch special from my desk chair.

"Buon giorno, Angelo," I said, using one of the few acceptable Italian expressions I had learned from my grandfather, "let me have two large black coffees."

"How's the elbow, Jake?"

I had taken a hard line drive to the elbow while playing first base in a softball game the weekend before. The ball was caught on the fly off my elbow by the second baseman. I was credited with an assist.

"It only hurts when I do this," I said, lifting my arm over my head.

"So, don't do that," Angelo said, trying to sound like Henny Youngman.

He sounded more like Walter Brennan.

"Did you hear about Judge Chancellor?" Angelo Verdi asked as he poured.

"He take another bribe on a parking ticket case?" I asked.

J. Andrew Chancellor was the most noted criminal courts' justice in northern California, if not in the entire state.

"He took a six-inch kitchen knife in the chest," said Angelo.

"I hope whoever stabbed him wasn't aiming for the heart, since he doesn't have one," I said. "Is he going to live?"

"Not anymore."

"Oh," I said.

"The story is he had just arrived home from a weekend at his cabin near Mill Valley and bumped into a house thief. Can you believe that, the judge killed without premeditation? That'll wind up in Ripley's Believe It or Not!"

"They catch the thief?" I asked.

"Right there in Chancellor's bedroom. The "Good Morning San Francisco" news guy said that the perp was trying to stuff the

8

judge's body under the bed when the heat showed up."

"How did the cops get there so fast?" I asked. "They must have had a week's notice."

"At least a week," Angelo said. "Lucky break though. Their list of suspects would have been longer than their log of unsolved cases. You're probably relieved that you won't have to tell the police where *you* were last night."

"And how. I'd almost rather take the rap than admit that I took my mother to see a Sandra Bullock movie."

"What's with the coffee, Jake, Darlene get stuck in Denver? I can't believe that Chancellor bought it that way" he went on. "It's like a guy who just negotiated a minefield getting hit by a bus on the other side. I threw in a hard roll."

Angelo Verdi was a master of the non sequitur.

"Darlene said she was staying the extra day to lick Bruno's wounds. I've been trying not to picture it," I said, grabbing the deli bag and heading for the door. "What do you think about the Giants and the Athletics in the World Series?"

"I don't know if I could handle the excitement," Angelo Verdi said. "The last time they played each other, in the eighty-nine series, an earthquake postponed game three for ten days. I'm making sausage and peppers for lunch."

I was halfway down the hall from the stairwell to the office when I heard the phone begin to ring. I had taken to walking up the two flights to the office lately, partly because I understood the benefit to my cardiovascular system and mostly because the elevator had the knack of absorbing the odors of whoever slept in it the night before. For some indefensible reason I decided to try to catch the phone call.

As I fumbled for my keys the deli bag dropped to the floor, landing neatly in a standing position.

I managed to get the door unlocked and grabbed the receiver of Darlene's desk phone in the middle of what may have been the fifth ring.

I had intended to greet the first caller of the month with the standard salutation, "Diamond Investigation, Jake Diamond speaking," but he didn't let me get the words out.

"Is this Jake Diamond?"

"Diamond Investigation, Jake Diamond speaking," I said. Give me a chance to slip it in and I will.

"This is Lefty Wright. You can call me Al."

"What can I do for you, Al?"

"Find out who really killed Judge Chancellor," he said.

The conversation consisted of a good amount of incoherent babbling on his side and exhortations to calm down from my end. If Lefty hadn't mentioned the name *Sam Chambers* in the midst of his jabber I would have done the smart thing.

I would have vehemently insisted he locate a good lawyer. And fast.

Sam Chambers was an old buddy and fellow movie bit-player currently residing at the California Men's Colony in San Luis Obispo on an armed-robbery conviction. To say that any friend of Sam's was a friend of mine might be stretching it, but the mention of Sam as a personal reference did warrant my consideration.

From what I could get out of Lefty on the telephone, he had helped Sam out of a tight spot at the Men's Colony a few days before Wright was released. Another inmate had provoked Sam into an altercation, which didn't take much, and the guards were on both of them within seconds. They were about to shackle the two for a trip to solitary when Lefty called one of the guards over and whispered into his ear. The guard let Sam and the other convict off with a warning.

"What did you say to him?" I asked Lefty.

"I told him he could have my autographed Mo Vaughn poster when I left."

In return for the assist, Sam offered Lefty the only thing he really had to give: the green light to call me if Wright was ever in a jam himself. It didn't take long.

I told Al that I would be down to see him at Vallejo Street as soon as I could, since we were getting nowhere on the phone.

I placed the receiver down, my impression being that Lefty Wright was innocent. The notion wasn't based on what he had said, most of which was unintelligible, but in the way he had sounded. The kid was clearly frightened to death. One of the things I have learned in this business, and in my personal experience as well, is that it's a lot scarier being accused of murder when you're not guilty.

It was at that point in my presumptive analysis that I remembered the coffee in the fallen paper bag, started toward the hall to pick it up and saw the dark brown liquid seeping into the office from under the door. Then I noticed the doorknob turning and instinctively ducked behind Darlene's desk.

"Sorry about that, Jake. Not a great place to leave your breakfast," said Vinnie Stradivarius, tracking in Italian roast and talking through a mouthfull of buttered hard roll. "Luckily this bread didn't get too soggy."

"Glad to hear it, Strings," I said.

I moved past Vinnie into the hallway to fetch a mop from the janitor's closet.

Vinnie just stood by watching me clean up the mess. I finally accepted that I was going to have to ask.

"Vinnie."

"Yeah, Jake?"

"Would you do me a favor?"

"Sure, Jake. Anything."

"Would you run down to the deli and grab a couple of coffees," I said, as nicely as possible. "And when you get back you can tell me what you're doing here so early."

Seeing Vinnie Strings awake before noon was a rarity.

"I figured you could use the help, with Darlene not back yet."

Great.

"Oh," I said, "well how about just getting the coffee then."

Strings looked at me as if I'd asked him to explain the theory of relativity and had warned him not to budge an inch until he did. I reached into my pocket, pulled out a five-dollar bill, handed it to him, and watched him skip off toward the elevator.

"Take the stairs, Strings," I cautioned.

I had quasi-employed Vinnie Strings to do odd jobs for me, hoping it would allow him less free time to get into trouble. On top of that, Vinnie hit me up for money so often that I thought

11

I might as well give him the opportunity to earn some of it. It was a rational and noble gesture, but not a very successful one on either count. Since I had inherited Vinnie from my old friend Jimmy Pigeon, I kept trying.

We sat over coffee for a while, Vinnie doing most of the talking, primarily about his consummate bad luck in picking horses. Like everyone who was hooked on playing the ponies, Vinnie Strings had a system. His was like a sewerage system. I asked him to stay by the phone, write everything down, and not try to solve any mysteries without me.

Then I headed over to the Vallejo Street Station to talk with Lefty Wright.

T h r e e

MY MENTOR, THE LATE Jimmy Pigeon, wisely suggested that before agreeing to accept a case I should always get the question that was nagging me most out of the way as soon as possible.

"So, let's see if I have this straight," I said, "Lefty is your given name and Al is your nickname."

"Correct."

Great.

Now I could move on.

"Okay, you're going for the Rolex and you trip over the body."

"Yeah. And I'm half wondering why his watch is lying there. Whoever iced him had to be waiting for him in the room," Lefty Wright said. "The poor bastard didn't even get his jacket off."

"And the knife that killed him?"

"It came from Chancellor's kitchen, had the judge's prints all over it, but the cops are ruling out suicide."

"And he was dead for how long?"

"I'm being told the body was still warm. And that's the thing. The judge gets home, gets a knife in the chest, and my timing is right on. I'm in the place for less than fifteen minutes and the police are all over me like it was Waco. If that isn't a setup then Nixon erased the tapes by accident. And the worst part is that I never saw it coming."

13

"So, who's the guy who sent you in and how do I find him?"

"Vic Vigoda, and I'm guessing that finding him is going to be tricky."

"Where would you start?" I asked.

"The way my luck has been going since I dropped off a balcony a few weeks ago, I'd start with the morgue."

"You should try being more optimistic."

"It's not in my nature. Look, you don't have to be Galileo to figure out that someone put Vigoda up to it. Vic could hardly spell his own name. And he's far from a saint, but he wouldn't have sent me in if he knew what was under the bed. Someone wanted the judge dead, and an idiot to take the rap. That's why I called you. Sam Chambers told me that you were skilled at rescuing idiots."

"Have you found a lawyer?"

"I have a lawyer, but she's not going to do me much good if you can't give her something to work with."

"I don't remember saying that I would take the case," I said.

"Who are you kidding? How could you resist?"

Lefty Wright was one perceptive felon.

Four

I WAS ALMOST OUT THE door of the police station when a winning figure came into view. A shoulder-length cascade of strawberry-blond hair topping shoulders in a well-tailored light gray herringbone suit, all held up by a pair of legs that would have made Betty Grable envious forty years ago. I walked up behind the apparition just as she turned around.

"Good morning, Lieutenant," I said, smiling my smile. "Nice threads."

"New tie, Diamond?" she parried.

Detective Lieutenant Laura Lopez had it all, striking physical beauty, street smarts, and my number.

"Congratulations. Your guys solved the Chancellor murder case in no time flat."

"They're not my guys, Diamond. Am I detecting a special interest in the case on your part?"

"The kid they have locked up is my client. He seems to believe that the real killer is still out there, and I'm inclined to agree. If you get a minute, talk to the kid and let me know what you think."

"I'll tell you what I think, Diamond, and then I really have to get to work. Lefty Wright is *it* until something better comes along. Wright is twice convicted for B and E, and he had a history with the judge. A good citizen who preferred to remain anonymous

15

heard a commotion, made a phone call, and the SFPD responded quickly and efficiently. That's straight from the mayor's press conference statement and was penned by some hotshot journalism grad student intern from the governor's office. The governor was a good friend of the late judge, and it is mandatory that an alleged suspect be in custody."

"And it doesn't matter that Wright has never pulled an armed robbery, or that in fact the kid is obviously harmless except to himself?"

"I'm afraid not."

"With the possible exception of my mother, everyone in the Bay Area had more reason to snuff Chancellor than some small-time crook caught with his paws in the safe."

"Which is exactly Wright's biggest problem. When everyone is a suspect, you have to like the one you've got locked up. Particularly when the governor of the state is scarier than Michael Myers."

"Wright is saying that a toad named Vic Vigoda lured him to the scene, that it was a setup. He thinks someone put Vigoda up to it because Vic is dumb as a rock."

"So I heard. We're looking for Vigoda, but I don't see how we'll prove he had anything to do with it unless he's a self-incriminating dumb rock."

"And that's the way it is?"

"I didn't write the book," she said. "You know me, Diamond. If I'm not happy with Wright as the perp, I'll do whatever I can do to straighten it out. However, to be perfectly sincere, without another lead it'll be a midnight walk in the park."

I did know the lieutenant, and I did know she would do what she could. I also knew that for the time being I'd be walking the park alone.

I thanked Lopez, just to be polite.

I walked back to my office.

I stopped into Molinari's to pick up some take-out for lunch, a sausage-and-pepper hero for Vinnie and a salad for myself. I had been trying to cut down on my consumption of meat, without actually knowing why.

I had some ideas about how to get started on Lefty's behalf, but I was tied up for the rest of the day. I was checking out a few other cases, one of them was taking me out to Marin County at three.

I would get Darlene busy on the Chancellor case as soon as she got back and in the meantime give Vinnie a chance to play detective. When I walked into the office with the food he was on me like a puppy.

"You had three calls, Jake. I wrote it all down, are you ready?" he said, shuffling his notes and visibly laboring to identify priorities.

"Take it easy, Vin, you're going to bust a vein. I brought you a sandwich."

"Sausage and peppers?"

"Yup."

Vinnie threw his scribbling down on the desk and reached out with both arms like a trained seal. I barely succeeded in popping open a soft drink and getting it into his hand in time to save him from gagging. I let him go through a few more sequences of filling his mouth to capacity and trying to swallow without suffocating, not daring to say a word. I hadn't touched the salad. He finally slowed down and managed to choke out a few words about the merits of the sandwich.

He took a deep breath, and as the color returned to his face I decided it was safe to speak.

"You okay, Strings?"

"Never better, pal."

"Ever hear of a guy named Vic Vigoda?"

"Vic Vigs? Sure, I know who he is," Vinnie said. "Are you going to drink that other Pepsi?"

"Go ahead," I said, shoving it over. "I was hoping you could try to locate him."

"Absolutely, Jake. I'm all over it."

I wasn't sure if he was referring to his commitment to the assignment or to his attempt at self-strangulation.

"Good. That would be a great help to me."

Not even the wolfing down of a huge greasy Italian sub made

Vinnie happier than an opportunity to help me. I only wished he were as proficient at the latter.

"What do you want me to do when I find him?"

I tried to think of a nice way to say don't do anything. I couldn't think of one.

"Nothing, Vin. I beg you. Just call me and tell me where you are."

"Sure, Jake. You're the boss."

I really hated that.

"Great. You have my cell phone number, right?"

"Write it down for me. Want me to get going?"

"No need to rush out, Vinnie. Why don't you take some more of that soda, take a quick peek at your notes, and tell me who called."

Strings relocated the three small slips of paper he had torn off the "While You Were Out of the Office" notepad I had given to Darlene on her first day of work. In five years she had never used it, except occasionally as a coaster. He arranged the notes in a row in front of him on the desk and started moving them around like a three-card monte dealer.

I basically liked Vinnie Stradivarius.

But he never made it easy.

Finally he chose the one that was now in the center, picked it up, reviewed it for a moment, and made his report.

"Sally called to say she would meet you at La Folie at eight for dinner."

Sally French had been my first client, my wife, my ex-wife, and, currently, my sort of steady female companion, in that order. We were taking it very slowly.

When Vinnie was sure that I understood the message, he continued.

"Jeremy Cash called to confirm your meeting with him today at his beach house at three," he said.

Vinnie sat, I waited.

I became tired of waiting.

"Well?" I said.

"Well, I guess I'll get out there and track down Vic Vigoda."

Vinnie crunched up the deli paper, tossed it into the waste-basket, and got up to leave.

"Weren't there three calls, Vin?"

"Oh yeah," he said, "Joey Russo called to tell you that he has two tickets to the play-off game against the Mets on Wednesday afternoon, if you weren't busy. He's at home if you want to call him back."

It hurt Vinnie just to say it.

"You know, Jake, if you can't make it I'd be glad to take your place. I'd hate for Joey to have to sit at the ballpark alone."

"Thanks, Vinnie, that's very considerate. I'll let you know."

That pretty much took care of new business, so I reminded Vinnie to do no more than call me if he spotted Vic Vigoda. I jotted down my cell phone number for the fiftieth time, and Vin-nie headed out the door.

I played around with the salad for a while but couldn't deal with it. I called Joey Russo to tell him that Wednesday sounded great.

It was nearing two in the afternoon so I changed my shirt and tried to hand press the wrinkles out of my suit jacket. I was off to see a rich man in the land of rich men and wanted to appear a little less as if I'd just crawled out of a sleeping bag.

I had even taken out the '63 Chevy Impala convertible for the occasion.

I hopped into the car and headed out Lombard toward the Golden Gate Bridge to see Jeremy Cash.

F i v e

JEREMY CASH HAD MADE LOTS of money writing books on how to make money.

In the early nineties, *How to Make a Million in Real Estate* and the subsequent *How to Make a Million in Foreign Real Estate* occupied spots on the nonfiction best-seller lists for nearly three years. Cash's *How to Make a Million in the Stock Market* held solid in the top ten for fourteen months until it was finally knocked off the list by Cash's *How to Make a Million on Internet Stocks*. His latest tome, *How to Make Millions Writing How to Make Millions Books*, debuted at number one and was currently holding the top spot, more than a year later. Jeremy Cash could hardly have done better conjuring up the adventures of a skinny English kid with large round glasses.

Most professional investors understood that Cash's books were better suited to the *other* best-seller list, since they read much more like fiction. But the uninformed public ate them up, and Jeremy Cash's uncanny ability to attract wanna-be millionaires was rivaled only by state lotteries and Regis Philbin.

Any rational thinking human being knew that if the advice in Cash's books could actually make you wealthy, Cash wouldn't be writing books about it.

Jeremy Cash had been in the headline news since the previous week when his twenty-three-year-old son, Freddie, had been kid-napped outside a health club in the Marina District, and a one-hundred-thousand-dollar ransom demand for his safe release followed. Cash had dodged every attempt by the local authorities and the FBI to get involved in the case. He had quickly rounded up the money and made the exchange, doing a better job at running the cops and the feds in circles than the kidnappers could ever have hoped to have done.

Less than forty-eight hours after the abduction, Freddie Cash was back at the country club for Sunday brunch with his father.

A week later, Cash bumped into my ex-father-in-law, Lincoln French, as the two jogged along Stinson Beach, where they both owned large homes. Cash casually asked Lincoln if he knew of a dependable and discreet private investigator. A few months ear-lier, for better or worse, Lincoln would have said no. But of late, my relationship with Sally's father had progressed from frigid bor-dering on nonexistent to tolerable bordering on amiable.

Lincoln gave Cash my number.

The question that intrigued me as I pulled the Impala into the circular driveway fronting the beach house was why Jeremy Cash was looking for a PI now that Freddie was back in the cradle. I imagined that the request for a meeting could have been totally unrelated to the kidnapping, but I somehow doubted it.

My musings were rudely interrupted when I stepped out of the car and a small ugly dog began snapping its jaws at my feet like a turtle. I was deliberating whether to jump back into the car or kick out at the puny varmint when a voice from the front door froze my attacker into a prostrate statue of an ugly little dog.

"Stay, Kafka!" was all Cash had to shout and the meta-morphosis was complete.

I stepped over the animal, who was lying there as motionless as a desk ornament, and moved to meet Jeremy Cash moving to meet me. Cash shook my hand firmly and then motioned toward the open door.

"Come, Kakfa," he called. I hurried ahead of them into the house.

Cash led us into his library, the dog and I exchanging untrusting glances all the way. Once Cash and I were seated opposite each other in matching leather armchairs, and he had poured a glass of Glenlivet for each of us, his pet took a spot near his feet and assumed the shape and expression of a gargoyle on the tower of Notre Dame. The animal remained so silent and motionless that I might have believed the ugly little thing would never move again if I weren't such a pessimist.

Cash lifted his drink, brought it up to his eyes, and looked at the twelve-year-old whiskey with great reverence before taking a healthy swallow. I took a quick swig of my own, just to be sociable. I would have preferred a shot of George Dickel Tennessee Sour Mash Whiskey.

"So, Mr. Diamond," he said, finally setting the ball in motion, "it was good of you to come. I suppose you are wondering why I called you here."

I had absolutely no comeback.

"Call me Jake," I said.

"You may have heard of the recent incident involving my son," said Cash.

Next he would ask me if I knew what day it was and if I'd ever heard of Barry Bonds. I thought about telling him to stop beating around the bush, but the single malt had numbed my tongue.

"Yes, and I was glad to hear that your son came through this terrible ordeal unscathed," I said lamely.

"I would like you to try to discover if my son was in any way involved in his own kidnapping," he said.

Cash had been slow out of the starting gate but he quickly had my full attention.

"Do you have reason to suspect your son?"

"Not really. I'm a naturally suspicious person."

"Is it the money?"

"Not at all."

"Then forget it," I said, and drained the glass.

"Mr. Diamond," he said, "I know what you're thinking."

Actually I was trying not to. Cash was determined to play it out.

"You're thinking that it's better if I don't know," he said.

"Something like that," I said, and then I reached for the bottle. "Do you mind?"

"Please help yourself."

I poured myself a tall one.

"Mr. Cash. Kidnapping is a serious offense, and I'm a PI, not a priest. Let's say, for argument sake, that your son was involved. If I found out, I don't know that I could keep it quiet."

"Even if no one asked?"

"I don't think I can help you, Mr. Cash."

"Mr. Diamond, I'm worried about my son. I believe that he may be in some kind of trouble. I have never denied him a thing. What concerns me most, if he *were* in some sort of dilemma, is his keeping it from me. I cannot understand why, if he were only in need of money, he would not simply have come to me."

This guy was talking about a hundred grand like it was pocket change.

"I'm not a psychologist, either. Why don't you just ask him if he needs help? You may be way off base. Unless you have something more than your naturally suspicious nature to go on?"

"I need to be sure that Freddie isn't in some kind of serious danger, and I need someone to help me find out without scaring him off. I can pay you very well, Jake, for your time and your discretion."

I rose from my chair; I wanted a cigarette badly. I began pacing, which brought the little gargoyle back to life. Kafka was eyeing my shoes hungrily and all I wanted to do was to say no thanks and get the hell out of there. Instead I beat the puny dog to it and stuck my foot in my mouth.

"I'll think about it," I said, in a voice that I sadly recognized as the stupid Jake Diamond voice.

"Thank you," Cash said.

I was about to make my getaway when I was pulled up short by a glimpse of a group of stunningly painted eggs sitting in a glass-doored cabinet between the crammed bookcases. I'll never learn.

"Are those what I think they are?" I asked.

"Fabergé. May I show you something?"

23

Some other time, I thought.

"Sure," I said.

Cash walked over to the display, carefully removed one of the gilded eggs from its stand, and called Kafka over to his side. The dog looked up at Cash and then neatly rolled over onto his back with his four legs pointed straight up in the air. Cash placed the egg on the dog's right front paw where Kafka balanced it deftly.

"You're going to love this, Mr. Diamond."

I was dubious.

The dog began passing the priceless Russian knickknack from one paw to another, counterclockwise, and after four rotations changed direction. I stood watching, transfixed, feeling as if I had stepped into the pages of a Carlos Castañeda book. Then my cell phone went off, the dog jumped, the Fabergé rose five feet into the air, and hung a U-turn toward the floor. I made a failed attempt at a lunging catch, and the egg hit the deck. It cracked open, spilling out its yolk, and Kafka quickly proceeded to lap up the yellow matter.

"I keep the real articles in my safe, of course," Cash said.

"Hold that thought," I said.

I flipped open the phone.

"Jake."

"Vinnie, I can't talk now," I said. "Call me back in about ten minutes."

I took one more look at the dog as if to etch in my mind the last time I would ever see the thing, thanked Cash for the drink, and made for the Chevy. I lit a Camel, took the far side of the circular driveway at about fifty, then headed for the bridge as if I were afraid it might vanish before I reached it. When the phone rang I pulled over to the side of the road, afraid that talking to Vinnie at the moment might cause me to drive into the sea.

"I got a lead on Vic Vigoda."

"Where are you?"

"I'm at Carlucci's Restaurant. The bartender here seems to think that Vigoda is playing poker tonight. I'm trying to get an address on the card game."

"I'll meet you in front of the office. Give me twenty minutes."

I raced to make it to the bridge before it disappeared.

Six

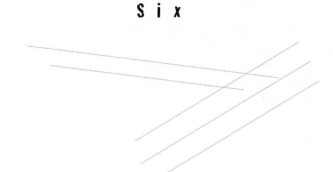

JEREMY CASH WAS A STRANGE bird. From the way he drank his whiskey to the way he parted his hair. I won't even mention his fingernails. As eccentric as the man was, and as much as I disliked little dog tricks even more than I disliked little dogs, it did seem as if Cash was seriously worried about his son. I hadn't said that I would take the assignment. On the other hand, in spite of my reservations, I hadn't said I wouldn't.

Usually when I don't refuse a case outright I find myself tip-toeing into it, either amazed at my faultless instincts or, more often, scraping it off my shoes.

I quickly moved the Cash question to the back burner when I spied Vinnie Strings shuffling from foot to foot in front of Molinari's.

"You could have met me at the restaurant, Jake. I would have bought you a drink," said Vinnie, leaning through the passenger window.

"I'm running late, Vin. Maybe another time," I said.

The odds that Vinnie Stradivarius would ever pay a bar tab would resemble the numbers in a DNA match. Moreover, I wanted to avoid being spotted by any of the Carluccis, either Mama Carlucci looking to give me a bowl of minestrone, or her maladjusted son, Tony, looking to give me grief.

"So, what about Vigoda," I asked. "Where and when?"

"Fort Mason. Probably not much before ten."

"You said Vigoda was off to a poker game, not a modern dance performance."

"One of the small theater groups down there raises extra dough renting out the space on their dark nights. The card players love it; they put the table right up on the stage and revel in the scenery. They should have a real ball tonight. *The Iceman Cometh* is running."

"Okay, I'll pick you up at nine-thirty or so. Need a ride home?"

"I'll wait at the office, or maybe I'll stop in and watch TV with Angelo."

Vinnie extracted himself from the window and I drove over to exchange the 1963 Impala for the 1978 Toyota Corona parked at the curb in front of Joey Russo's house on Sixth Avenue between Clement and the park.

When I made the turn into the driveway, I saw Joey and his son-in-law, Sonny the Chin, sitting on the front porch. I deposited the Chevy safely into the garage, then walked back out and joined them.

"How's the elbow, Jake?" Joey asked.

"Good," I said.

I made up my mind that the next time I got a boo-boo, I wouldn't complain about it so much.

"Did you eat?" asked Joey.

"I'm having dinner with Sally."

"That's nice, Jake, I'm glad to hear it. Have time for a beer?"

"Sure," I said.

Sonny rose and glided into the house.

"Any ideas who might have snuffed Chancellor?"

Joey liked it when I just came out and asked.

"Too many. Why the interest?"

"I'm trying to help someone out of a jam."

"Who would that be, if you don't mind me asking?" said Joey.

Sonny reappeared and handed us each a bottle of Miller Genuine Draft.

"Lefty Wright. Calls himself Al."

"Small time break-in artist?" asked Sonny.

"That's him. He was found in the room with the judge's body."

"Lucky break," said Sonny.

"The cops are trying to drop the murder in his lap. Thing is, the kid is all wrong for it, and I'm pretty sure that even the SFPD detectives are hip enough to see that. But Governor Krupp is looking for the quick fix, and Keep the Governor Happy is the new state motto."

"So you find the real assassin and save the day?"

"That's the general idea, Joey," I said.

"Snooping into who may have killed Chancellor will be a lot like looking for a needle in a stack of needles crawling with rattlesnakes."

"That's one way of putting it," I said.

"Sounds like fun," Joey said. "What can I do to help?"

"I'm not quite there yet, I'll let you know."

"Don't hesitate."

For a long time I'd been leery of calling on Joey Russo for help. He spooked me at first; I'd probably seen too many Scorsese movies. I'd since smartened up.

I stayed long enough to finish a beer with Joey and Sonny, talking Raiders and 49ers. I peeked at my Swatch; I needed to get home in time to freshen up for dinner. I thanked Joey again for the invite to the opener of the division series; he said he would pick me up at my office on Wednesday afternoon before the game.

I climbed into the Corona and headed for my apartment in the Fillmore. I had inherited the Toyota from my father in the late eighties. It was the vehicle that had carried me from a fairly successful though far from lucrative Off-Off-Broadway acting career to a mediocre stint in Hollywood.

The two questions I'm most often asked by those first learning of my profession are were you a cop before you became a PI and what kind of heat do you carry.

The closest I ever came to being a cop was playing one in a low-budget thriller. I was killed in the first reel.

I own a few guns, keep one at home and one in the office,

but they very rarely make it out of their respective desk drawers.

I don't go around bragging about what I do. It's just a job, with very flexible hours, which I enjoy and sometimes do it well. There's nothing all that glamorous about it. It's not what I wanted to be when I grew up. Like most kids growing up in Brooklyn, I wanted to be a baseball player.

I picked up my mail from the box outside the front entrance and walked up to my apartment.

I jumped into the shower, climbed into my best suit between sips of George Dickel on ice, and left to meet Sally at the restaurant.

La Folie on Polk Street was Sally's favorite spot. The last time we had planned dinner there was three years ago, to celebrate our second wedding anniversary. We never made it there that night, and never made it to our third anniversary.

Sally had recently broken off her engagement to Dick Spencer, a lawyer in Los Angeles, after discovering that he was fooling around with his secretary. All things being relative, I suppose that Dick's indiscretions had me looking more like the frying pan than the fire.

Sally French remained one of the most attractive women I had ever set eyes on. I hoped that the second time around I would be smart enough to appreciate her other qualities as well.

The smile she gave me as I approached the table allowed me to believe that anything was possible.

"You look terrific, Sally," I said, stooping to kiss her on the cheek and then seating myself across the table.

"Don't you ever get tired of using that line every time you see me?" she asked.

"When I do, you'll be the first to know," I said.

We spent a couple of very pleasant hours over lots of expensive food and wine. When we were done with coffee and desert it was nearly ten, and the last thing I wanted to do was to try to crash a poker game with Vinnie Strings.

"I have to go to work," I said.

"Be careful on the job," she said.

It was the first time that I could remember Sally referring to what I did for a living as legitimate employment.

Thirty minutes later I pulled up in front of my office in North Beach. I had called ahead on my cellular phone and Vinnie was waiting out front. Strings climbed into the Toyota and we drove out to the theater at Fort Mason.

"Think we'll be able to get in?" I asked.

"Odds are against it," Vinnie said.

We didn't get in.

"Can you tell me if Vic Vigoda is in attendance?" I asked the Neanderthal at the building entrance.

"You just missed him," he grunted.

"Think he was leveling with us?" I asked Vinnie on our way back to the car.

"I wouldn't bet on it," said Strings.

And Vinnie would bet on just about anything.

We sat in the Toyota for an hour or so, but I was fading fast.

"How would you like to hang here and see if Vic walks out?" I asked.

"You want an honest answer?"

"No, thanks."

"Sure I'll stay, Jake. Only, could you spare twenty for a cab ride home?"

"Did you move to Santa Rosa since the last time I checked?" I asked.

I handed him two tens.

"What do I do if he shows?"

"Try to follow him somehow and give me a call."

I drove back to Fillmore Street, miraculously finding a parking space across from my apartment building.

I was asleep less than five minutes after setting my head on the pillow.

S e v e n

I WOKE UP FAMISHED, AS I often did after continental fare. I thought I would give Darlene some time to settle back in. I went looking for real food.

After a bacon and swiss omelet, home fries and onions, buttered sourdough toast, and a quart of coffee laced with half and half at the Home Plate on Lombard, I headed to Columbus Avenue and crawled up the stairs to the office.

I walked in a few minutes after ten. Darlene took one look at my complexion and volunteered to take my blood pressure.

"Way to go, Jake."

"You have no idea how glad I am to see you," I said.

"Give me some credit, Jake. I know exactly how glad you are," Darlene said, "and do me a favor. The next time you have Vinnie sitting in, put him at your desk."

"What makes you think that Vinnie was here at all, let alone at your throne?"

"Well, Watson, I first became suspicious when I found my chair readjusted into a position that could only be suited for Gumby. The piece of grilled green pepper on my Scotch tape dispenser clinched it. Here's a present for you," she said, handing me two fifty-yard-line tickets for the Sunday game between the Oakland Raiders and the Niners.

"What's this for?"

"From Bruno, to thank you for giving me the extra day off."

"Why does he think that I have anything to say about when you come in and when you decide not to?"

"Because I like him thinking it. I already made the coffee, anything else I can do for you today?"

Darlene was in rare form. It must have been the altitude in Denver.

"Did you hear about Judge Chancellor's demise?"

"As a matter of fact, Angelo Verdi was bending my ear this morning when I picked up your hard roll. I put it on your desk. Maybe it will sop up the cholesterol."

"Any calls?" I asked, trying to change the subject.

"The clinic, they can do your cardiogram at two," Darlene said, not changing it.

"Give me a break, Darlene."

"That's exactly what I'm trying to do, Jake. Jeremy Cash called. He said that if you want to get a peek at Freddie, the kid will be at Club NV tomorrow night."

"Great, just what I need, A client who informs on his own son and an excuse to take in some Wednesday night disco," I said.

"Isn't Freddie Cash the rich kid who was kidnapped?"

"Yeah, his father wants to know if the kid abducted himself."

"Sounds like a wonderful relationship. Are we taking the case?"

"I'm not sure yet, but we are looking into Judge Chancellor's murder for the kid they have locked up. I need you to find out all you can about the cases that Chancellor was sitting on, going back at least a year, particularly any he didn't have a chance to finish."

"I'll give my cousin a call. Vinnie phoned. I'm not sure if he was awake," said Darlene. "He asked me to tell you that he never spotted Vic Vigoda last night but he'll get back on it later today."

I wobbled back to my desk for the Mylanta.

For reasons beyond economics, I prefer working on more than one case at a time. When I'm occupied exclusively with one case

I tend to take it too seriously, often attributing undue urgency to its resolution.

Then again, the more I thought about it, the more I began to lose interest in Freddie Cash. From what I had learned about the kid, in the news coverage of the kidnapping, he was basically a spoiled brat.

Jeremy Cash's bankroll had purchased Freddie's acceptance to an Ivy league college. Freddie had been a poor Business major with a minor in theatre arts. His college acting notices made my short stage career sound Obie Award winning.

Freddie had recently been admitted into a top-rated law school, which probably cost his father a few Fabergé eggs. If Freddie had ripped off his own father and Jeremy Cash wanted me to bust his own son, I wasn't tripping over myself to get in the middle of such heartwarming family dynamics. To call it a can of worms would be like calling the Middle East a hot spot. I thought I might be wise to reconsider the Cash investigation.

I walked back to Darlene's desk just to get my blood circulating.

Darlene said that she was going out to lunch with her cousin Edie, who clerked at the criminal courts building. Edie wasn't very familiar with Chancellor's caseload, but she was tight with one of the late judge's assistants, Buzz Stanley.

"Buzz Stanley?" I asked.

"Valley boy, star wide receiver for UCLA before he destroyed his leg in the ninety-four Rose Bowl. Buzz is studying law part time at Berkeley and was assisting the judge between classes. Stanley probably loses his job when they replace Chancellor, but while Buzz is hanging on, Edie can do some fishing."

I didn't have anything close to good news for Lefty, but I figured that just a look at a friendly mug might help him get through another day.

"If Vinnie calls before you leave and has anything on Vic Vigoda, leave me a note," I said. "If Vinnie happens by, throw a drop cloth over my desk and sit him back there."

"Doesn't Vic Vigoda run errands for Tony Carlucci?"

"It wouldn't surprise me," I said.

"If you're going to visit a client, Jake, I hope you have a spare tie in your file cabinet."

"What's wrong with the one I have on?" I asked innocently.

"Everything," said Darlene.

When I reached the Vallejo Street Station I thought I'd drop in on Lieutenant Lopez. Maybe she could give me a word of encouragement to pass on to Al Wright.

I couldn't have been more wrong.

"The arraignment is in the morning," she told me.

"Lefty said he had a lawyer, who is she?"

"Kay Turner, she's actually a public defender," said Lopez. "Turner is actually a pretty good one, but her opposition is deadly."

"Who's prosecuting?"

"Lowell Ryder," Lopez said.

You learn something new every day, never knowing when it will come in handy.

I had come across Ryder's name only the day before, in the Metro section of the *Examiner*. With the election less than five weeks away, Lowell Ryder was on his way to becoming the youngest district attorney in San Francisco history. An honors graduate of Stanford Law School, Ryder had been raised in a small rural town east of Sacramento. He'd climbed the ladder with absolutely no political connections; his father was an avocado farmer.

Ryder moved quickly from DA offices in Stockton to Oakland to San Francisco, where longtime Chief Prosecutor Harmon Kramer took to Lowell like candy, appointing him assistant DA two years earlier at the age of thirty-two. The polls had Ryder twenty points ahead of his opponent.

"I thought that Ryder was super smart," I said.

"They don't call him Wonder Boy for nuthin'," Lopez said.

"Then why would he take on a case he can't win, so close to the election?"

"He wouldn't," said Lopez.

"Oh."

"You can bet your cravat collection that Ryder wouldn't touch it unless he was confident that it was a slam dunk."

"I can't wait to tell Lefty," I said.

"I meant what I said yesterday. You come across something I can work with and I'll run with it," she said.

"You'll be the first to know," I promised. "Any luck locating Vigoda?"

"Not yet, but don't count on Vigoda solving the case for you."

I didn't see how the DA's office thought they had a case. If Wright had just emptied the safe, stuffing his pockets full of cash while juggling a thirty-eight snubnose and a flashlight as Chancellor walked in and surprised him, where did he find the extra hand to stab the judge? Why would Lefty even pick up a knife on his way through the kitchen? He was already in possession of a lethal concealed paint scraper.

It was illogical.

But from what I had heard so far from Lopez, the prosecution was going to base its arguments on motive and opportunity and leave logic to the fickle.

So much for hoping to offer Lefty a little encouragement. I figured that a look at my friendly mug might not be quite enough to make his day. I decided to postpone my visit until I had better news. I hoped that with some luck I would be back to see Lefty again before the end of the month.

I tried to track down Vinnie Strings with no success. I could only wish that he was staying out of trouble. He was either out scouting for Vic Vigoda or blowing his weekly stipend on some nag at Bay Meadows Race Course in San Mateo.

I was anxious to hear if Darlene had learned anything from her cousin, but it was nearly four in the afternoon when I called the office and she wasn't back yet. I saw no reason to go back there myself, since the answering machine was already fielding calls.

I left a message for Darlene to phone me at my apartment.

When I reached home I took a shower and poured a bourbon to clear my head.

The combination put me to sleep in my living room chair.

The call from Vinnie Strings woke me up at half past eight.

"They just fished Vic Vigoda out of McCovey Cove," he said.

More real bad news for Lefty Wright, not to mention what Vigoda's day must have been like.

I had promised Lefty Wright that I would be there for the arraignment.

After hearing from Vinnie I decided that Vic Vigoda, Freddie Cash, and the late judge could well be spared my concern until after the arraignment and the baseball game.

I picked up *The Count of Monte Cristo* and read until I couldn't read anymore.

Eight

I WAS DOWN AT THE criminal courts building on Van Ness at eight-forty-five for the arraignment, which was scheduled for nine. I went directly to the rear entrance. Hank Strode, the security guard stationed there, was an ex-cop from Santa Monica and an old acquaintance from my days working for Jimmy Pigeon. Hank bore an uncanny resemblance to the African American actor Woody Strode, who was featured in a slew of classic Westerns, always standing in the shadows with a very big rifle draped across his arm, ready to back up John Wayne or William Holden if the odds turned against them. When I first met Hank, I asked if he was related to the actor.

"No," he said, "how about you? You look a lot like Neil Diamond to me."

I got the point, and we became friendly when Hank retired and came up to San Francisco. And I never had to empty my pockets when I came in the back way.

I spotted Al Wright as soon as I entered, standing handcuffed between two large police officers who watched his every twitch as if he were John Dillinger. A petite blonde who looked as if she should be in the next building taking the written test for her driver's permit, stood talking with Lefty. I guessed it was Kay Turner.

"Ms. Turner," I called to her, when Lefty had been escorted into the courtroom, "I'm Jake Diamond."

"Mr. Diamond, I'm glad you're here. I was hoping that we could talk after the arraignment."

"Sure. Are you going to be able to get bail for the kid?"

"It's unlikely. Not with this prosecutor and this judge."

"Who's the judge?"

"Adam Morgan, who's known in the public defender's office as 'His Horror.' "

Fabulous.

"I was at least hoping to delay the start of the trial," she said, "to give us more time to locate Vic Vigoda, but our star witness became immaterial last night."

"I heard. The PD have any ideas about who dropped Vic in the bay?"

"No, but I may have," she said. "Can we talk after they railroad my client."

"Sure," I said.

I liked her attitude. Whether it would benefit Lefty was another question.

Kay Turner had called it perfectly. The arraignment was as quick as the Japanese bullet train. No bail, no continuances, no nonsense. Lowell Ryder didn't waste a breath, and Judge Morgan more or less told Kay Turner to save it. They whisked Lefty Wright out of the courtroom for the return to the jail so quickly, it was like watching a reel of the Keystone Kops. I stood waiting for Kay Turner to meet me at the rear exit, taking the opportunity for a short chat with Hank Strode while I loitered.

"So, who do you suppose killed Judge Chancellor?" I asked Hank, jokingly.

"It wasn't that poor kid they got locked up at Vallejo, that I can tell you," Strode said. "It surprises me that Ryder wants to prosecute. I'd have thought Lowell would give the kid a medal."

I was about to ask Hank what he meant when Kay arrived, trying to stand tall after the beating she had taken in court.

I thanked Hank as we left the building, not quite sure what I was thanking him for.

Kay Turner led me to a coffee shop at Hyde and Turk, near the Federal Building. A look at the clientele had me fairly convinced that it was a lawyer hangout, but not of the four-hundred-dollar suit variety. The place oozed of nostalgia.

The classic coffee shop preceded and for the most part outlived the coffeehouse of the sixties and seventies and, in a scattering of urban neighborhoods and small town Main Streets, has somehow managed to survive the onslaught of the culturally irrelevant contemporary phenomenon known as the coffee bar.

The coffee shop was traditionally a long, narrow affair with booths on one wall and a counter opposite. The Turk Street coffee shop was no exception. Behind the counter were men in grimy white uniforms moving at the speed of sound.

The coffee was brewed in huge urns, gallons at a time. The grill was piled high with fried potatoes and onions, brittle bacon, and eggs in the process of being prepared in every conceivable way. Large stainless steel contraptions toasted six slices of white bread simultaneously, which were generously covered with swipes from a block of butter the size of Vermont. Underneath scratched and foggy Plexiglas domes sat barely visible wedges of cream pies—banana, chocolate and coconut—guaranteed to satisfy the daily calorie requirements of a rhinoceros.

"So," I said, as a waiter brought coffee in ceramic cups that took two hands and a grunt to lift, "you said you had some ideas about who may have sent Vic Vigoda the way of the Titanic."

"I'm thinking it was someone involved in the murder of Judge Chancellor."

I prayed she was pulling my leg.

"I had the same thought myself," I said, seeing no real reason to be rude.

"What I mean to say is that Vic Vigoda may still have something to tell us about who killed the judge," she said.

And of course she had a very good point.

The end of the road for Vic might open up a whole new avenue of investigation. But what happened to Vigoda made going down that path feel a whole lot scarier.

"Look," I said, "I think it's pretty obvious that Al Wright is innocent and has been elected to hold the bag. I'd like to be able to help clear things up because I like the kid, and that kind of arrogance really gets my goat. As to whether I'm willing to cross a swamp to get there, I may have to give that question some further thought."

"I perfectly understand, Mr. Diamond," Kay Turner said.

Which was exactly what Turner needed to say to push me right into the swamp. I could only wonder if she had hit the target blindfolded or had done her Jake Diamond 101 homework.

I would send Vinnie out to beat the bushes for any clues as to who may have been the last to see Vic Vigoda on dry land. I would sit down with Darlene for a recap of her extended lunch engagement with cousin Edie and find out what, if anything, Buzz Stanley might add to the equation. I would revisit Hank Strode and attempt to decipher whatever it was he was hinting at earlier.

But before I raced into any of that, I would spend the afternoon at Pac Bell Park with the only person I knew who could stop me spinning my wheels.

Joey Russo was taking me out to the ballgame.

N i n e

Pacific Bell Park WAS BUILT at the cost of three hundred nineteen million dollars on a thirteen-acre triangle of land bordered
by Channel Street, Sixth, and Third Street, where it continues
from downtown across the Third Street Bridge. The short, narrow
inlet coming off the bay between the docks south of the Bay
Bridge, where the Embarcadero ends at King Street, was chris-
tened McCovey Cove in honor of the other Willie. Since the opening of the new ballpark in April, homerun balls hit over the right
field wall and landing in the brink have been retrieved by dogs
diving off boats that cruise the inlet. It was during a baseball
retrieval practice session the evening before that one of the diving
canines surfaced with a leather wallet containing two thousand
dollars in soggy cash and a driver's license displaying a photo of
Vic Vigoda.

It was my first visit to Pac Bell Park, and Joey Russo gave me
the grand tour. The upper deck high above home plate offered
a panoramic view of downtown San Francisco, the Golden Gate
Bridge and Alcatraz Island to the northwest, the Bay Bridge and
downtown Oakland to the east. Food concessions featured everything from hot dogs to regional Italian pasta dishes.

"Remind me to pick up a portobello burger for Darlene before we leave," I said, as we walked back down to our seats on the first-base line.

We stayed locked on the game through the early innings, but by the seventh it looked bleak for the boys from Queens.

Born and raised in Brooklyn and having been on hand at Shea Stadium with my father and grandfather on the day the Mets knocked off the Baltimore Orioles when I was an impressionable nine-year-old, I was covertly rooting for the New York team.

Joey, from whom I held no secrets, was well aware of my sentiments. Joey decided that it might be a good time to shift focus.

"Well, Jake, what's the plan now that hopes of getting any answers directly from Vic Vigoda are all washed up?" he asked.

"I'm wide open, Joey."

"There's a line you hear in a lot of movies and TV shows. The cop asks the suspect if he killed the victim and the suspect answers, 'I wish I had, but somebody beat me to it.' The judge never won any popularity contests. We're fishing for suspects in a very well-stocked pond, if you'll permit the metaphor. We need to throw back the little ones."

I couldn't have said it better.

But I could reiterate, just to prove to myself that I was following his drift.

"So, what we're looking for is whoever was most threatened by Chancellor's continued longevity."

"Very seriously threatened, if not mortally threatened."

"That could narrow the field, but it doesn't move us along much."

"One step at a time, Jake. One step at a time."

"And the first step?" I asked, taking every advantage of Joey's lucidity.

I often thought that Joey loved detective work better than I did.

"Let's bring a portobello burger back for Darlene and find out if she learned anything provocative from her cousin Edie."

The Mets lost 5 to 1.

We grabbed a mushroom sandwich and went back to the office.

Making jokes at my expense was nearly a national pastime, and Darlene was a Hall of Fame inductee. On the other hand, poking fun at Joey Russo was not a good idea unless you were someone he really liked a lot.

"If it isn't Don Vito and Freddo," Darlene said when we walked into the office.

Joey got a kick out of it.

"What happened to you yesterday?" I asked, dropping the sandwich on her desk, "I didn't realize you were having lunch with Edie in Guam."

"We ran into Buzz Stanley on our way back from the Herbivore Restaurant. It cost me all afternoon, part of the evening, and a hefty bar bill at the Saloon to move him past his glory days on the gridiron to talk about his former employer. I had to drink orange juice from a can. Is this one of those portobello numbers from the ballpark?" she asked, fumbling with the paper bag.

"Yeah," I said.

"Hope you brought a side of grape seed vegenaise to go with it."

"So who killed Judge Chancellor?" Joey asked, trying to get us back on track.

Darlene had taken the sandwich out of the bag, and finding no condiment walked over to the small refrigerator for her egg-free mayo. Don't ask me how they make it.

"Edie and Buzz each had a few theories, ranging from jealous husbands to pro-life activists to a certain ex-convict televangelist," she said. "Which would you like to hear first, the far-fetched or the hallucinatory?"

"Do this for me," Joey said, "eliminate everyone Edie and Stanley mentioned who, one, would not have had access to Vigoda's complicity and who, two, could not possibly have tossed Vigoda into the bay as an encore. Then tell us who's left on the roster."

Darlene thought about it for approximately a split second.

"No one," she said.

"Okay, now we're getting somewhere," said Joey.

"Great," said Darlene.

"Jake. How about Hank Strode? Anything there?"

"I don't know. I got the feeling he was alluding to something."

"About?"

"About Chancellor and Ryder maybe not being bosom buddies."

"Sum it up."

"I just did."

"If you'll allow me to be presumptuous," Joey continued, "I think we have two options."

Joey was in the zone.

And he had a captive audience.

"Be as presumptuous as you like," I said.

"Go for it," Darlene said.

"We forget about trying to find Chancellor's murderer and concentrate our efforts on helping Lefty's defense show reasonable doubt. The kid didn't have a drop of blood on him. And if Chancellor walked in and surprised Lefty in the act, why was the watch on the floor? I think that whoever iced the judge was waiting for him and was there to kill him. Lefty had no real motive, has no history of violence, and he could have got out without having to kill anyone."

"Unless Chancellor surprised *him* with the knife, there was a struggle and the judge took it in the chest," said Darlene, playing mock prosecutor.

"Okay. But if the Rolex was found on the floor, it doesn't add up. If the judge lost it in a struggle, Lefty would have scooped it up. And why would Lefty hang around to shove the judge under the bed? No, I believe if we concentrate on clearing Lefty we don't have to actually come up with the guilty party."

"What's the other option?" I asked.

"We admit that the hunt has less to do with Lefty than with our own love of the game," said Joey, "that we're as much interested in solving the murder as we are in clearing Lefty, in which case it's time to stop scratching the surface and start seriously digging."

"What's your gut feeling?"

43

"I'm Italian, Jake. I don't have gut feelings. They're all right out here on the surface. All I can tell you is what I think would be more dangerous but a lot more fun."

"Where would you start digging?" asked Darlene.

"Well, and you won't like this, Jake, I think we need to talk with Carlucci."

"I labor at avoiding Tony C. every day that I walk down Columbus Avenue."

"I'm talking about John Carlucci."

"I thought Johnny Boy Carlucci was safely locked up in San Quentin," I said.

"He is."

"What could John Carlucci tell us about what happened with Chancellor?"

"If I knew that, we wouldn't have to go out there and ask him."

"And why would he even talk with us?" I asked.

"Because he thinks he owes us one, for helping his brother Tony locate the rat who put him in the joint."

"What ever happened to Frank Slater?" Darlene asked.

"You don't want to know," said Joey. "Look, Jake. It's not going to hurt to talk to Carlucci. We have nothing to lose. Or I could go home and mow the lawn and you can wait here for the next chump who walks in suspecting that his wife is screwing the guy who mows *his* lawn."

"Or better yet," said Darlene, never missing a chance to drive a point home, "you can go find out if Freddie Cash kidnapped himself."

"What's that about Freddie Cash?" asked Vinnie Strings, bopping into the office.

"You just wake up, Vin?" I said.

"No, Jake. I was out at Bay Meadows trying to get my mind off what happened to Vic Vigoda. I heard that the fish ate his eyeballs," said Vinnie. "What kind of sandwich is that Darlene?"

"Does it really matter now?" said Darlene, pushing it aside.

"I think I'll get going," said Joey. "I've got a nice piece of salmon in the refrigerator to reconsider. Call me if you want to go out to Quentin tomorrow, Jake."

"Who won the ballgame?" asked Vinnie after Joey left. "What's at San Quentin?"

"Vinnie do you have any idea how annoying it is when you persist in asking more than one question at a time?" Darlene ranted. "How did you do at the track today, Vin? Is that a new shirt? What are you doing for dinner? Have you seen the new Robert DeNiro movie?"

"All right, Darlene," I said. "You made your point."

"Only time will tell."

"So I guess I need a new assignment," Vinnie said. "What can I do? What are you doing for dinner, Jake?"

"That didn't take long," said Darlene.

"I think I'll go home, pop something frozen into the oven, and read about Edmond Dantès," I said. "Check back with me tomorrow, Vinnie, and I'll find something that you can do to help."

Darlene looked at me like I was insane.

"You got it. What were you saying about that Cash kid who was kidnapped?"

"It's not important, Vin."

"Okay. I just thought it was funny you mentioned him, since I saw him walk out of the poker game the night I was watching for Vic Vigoda at Fort Mason."

I wasn't sure that *funny* was the right word for it.

"You don't say," I said.

"He just said it," said Darlene.

"It's a figure of speech, Darlene."

"So I'm told, but what does it mean?"

"Maybe talking with Freddie isn't such a bad idea," I said.

I was hoping that Darlene would quit it.

"You'll find him at Club NV at around ten tonight," said Darlene. "Don't you have some of Jimmy Pigeon's old polyester shirts and his disco boots?"

"Give me a break, Darlene."

"Can I go with you, Jake?" asked Vinnie Strings.

"I'm not sure I'm up to it, Vin. I'll think about it over a Swanson's Hungry Man and Alexandre Dumas. If I decide to break out the bell-bottoms, I'll give you a call."

Yeah, sure.

Ten minutes later we all left the office and went our separate ways.

My separate way pulled me up short in front of Molinari's. I was hungry, in spite of Vinnie's allusion to McCovey Cove fish food, and the business about frozen TV dinners was a ruse. I had decided I would try to catch Freddie Cash at Club NV, and conveniently forget to call Strings. I thought that a wedge of eggplant parmigiana might put me in better shape to deal with Donna Summers's greatest hits. A single moment's hesitation in front of Molinari's door was all it took to be spotted.

"Diamond, you're a detective, maybe you can explain this."

Tony Carlucci strutted up to my side wearing his celluloid smile. Tony thought that just because he was five foot six and Italian American he looked like Al Pacino.

I remembered that Joey wanted to take me to San Quentin to chat with Tony's brother John, so I tried to grin and bear it.

"How's your mother, Tony?"

"Great. She keeps asking when you're going to drop in for dinner. She's worried that you don't eat."

I was losing my appetite rapidly.

"Soon," I said, closing my eyes quickly and wishing that I would disappear.

"You're a detective, maybe you could explain this."

The conversation had gone full circle.

"Okay, Tony, I'll bite."

"Why was Judge Chancellor trying to get in touch with me just before he bought the farm?"

"Was he?"

"The very afternoon. I was at the track. Mom said that Andy called from his cabin, asking for me."

"Andy?"

"Me and His Honor went back some, but that's another story. Anyway, I tried to call him at his place up the coast, but he was gone, probably on his way back down here. I called him at home later in the evening and some dick answered the phone. Needless to say I didn't identify myself."

"Why are you telling me this, Tony?"

"I heard you were interested."

"From who?"

"My bartender said that Vinnie Strings was around, asking about Vic Vigoda. I put two and two together."

I didn't think that Tony could count that high.

"So what do you think Chancellor wanted?"

"There you go, Diamond, get past the rhetoric and right down to the investigating. Thing is, I'm not sure," said Carlucci. "The last time I spoke with the judge, a week ago in case it's relevant, he indicated that he needed some research done and thought I could help."

"But you never got to the details."

"Bingo. The judge never got around to it."

"Why are you telling me this, Tony?"

I was repeating myself.

"I don't like what happened to Vic Vigoda."

"And what makes you think that what happened to Vigoda had anything to do with what happened to Chancellor?"

"Because you do, Diamond, and you're the best."

I was beginning to feel nauseous.

"I'm flattered, Tony," I said. "Is that it?"

"You talked with Lefty Wright. He told you that Vic turned him on to the score at Chancellor's place. I can verify that for what it's worth, though it seems that the police don't give a shit. Vic was throwing money around that night, feeling pretty good. Then the word came down that the judge was zapped and Vic turned white. I'm no Marlowe, but I'd bet the restaurant that Vigoda didn't know that part of the deal. Vic was a mixed-up kid, and for enough dough he would have sent his mother in there without asking too many questions, but he would have drawn the line if he suspected that he was setting Lefty up for a murder rap. Of course, that's just my opinion. I could be wrong."

"And that's it?"

"In a nutshell."

"Any reason to believe that your brother John knows anything more about it?"

"Sounds like an idea Joey Russo might come up with."

"Anything to it?"

"Well, Joey knows what I'll humbly admit, that my brother John knows more about everything than I do. And Joey also knows that if Chancellor wanted me to do something for him, he'd have to get John's okay first."

"Well," I said. It was the best I could come up with.

"Don't worry about thanking me, Diamond. I'm just trying to be a good citizen."

I considered asking Tony Carlucci if he was attempting to endear me to him, but the thought was too scary.

"Tell your mom I'll be in soon."

"You wouldn't want to make a liar out of me in front of my mother, Jake."

"Don't say anything. I'll surprise her."

"Can I buy you a slab of eggplant?" Tony said, nodding toward the deli door.

Standing on Columbus Avenue with a psychic mobster, disco night at Club NV was looking better every minute.

"No thanks, Tony. I'll see you around."

"Only if I see you first, right Diamond? It's all right, don't say a thing. I'm used to it. I've been misunderstood all my life."

With that, he turned on his heel and did his best Jimmy Caan gait back toward his restaurant. I watched him cross Green Street and I ducked into Molinari's. Luckily, Angelo's son was at the counter and he wasn't a blabber. I opted for a veal parmigiana hero and a six-pack of Sam Adams.

I headed back to my apartment, washed down the sandwich with a couple of beers, and decided I would run over to Club NV at nine-thirty, try to catch Freddie Cash before he went in.

I was outside the club at half past nine, watching out for Freddie Cash. I knew that I wouldn't have any trouble recognizing him. I had seen his picture in the *Examiner* after the kidnapping and he looked so much like his old man the two could have done an Ivory dish-soap commercial.

At nine fifty, I caught sight of Cash moving in my direction, alone. There were a number of ways to go. I went with blunt.

"Freddie," I said, as he came up to the entrance.

"Yes?"

"Your father wants to know if you kidnapped yourself."

I've learned quite a bit about reading a person's reactions in my years in the PI business.

It didn't do me much good with Freddie Cash.

"Would you mind coming inside with me, Mr. . . . ?"

"Diamond, Jake Diamond."

"Mr. Diamond, I'd like to show you something. I'd prefer it not be out here on the street."

"I don't know if I could handle the tunes," I said.

"Don't worry, we can avoid the dance club. There's a private get-together in one of the events rooms. We can talk there."

"After you," I said, and followed him into the building.

A few minutes later we stood alone in a small side room off the main party area. The larger space, set up with a bar and tables of cocktail foods, was quickly filling with attractive men and women moving around rubbing elbows.

"Mr. Diamond," Freddie said, closing the door that adjoined the two rooms, "I can't tell you how sorry I am to hear that my father suspects me. I'm quite speechless."

"I think it's more worry than suspicion, Mr. Cash. Give me something that I can use to ease his troubled mind and we can wrap this up before the miniature quiches get cold."

When he reached down to untie his shoelace I nearly forgot what the hell I was doing there. When he removed the shoe and then the sock from his left foot I almost bolted. When I noticed that the little toe was missing, it brought to mind the plate of popcorn shrimp I had noticed on my way in.

"I didn't want my father to have to see this," he said.

Thoughtful kid. The privilege was all mine.

"Your kidnappers did that?"

"They were going to send it to my father. I told them that it really wouldn't be necessary, but I think they had their minds set on it from the start and were incapable of improvising."

"What happened to the toe?" I asked. I couldn't say why.

"They were nice enough to offer it to me before the exchange. Had it in a small leather earring case, on a bed of cotton. I passed."

"I'm sorry."

"Not your fault. Do you think you can convince my father that I wasn't involved without bringing up the little piggy that went to market?"

"Yeah, I think so."

"Thank you."

"So, come here much?" I asked, just to give him time to dress.

"I'm here for the soiree in the next room," he said, "a fundraiser for Lowell Ryder."

"Oh?"

"He's going to be the best DA this city ever had," Freddie said.

It wouldn't take much.

When he had the sock and shoe replaced, I was maneuvering for escape. I followed him back through the larger room, which was reaching capacity.

"Shrimp?" The question came from a perky brunette, holding out a platter. She wore a miniskirt decorated with the California State emblem.

"No, thanks," I said as politely as I could, and turned my attention back to Cash.

"Freddie, ever play poker with a guy named Vic Vigoda?"

He looked as if someone had just lopped off another toe.

"I can't say that I have, Mr. Diamond," Freddie stuttered, after finally finding the power of speech.

I decided to let it ride for the time being.

I needed air more than I needed dubious answers.

Ten

I ARRIVED AT THE OFFICE at nine the following morning. Darlene was already there and coffee was up.

"Good morning, Darlene."

"Good morning, Jake. How did it go last night?"

I filled her in on my talk with Freddie Cash.

"Ouch. Hard for him to do the Disco Duck, I would imagine."

"You make a good point," I said.

"That's what I'm here for, Jake," she said. "What point is that?"

"Freddie wasn't limping, not favoring the foot at all. It didn't register last night, and I'm no physical therapist, but I would think that if Freddie just lost a toe it would take longer than a week for him to get accustomed to it."

"My point exactly," Darlene said, smiling.

"See if you can get his father on the phone for me," I said. "Please . . ."

I walked back to my office. Darlene was buzzing me before I made it to my chair.

"I've got Jeremy Cash on the line, Jake."

"Mr. Cash, Jake Diamond."

"Yes, Mr. Diamond. What can I do for you?"

"I had a little man-to-man with your son last night."

"And?"

51

Something was bothering me. I began to wish that I hadn't called Cash, that I had waited to figure out what was it was.

I decided to let it be too late.

"I don't think your son was involved," I said.

"Could you share your reasons?"

I suddenly realized why I should have waited to call Cash. I hadn't taken the time to fabricate an answer.

"The kidnappers amputated one of your son's toes."

"My God."

"Freddie didn't want you to know about it, I sort of promised him that I would try to delete it from my report."

"I understand. Thank you for telling me. It is a horrible way to be assured of his innocence, but confirmation nevertheless. What do I owe you, Mr. Diamond?"

"I'll send you a statement, Mr. Cash, unless there's something more I can do."

"No. I'm quite satisfied. Thank you and good day."

And that was that.

I walked back out to the reception area.

"Darlene, send an invoice to Jeremy Cash when you get a chance."

"That was easy."

Too easy.

"Give Joey Russo a call, tell him I'll touch base later about a visit to San Quentin. And see if you can scare up Vinnie Strings."

"Vinnie unplugs his phone every night, at least until after noon."

"Maybe he forgot," I suggested. "I'm going to see Al Wright and then over to chat with Hank Strode."

I left the office and headed over to Vallejo Street Station.

I was put into an interview room with Lefty. He looked as if he were late for his own wedding. He drummed the table with his fingers.

"It's not looking too good, is it Jake?"

"This will sound strange, Al, but I believe it's looking better for you every day."

"I don't get it."

"I'm not so sure I get it myself. But the DA's office and the SFPD brass are boasting about how quickly they got their man and what a cinch the trial will be. I don't see it. I don't see how they can make this case. It's all circumstantial."

"I was at the scene, nose to nose with the judge. Bad circumstances."

"Granted. I just don't think it's enough to get a conviction. I think you have reasonable doubt squarely in your corner and Vic Vigoda's death doesn't help the prosecution any, it presents more questions than it does answers. What's more, and here's the part that has me talking to myself in public, I'm almost sure they know it."

"You're saying that they know they can't win? It's not very good politics to spend taxpayer money on a losing cause, especially at election time. What's the angle?"

"A homicide detective down in LA once told me that if you don't get your hands on the killer within the first forty-eight hours, the chances become very slim."

"Well, I had hands all over me in less than forty-eight minutes."

"And for the past three days nobody is looking for Chancellor's killer except me. I think that you're in here until the trail is ice cold, and then you'll get cut loose."

"Do you know what you're saying? You're saying that I'm here to pull the cops off the trail. I get it. But that means somebody is pulling a scam—more than one somebody, maybe, and you're forgetting something, Jake. Cutting me loose with no one to convict is not going to make the governor too happy. I think you're giving the cops a lot of credit. I think I'm here because they're too dumb to find the real killer and everybody is scared shitless of getting the governor mad."

Lefty Wright was sharp as a tack.

"Are you playing devil's advocate?" I asked.

"I believe that we both are," Lefty said, "but that's what makes human dialogue so invaluable."

"Anyone ever tell you that you're very well spoken?"

"Yeah. My ethics professor at college."

"How did you wind up choosing burglary as a vocation?"

"My ethics professor at Yale. I broke into his house for the questions on the final exam. After that, I never found anything else I enjoyed more."

"Do you think I'm grasping at straws?"

"More like clutching at them. In any event I appreciate the gesture. If you came here today to try to give me hope, I accept."

"So."

"So? I'm hanging in, Jake. And if you're right and they decide tomorrow that it's time to drop the charge to breaking and entering, I won't complain. But I'll always want to know who set me up, so that I can properly express my indignity. So? If you decide to stay on the case I wouldn't object to that, either."

"I'm on it, Al," I said.

I left Lefty for my date with Hank Strode.

I had called Hank earlier and invited him to join me for lunch. I took a peek at my watch and saw that I had forty-five minutes to kill before we met. I decided to check in on Lieutenant Lopez while I was at the station.

Then I looked at my watch again and remembered the Rolex.

Lefty said that he was going for the Rolex when he tripped over the judge's body. As Joey had suggested, if Wright had been surprised by Chancellor, killed the judge, and removed his watch, the Rolex would have been found in Al's pocket with the gun and the cash, not on the floor. I was sure that Kay Turner could do something with that and made a mental note to give her a call after lunch.

I went up to the desk sergeant and asked to see the lieutenant. Before he could respond, a voice beside me caused me to gulp.

"The lieutenant is out on a call, Diamond, maybe I can help you."

I slowly turned to the familiar voice and braced myself for the familiar visage. Detective Sergeant Johnson had a face that only a mother could love. I won't try to describe the back of his head.

"I wanted to chat with the lieutenant about the Chancellor case," I said.

Johnson's face looked badly out of focus. The sad thing was that it had nothing to do with my eyesight.

"What about it?" he asked.

What the hell.

"I was wondering what she thought about the Rolex."

"Which Rolex would that be?"

I had some time before meeting Hank, I figured I might as well squander it.

"The judge's Rolex. It was sitting on the floor in his bedroom when your boys stormed the place."

"I don't remember anything about a Rolex," Johnson said.

"I don't mean to question your powers of recollection, Sergeant, but do you think you could check?"

"It's not exactly my job to indulge your whims, Diamond."

"Forgive me Sergeant, I haven't had time to study your job description. I only asked because you volunteered assistance. It can wait until I catch up with Lieutenant Lopez."

"You just love getting the hair on the back of my neck up, don't you Diamond?"

"Absolutely not, Sergeant," I said, trying not to envision it.

Johnson let me wait it out for almost a full minute.

"Sullivan," he said to the desk sergeant, "put down the doughnut and get on your PC. See if there's any mention of a Rolex in the Chancellor crime scene report."

Johnson and I stood fidgeting and avoiding eye contact while Sullivan did his research. I hummed "California Dreamin' " silently in my mind to pass the time.

"Nothing," said Sullivan finally.

"That satisfy your curiosity, Diamond?" asked Johnson.

"Actually it makes me wonder which of your colleagues decided that it wouldn't be missed."

"Are you suggesting that one of the attending officers stole a watch?"

"Don't tell me it doesn't happen."

"What proof do you have that there was a Rolex there to begin with?"

"Just the word of a murder suspect. But if it was there, whoever grabbed it was adding evidence tampering to grand theft wristwatch."

"That's a serious charge, Diamond."

"That it is, Sergeant Johnson, and tough luck for Lefty that I have no way to follow it up. Right?"

"I don't know," he mumbled.

I could feel the nibble. I quickly took in some line.

"Then again, the lieutenant did express her willingness to dig around if I could hand her a shovel. Tell her I'll call later. Maybe she'll think it's worth looking into."

"I'll look into it, Diamond," he said. "Just do me a favor and keep your theory between us until you hear from me."

"Fair enough, Sergeant. Thanks."

"Don't thank me, Diamond. And wipe that big-game fisherman grin off your face. Don't think you're smart enough to play me without the sheet music."

So much for the brilliant strategist attitude.

"My mistake, Sergeant. I forget humility from time to time."

"Well, then, it's a good thing you have my handsome face to remind you."

"Yes it is, Sergeant," I said.

Suddenly he was much easier to look at.

"I'll be in touch," he said, and turned to walk away.

I continued on to the courthouse.

I told Hank that lunch was on me. Cuisine and venue his choice. At ten past noon we sat on a park bench across from the Hall of Justice, each holding a hot dog from the nearby stand, napkins tucked under our legs against the wind.

I took a gulp of my Orange Crush and got to it.

"Hank, tell me about Chancellor and Ryder."

"They didn't get along."

"So I've heard. Can you be more specific?"

"I don't know, Jake. There was something between them, but I really don't know what it was."

"Fine," I said, "disclaimer noted."

"Okay, for what it's worth. Last week, just before Judge Chancellor took the long weekend at his cabin, I asked him what he thought of the prospect of Lowell Ryder as the next DA. I'd seen the two go at each other, in the courtroom and in the hallways, so I pretty much knew where Chancellor stood. We were on the elevator alone, it was too quiet for me, I guess that I just asked the obvious to make conversation. His answer surprised me."

"Which was what?"

"The judge said that Lowell Ryder would never be San Francisco DA. Those were his exact words, with an emphasis on the *never.*"

"Do you think it would have worried Ryder any?"

"I doubt it. Ryder is so favored I can't see how Chancellor could have touched him, even with the help of the Judge's buddy, Governor Krupp."

"What do you think motivated Chancellor's vehemence?"

"I really couldn't guess, Jake."

"Couldn't or wouldn't, Hank?"

"Can't say, Jake. Not enough information."

I popped the last of the hot dog into my mouth, wiped the glob of mustard from my lip, drained the orange soda, and thanked Hank for his time.

The bad taste in my mouth had nothing to do with the meal.

Eleven

D<small>ARLENE," I SAID, WALKING</small> into the office, "I need you to get together with Buzz Stanley again."

"Please, Jake, have mercy."

"We need to know if there was anything in the wind about
trouble between Lowell Ryder and Judge Chancellor. It's a shot
in the dark. Run it by your cousin Edie, as well. Did you reach
Vinnie?"

"No."

"Keep trying. How about Joey Russo?"

"He said you can call him whenever you're ready to go to San
Quentin," Darlene said. "Joey said that Johnny Boy Carlucci isn't
going anywhere."

"I'll be in my office," I said, moving toward the back.

I walked through the connecting door and shut it behind me.
I opened the two large windows to let out the stale air and let in
the noise from the avenue below. I flipped the switch on the pole
fan and pointed it toward my desk chair and the window behind
it. I hoped it would clear the atmosphere. I sat and lit a Camel
to test the theory.

I called Joey Russo.

"How does this afternoon sound?" I asked.

"Works for me. I'll pick you up at four," he said.

I grabbed a flyer off a pile on the desk, advertising a new sandwich joint up the street, and turned it to the blank side. I drew two vertical lines down the sheet, dividing it into three approximately equal parts.

I wrote a heading at the top of each column.

It was inventory time.

Things I think I know

Lefty Wright didn't kill Judge Chancellor.
Someone paid Vic Vigoda to lure Lefty to the scene.
Vic Vigoda played poker.
Vic Vigoda was expendable.
Someone lifted the Rolex at Chancellor's place.
Freddie Cash played poker.
Freddie Cash had nine toes.

I walked back out to Darlene's desk.

"Darlene," I asked, "how could we find information about Freddie Cash's medical history?"

"That's not always easy," she said. "Medical records are for the most part treated as confidential. If we knew his PCP, maybe I could convince a gullible receptionist that I'm with an insurance company doing some background and ask a few questions. Do we know his PCP?"

"I don't even know what that is, Darlene," I complained. "It sounds like an automobile valve."

"Right. I forgot that you stopped going to the doctor when the idiot kept insisting that you quit smoking. Primary care physician. Didn't you mention that Freddie was in law school?"

"Yes."

"Then he would have taken some kind of physical examination," Darlene said. "I'll see what I can find out."

"Good."

"What are we looking for?" she asked.

"A toe count," I said.

I went back to my list.

I walked back out front, poured a cup of coffee, and walked back to my desk. As I sat down I could hear the new tenant in the office above doing what could only be jumping jacks. A piece of paint from the ceiling dropped onto the middle of the desk.

I designated the third column "Things I'll never know." Instead of getting started on what could have easily been the longest slate, I reviewed the progress on column two.

Sergeant Johnson was looking into the missing watch. Darlene would be looking into Freddie's toe count and Chancellor's problem with Ryder. I could put Vinnie on the poker question, try to confirm if Freddie and Vic had ever sat at the same table.

Just before four, Joey picked me up.

"When we see Carlucci, let me do all the talking," Joey said as we pulled into the parking area at San Quentin.

Twenty minutes later Joey and I sat in metal folding chairs in the corridor outside John Carlucci's prison cell. On the other side of the bars, Carlucci paced, ranting about the 49ers' offensive line in a high-pitched goodfellas' voice.

Joey patiently waited for Carlucci to shut up.

The guard who had set us outside the cell had admonished us to refrain from reaching between the bars for any reason.

I felt as if we were in a movie scene, a cross between *The Silence of the Lambs* and *My Cousin Vinnie.*

When we finally got down to business, John Carlucci made it clear that there was no grass growing between his toes.

"Judge Chancellor was never what you would call San Francisco's most beloved citizen," said Carlucci.

"I can't argue that, John. We were hoping for something a bit more concrete."

"Joey, look at me. I'm sitting here in a cage. How would I know any more about what's going on out in the street than you guys do?"

It was a trick question, and Joey treated it as such. With a cherry on top.

"You could be in Siberia, John, and know more than we do."

Carlucci ate it up.

"Chancellor was in to visit me less than a week ago. They gave the judge a much nicer chair, by the way. The judge said he had obtained a lead on information that he wanted explored. Chancellor said he wanted to ask my brother Tony to do the looking, and he came to get my blessing."

"Did he give any particulars," Joey asked, "about what he wanted explored?"

"Chancellor said he was trying to locate someone," Carlucci said, "that he had some kind of document that might help in the search. I stopped the judge before he went any further. I wasn't really interested in the details; I have other things on my mind, like when the prison cafeteria will serve creamed spinach again."

"That was it?" I blurted.

Joey cleared his throat.

"I told Chancellor he could go ahead and see my brother about it, and I quoted him a price for services," said Carlucci. "I guess he never got to talk with Tony."

"A document?" Joey said.

"That's all I can tell you, Russo. It must have been something pretty important to the judge, because he was willing to pay ten thousand for the research. If it were that valuable an item, I would have expected the police would have found it in his safe. Did the kid they have in jail empty the safe?"

"According to what Lefty Wright told Diamond," Joey said, "Wright took cash, a gun and a gold chain, and left some other jewelry and coins."

"What about papers?"

"Papers?" asked Joey.

"A will, insurance policies, birth certificate, passport, personal papers, whatever?" said Carlucci.

61

"Lefty never said anything about any papers in the safe," I said.

Joey gave me another look to remind me that we had agreed he would be doing the talking.

"Look, I'm not the detective here," said Carlucci, "but let's assume that the judge wasn't killed because he surprised your boy Lefty in the act. Let's assume that the kid is alert enough to hear Chancellor coming and coolheaded enough to get out of the place without having to knife the poor bastard. I mean that's what all this is about, am I right?"

"Yes," said Joey.

"If Chancellor was killed to keep him quiet about something in this document he alluded to, then whoever killed him wouldn't leave the thing behind. If there was nothing in the safe that fits the description, then someone grabbed it or it's still in Chancellor's house, at his office, or at his place in the woods."

Joey looked as if he had another question or two, but when Johnny Boy raised his hand in front of his face, Joey remained mute.

"Now, if you'll excuse me," Carlucci said, "I think it's time for the poison they call dinner around here."

"Thanks, John," Joey said, and almost dragged me out of the cell block.

"Do you think Carlucci has any idea what he's talking about?" I asked Joey as we walked to the car.

"It's not out of the question," Joey suggested. "Where to?"

"How about Vallejo Street Station? I'd like to ask Lefty about Judge Chancellor's personal papers."

T w e l v e

JOEY DROPPED ME IN FRONT of the Vallejo Street Station a few minutes before six. I knew his wife would be waiting for him for dinner, so I thanked him and told him that I would walk back to my office from there. I asked the desk sergeant if I could speak with Lefty Wright and was told to take a seat. Five minutes later Lieutenant Laura Lopez came up behind me.

"Got a minute, Diamond?" she asked.

"For you, Lieutenant. Anytime."

I followed her to her office on the second floor.

"I need your help, Jake," she said, when we were seated across her desk.

The use of my first name was suspect.

"Oh," I said.

"I have a lab report here," Lopez said, tapping a folder on the desktop, "which suggests that the money found on Lefty Wright at the Chancellor house didn't come out of the safe."

"I don't follow," I said. Since I didn't.

"The bundles of money had traces of soil and grass stains and were slightly damp. The crime scene investigators are positive that the cash was sitting outside the house under a fieldstone below the entry window. Your boy had the money before he went in."

I wasn't a lawyer and I wasn't in court, but I knew enough not to ask a question that I didn't know the answer to.

"Why would Lefty have gone in, if it wasn't for the cash that wasn't in the safe?" Lopez said, asking for me.

"I don't know," I confessed.

"I've got a couple of ideas. One, Wright went in to wait for Chancellor with intent to kill. Two, he went in for something else in addition to the five grand outside. Since nothing was found on him to support the latter, you can see where this hurts his murder defense. In any case, he knows more than he's telling us, and more than he's telling you by the look on your face."

I'm sure it was really something. I wanted to ask her why she was being so candid, but I felt pretty certain she was about to tell me.

"So, as I said, Jake, I could use your help," she continued. "I tried reasoning with Wright earlier, and he's not being smart. Talk to him."

"With all due respect, Lieutenant," I said, "I'm not in the business of grilling my clients for the police."

"I understand that, Diamond. But I'm assuming that you are in the business of trying to help your clients, and you have one downstairs that needs a lot of help. Give it some thought."

"Can I see him?" I asked.

"Sure."

"In private?"

"I'm being cordial, Diamond. Don't insult me."

"Sorry."

"Get out of here. If you hurry Lefty might share his dinner with you," she said, and put her face into the crime scene report until I was out of the office.

A uniformed officer locked me into the cell with Lefty and told me to yell when I needed out.

"Would you like half of this burrito, Jake," Lefty asked when the cop left.

"I was hoping for the whole enchilada, Lefty," I answered.

"You've been talking with Lieutenant Lopez."

"Actually, Lopez did most of the talking. I more or less sat there looking like an idiot. I don't particularly care for being played by my own client," I said, "it sort of defeats the purpose."

Wright began to say something but I stopped him.

"Look, Lefty, here's the deal. If you really need my help, tell me everything and give me a fair chance to decide. If you don't need my help, take it easy and good luck."

"Vigoda came to me with an offer of fifteen thousand dollars to pull something out of Chancellor's safe," Lefty said. "Five grand down, outside the house, and the balance later. I suppose Vic got a fee for finding someone for the job, which didn't do him much good. I was supposed to be out by eight, but when I first went there at just after seven, the neighbors had a party going so I had to leave and come back."

"What were you after?" I asked.

"There was a metal document box. I was told that I would find a nine-by-twelve-inch envelope. All I had to do was to get it out of the safe, and I'd collect another ten grand."

"Did you find it?"

"There were no envelopes at all, so I turned to leave. I spotted the watch and went for it. And then the cops showed up."

"The Rolex was never reported found, Lefty," I said.

"It was there, Jake. Someone lifted it. It might have been one of the cops who arrived first. One of them was cuffing me where I lay on the floor; the other may have grabbed the Rolex."

"Do you know the names of the cops that came in first?" I asked.

"No, I was facedown on the rug. I only know there were two cops to start, but by the time they let me up, the room was full of them."

"How were you supposed to identify the envelope?"

"There wasn't a single flat envelope in the box, Jake. I doubt there ever was one," he said, "I was just sent in to take the murder rap, I guess."

"That doesn't answer the question, Al. It could have been a box full of flat envelopes. Were you given a name to look for or any other identifying information?"

Lefty paused to think about it. I wondered what there was to think about.

"Alfred Sisley," he finally said, "for what it's worth."

"And that's all of it?" I asked.

"That's all I know, Jake," Lefty said, "and with Vigoda gone, it's probably all we'll ever know. What are you going to do?"

"I'm not sure there's anything I can do, Al," I said.

And that was the best I could leave him with.

I walked out of the police station and lit a cigarette. I thought about the Rolex and the envelope. I believed that the watch had been there on the floor. If one of the police officers lifted the Rolex it could have been a simple theft with nothing more sinister attached to the action. But it didn't explain the envelope that Lefty said he was being paid fifteen thousand dollars to take out of the safe. If someone set Lefty up by sending in the cops to bust him at the murder scene, and Lefty is carrying the envelope, then the police get the envelope also. And that only works if the cops that went in first were meant to take the envelope from Lefty before he got it out of the house.

And if there was something in an envelope that was threatening enough to kill for, and it wasn't in Chancellor's safe, then where was it, and who might still be out there looking for it?

And who the hell was Alfred Sisley?

I needed to find out who the first two officers at the scene were. I stamped my cigarette out on the ground and turned to walk back into the building to ask Lopez.

Instead, I turned again and walked down the steps of the police station.

I walked back to my office on Columbus Avenue to call and ask Kay Turner.

I couldn't track Kay down so I left a message with her answering service.

I sat at my desk and realized I hadn't eaten since breakfast. I went down to Carlucci's Restaurant for a bite to eat. Maybe I could kill two birds with one stone.

I sat at a small table across from the bar over a plate of ziti with meatballs and a glass of red wine, hoping for a change that Tony Carlucci *would* find me. When I heard his voice behind me I tried to convince myself that I was a lucky guy.

"Why so late, Diamond? My mother is going to be very disappointed that she missed you."

"How are you, Tony?" I asked.

"I'm touched that you would ask, Jake. What do you want?"

There was no sweet-talking Tony Carlucci.

"I was hoping you could tell me how to find Chancellor's cabin," I said.

"Doing a little real estate speculation, Diamond?"

"Just thinking about something your brother John mentioned this afternoon."

That seemed to satisfy Carlucci, and he gave me directions to Chancellor's retreat in the woods. I finished my meal, picked up the Toyota, and headed out toward the Golden Gate Bridge.

Judge Chancellor's cabin was just outside the town of Mill Valley, north of Sausalito, in Marin County. I drove through the town and found the road where Tony Carlucci told me I would find Chancellor's place.

Mount Tamalpais loomed in the near distance.

I reached an intersection at which a sign indicated Muir Beach to the left. I turned right onto a wooded dirt road and drove about a quarter mile. I caught sight of a lit cabin ahead on the left and killed my headlights, able to see the road ahead by moonlight.

The judge's cabin was a few hundred feet farther down on the right. I was pleasantly surprised to find the front door unlocked, then unhappily surprised by the voice behind me.

"No one home," the voice said.

I turned and saw a rifle pointed at me, chest high.

"My mistake," I said.

"You a cop?" the man asked.

"Private investigator."

"Have some ID?"

I showed him my investigator's identification card. Thankfully it was enough to inspire him to lower the weapon.

"Bob Gentry," he said, holding out his hand. I didn't hesitate to take it.

"Jake Diamond," I said. Of course, he already knew that.

"What are you after, Mr. Diamond?"

I thought that honesty might be exactly the right policy.

"I'm working for the man who the police are holding for the murder of the judge. I don't believe he's guilty. I was hoping to find something to help the cause."

"You won't find anything helpful in there," said Gentry.

"Why is that?"

"Someone would have beat you to it. A San Francisco cop as a matter of fact, or so his uniform and badge would suggest. Came out the night that Judge Chancellor was killed, it was the first I heard of the judge's death. The cop was in there for more than an hour. I doubt you could do much better."

"Catch his name?"

"Yeah."

"Remember it?"

"Hard to forget. Katt it was. Tom Katt."

"Did you know the judge well?" I asked.

"Sure, we've been neighbors here for years. Always played a few games of chess when he came up from the city," he said.

"He come up often?"

"Almost every weekend."

"Did you see Judge Chancellor that weekend?"

"We spent most of Sunday together. He left around seven or so, said he had to find someone and decided to go back early."

"Mention a name?"

"No."

"Chancellor ever mention someone named Alfred Sisley?"

"No."

"Have any idea who might have killed Chancellor?"

"No."

"Seen anyone else here that didn't belong, before or after Chancellor's death?"

"No, and I would have. I keep a pretty good eye on our little neighborhood."

I was sure he did.

"Maybe you could give me a call if you see or hear something," I said, handing him one of my cards.

"Maybe," he said, dropping it into his shirt pocket.

"Mind if I take a look around, anyhow? Just for the hell of it," I asked.

"I'd rather you didn't," he said, nodding toward the rifle. "Nothing personal, you understand."

"I do," I said, and made for my car.

"Well, good talking to you, Mr. Diamond. Have a safe ride home."

"All right, then," I said, "thanks for your help, Mr. Gentry."

"Good luck," he said.

I climbed into the Toyota, jockeyed the car around, and headed back out to the main road and through town to Sausalito and the bridge.

I had a pretty strong feeling that I was going to hear the name Tom Katt again.

There was no return call from Kay Turner when I reached my apartment, nor was there one on the office machine. It was late enough to justify saving the report to her until morning.

It had been a long day, but I wasn't sure that I would fall asleep if I hit the rack.

I poured a glass of Dickel on ice and read *The Count of Monte Cristo* until I was fairly confident that if I stretched out in the bed, sleep would take me.

It did.

Thirteen

I WALKED INTO THE office Friday morning at nine.

"Kay Turner called, Jake. She said she was off to a meeting with Judge Morgan and Lowell Ryder this morning to discuss the possibility of bail for Lefty. She said she would call you after the meeting."

I walked over and poured a cup of coffee.

"Have you talked with Buzz Stanley?" I asked.

The phone rang before she could answer.

"Speak of the devil," she said, with her hand over the mouthpiece. "Okay, Buzz, calm down."

"What is it?" I asked.

"Buzz says that he showed up at Chancellor's office this morning and found the place turned upside down."

"Ask him if he knows where the Turk Street coffee shop is and if he can meet me there in fifteen minutes."

"He said he'll be there," Darlene said, hanging up the phone. "Watch what you eat, Jake."

I refrained from saying that I would watch it all the way from the plate to my happy mouth.

"If Kay calls, give her my cell phone number," I said, and ran out to meet Buzz.

"So," I asked, hungrily eyeing a sausage link, "what do you think whoever rifled the office was after?"

"I don't know," said Stanley.

"Do you know anything about a document the judge may have received recently? Maybe in a large envelope. Something he thought important."

"There was an envelope, now that you mention it, brown manila, nine by twelve," said Stanley. "It was delivered about two weeks ago. I remember because the judge snatched it off my desk while I was going through the other mail and immediately locked it in his desk drawer. And I'm pretty sure it was the same envelope that I saw him stuff into his briefcase the following week, before he left for the long weekend at his cabin."

"Did you notice anything written on the envelope," I asked, "like a return address, for instance?"

"I can't remember."

"Come on, Stanley, think. Nothing? A name? Anything?"

"I don't know," he said, "you're shouting at me."

"I'm sorry. Did Chancellor ever mention someone named Alfred Sisley?"

"Not to me."

"Do you know why the judge was set against Ryder's bid for the DA's office?"

"It was personal," said Buzz. "Chancellor had a very close friend, Alan Jameson, who committed suicide six months ago. The judge blamed Ryder for the man's death."

"Why so?"

"Jameson was accused of insider trading, based on information he may have had about the sale of the company he worked for to a large conglomerate. Jameson always insisted that he had no prior knowledge, but Ryder went after him with both barrels. It was a very high profile case. Ryder must have figured that a big splash would kick start his bid for the DA's office. Chancellor pleaded with Ryder to drop the charges. He told Ryder that he was positive that Jameson was innocent and that Jameson was prepared to donate his profits to charity to prove good faith. Ryder went ahead, Jameson was convicted, sentenced to eight years in prison, and shot himself before reporting for lockup."

"Why didn't Chancellor appeal to his buddy, the governor?"

"The judge enjoyed his job, and rumors were circulating that Chancellor may have been involved in the stock scandal, since he was close to Jameson personally. It wouldn't surprise me if they came from Ryder. I guess that Chancellor was afraid to be too vocal in Jameson's defense, fearful of guilt by association."

"I can see why Ryder would be on the top of the judge's shit list."

"When Jameson killed himself, I could see that the judge felt guilty about not fighting harder for the man. That whole week after it happened, Chancellor was walking around the courthouse like a zombie. The judge would have done anything to derail Ryder's candidacy, but he didn't have enough clout."

Except that just before the judge was killed, Chancellor had told Hank Strode that Ryder would never be elected.

"So," I said, "you feel confident that if someone was looking for that particular envelope, it wouldn't have been found in Chancellor's office."

"I'm almost positive that the judge took it with him that day. It was the Tuesday before he died," Buzz said. "On Wednesday he went to San Quentin to visit a prisoner, and the next day he went up to his cabin."

My cell phone rang. It was Kay Turner.

"We have a bail hearing set for this afternoon, Jake," she said. "It looks good. I think Lefty will be out for the weekend."

"Why the change of heart?" I asked.

"I don't know. The judge seemed to think that Lefty wasn't a flight risk, and Ryder didn't really argue much."

"Well, it sounds like good news," I said, wanting to believe it. "What time is the hearing?"

"Four."

"I'll be there," I said. "Do you have a copy of Lefty's arrest report handy, Kay?"

"Yes."

"Who were the two officers first on the scene at Chancellor's place."

"Let's see," she said, "one was Philip Moss and the other was, I have it right here somewhere."

"Tom Katt?"

"Yes, Officer Thomas Katt, how did you know?"

"Wild guess," I said, "I'll see you at the hearing at four."

I thanked Buzz Stanley, apologizing again, and went out looking for Katt.

I went right up to the desk sergeant at the police station and asked to speak with Officer Katt. I was told that Katt would be coming on duty at three. I decided that asking for a home phone number or address would be a waste of breath.

I thought about bringing my suspicions to Lieutenant Lopez, and I came to regret that I hadn't.

Instead I called Joey Russo to ask if he had any way to get the information.

An hour later I was back at the desk in my office when Joey called with Katt's home phone number and street address.

I dialed the number.

He answered on the first ring.

"Officer Katt," I said, "this is Jake Diamond. I was hoping that you had some time to talk, as soon as possible."

"What do we have to talk about?" Katt asked.

"A Rolex and an envelope," I said.

There was a good long pause before he answered.

"I get off duty at eleven," Katt finally said. "I'll meet you in front of the station if you want."

"See you then," I said, and hung up.

At ten minutes to four I arrived at the courthouse for the bail hearing. Kay Turner came running up as soon as she spotted me. She was breathing as if she had taken a right to the abdomen from Lennox Lewis.

"Jake, Lefty is dead! They're saying he was killed trying to escape."

"Slow down, Kay," I said.

"Lefty was being transported to court from the jail and grabbed for the officer's gun in the parking garage. The gun went off and killed Lefty."

"That's ludicrous, Kay. What officer?"

"Thomas Katt."

"Were there any witnesses?"

"Not that I've heard," she said.

I felt as if I had been hit by a wrecking ball, which was trying to make contact with good sense and caught me blocking the way.

I could think of no reason why Lefty would try to escape.

I spotted Lieutenant Lopez and Sergeant Johnson coming in through the front entrance.

"What's this all about, Lopez?" I asked. "Where's Katt?"

"He's at the station, being interviewed by Internal Affairs."

"Lefty was assassinated, Lieutenant," I said. "I wouldn't let Katt out of my sight if I were you."

I turned away before she could think up a response.

I left Kay Turner standing there; she was still having trouble breathing.

I went out the back way past Hank Strode, who didn't say a word.

I headed straight for Katt's apartment on Divisadero Street.

The apartment building at Divisadero and McAlister was in the Western Addition on the other side of Alamo Square from my place on Fillmore Street. The front door off the street was unlocked, but Katt's door was locked fast and constructed of metal.

I went around back and climbed the fire escape to Katt's kitchen window. The window slid open easily, and I climbed in.

I passed through the kitchen into the next room and stood face-to-face with a German shepherd as large as a pony. We looked at each other for a full thirty seconds, each standing perfectly still. Then the dog moved slowly toward me. I reached out my hand wondering if I would ever see it again.

The dog gave my fingers a few good sniffs and then soaked my palm with his large warm tongue. I wiped the hand on his forehead and started going through the apartment.

In the top drawer of a dresser in the bedroom, under ties, handkerchiefs, T-shirts, and jockey shorts I found ten thousand dollars in fifties and twenties. I moved on to the other drawers. I was looking for a gold Rolex.

Something told me that I didn't have much time, so I went through the remaining rooms quickly, looking for anything that might help identify who it was that Katt, Vigoda, and Lefty, whether he knew it or not, was working for. I found nothing.

The dog tailed me, nudging me occasionally with his large snout.

When I was feeling too anxious to stay any longer I headed back to the kitchen with every intention of leaving the way I had come in. The dog followed me and took a drink from a large bowl of water. I heard a key being turned in the front door and was rushing for the window. Then I heard a gunshot. I froze, not knowing which way to go, checking myself for leaks. I heard something hit the door, and then the floor, hard. The dog was barking and I heard footsteps running from the door. I moved to the front window to see if I could catch sight of anyone going out. Nothing. I heard a door slam down in the alley, but when I made it back to the kitchen window it was too late.

I went back to the front door, slowly unlocked the deadbolt and opened the door. The key was in the lock. A body lay in the hall. He was as dead as Jesse James.

The name tag on his chest read Thomas Katt.

I walked back to the kitchen and put in an anonymous phone call to the police.

I looked down to find the dog looking up at me. I bent down, picked up the water bowl, dumped its contents into the sink and headed for the front door with the empty bowl in my hand. I grabbed the leash I found hanging on the doorknob and went out into the hall.

"Let's go," I said, as I stepped over the body.

The dog looked back into the apartment for a moment, stopped for a quick whiff of Katt's corpse, and then turned and followed me out to my car.

I stopped into a 7-Eleven for dog food and drove over to Darlene's house on Buena Vista. I carried the bag of food, the bowl, and the leash to Darlene's door with the dog at my heels.

I rang the bell.

When Darlene came to the door she looked from me to the dog and back to me again.

"What's wrong, Jake. You look terrible."

"I'm sure I do," I said. "Can we come in?"

"Of course," she said.

"Darlene, do me a favor," I said, filling the water bowl and placing it on the floor in her kitchen. "See if you have something to put this food into. And see if Sonny and Joey are interested in the game on Sunday. Tell anyone who cares that I'll be out of touch until Monday morning."

I handed her the two football tickets and walked out without another word.

THE ROUND TABLE

On the stage he was natural, simple, affecting;
'Twas only that when he was off he was acting.

—OLIVER GOLDSMITH,

RETALIATION

Fourteen

Lefty Wright's death hit me hard.

And that surprised me.

I really didn't know him well, but I had come to like him.

Lefty was a bright kid, he was covertly optimistic. Lefty wasn't an innocent, but he was fairly harmless. He did what he did well. Professionally, carefully, and with no malice intended. Lefty never tried to rationalize his actions with lofty notions like the egalitarian redistribution of wealth.

I was convinced the moment I met Lefty Wright that he would never physically hurt a soul.

I had a pretty strong feeling that Lefty wasn't done with me yet.

My first impulse was to jump in feetfirst.

I wanted all the answers and I wanted them yesterday.

I wanted to confront, accuse, alarm, and convict the culpable. I wanted to release the hounds. I wanted to be the thorn in the side, the righteous bust, the roadblock to the clean getaway, the unforeseen contingency.

I needed to hold my horses or I would find out the hard way.

I wanted to stop feeling partly responsible for what happened to Lefty.

I decided to take the weekend to mull it over.

I checked my provisions. A full fifth of Dickel, a half carton of

Camels, a ton of frozen leftover pasta from my mother's kitchen, and *The Count of Monte Cristo.*

I was ready to hunker down in my capsule for two days with all I needed to survive until splashdown Sunday night.

I broke the seal on the bottle of bourbon, fired up a cigarette, and picked up the Dumas book.

I don't remember much about the next forty-eight hours. I managed to feed myself, devour five packs of smokes, knock off most of the bourbon, spend short fitful periods of time in bed, and read when I could hold the book open.

In waking and sleeping dreams I found myself incarcerated in the Château d'If. The island prison off the French coast near Marseilles was the Alcatraz of its time. A life sentence was exactly that. No one departed alive.

Another prisoner had dug a tunnel out of his cell in an attempt to escape, which ineffectually dead-ended at my cell. He looked very much like Lefty Wright, and though no closer to freedom, the man reveled in our companionship, having been isolated from human contact for many years. We took turns making the arduous trip between the two cells and shared dreams of salvation.

One evening I crawled through the close tunnel only to find him lying lifeless in his cot, his body tied into the long canvas bag that would serve as his coffin. Shortly his remains would be taken by guards to the island cliffs and dropped into the sea below.

I lamented over the loss, over my return to solitude.

And then, at the very height of hopelessness, I saw what could only be seen from that desperate altitude.

I untied the ropes that bound his shroud and pulled his body through the narrow tunnel and into my own cell. Then I returned, crawled into the body bag, retied the ropes, pulled my hands inside, and lay waiting. Finally, after what seemed the better part of my life, I felt myself being lifted from both ends. I was carried out of the cell and down the long stone corridor. I felt the cold wind and knew that we were outside. I heard the men struggle with my weight up a steep hill and place me on the ground.

I heard the sound of the sea beating violently against the shore below. Soon I felt hands on my legs and shoulders again. My body took on the motion of a pendulum as they swung me forward and back between them.

I experienced the release that sent me sailing upward and outward and felt myself dropping through the air, forever.

And my body plunged into the frigid ocean.

And the glass of bourbon dropped from my hand.

And I filled the bathtub with hot water and climbed in to stop my shivering.

And it was Sunday night.

And from the bath I could hear the television. The Mets had eliminated the Giants from the playoffs.

And I dried my body, and dried my eyes, and ate cold ziti.

And I drank strong coffee.

I sat up and read Dumas until I was too tired to sit. Edmond Dantès had made it safely to the mainland. And he swore that he would find the men who had framed him and imprisoned him and stolen his youth. And he would have them pay.

And I swore that I would try to do the same for Lefty Wright.

And I went to my bed and fell into a dreamless, guiltless sleep.

Fifteen

WHEN I WALKED INTO THE office on Monday morning I found what was by normal standards a full house. Darlene Roman, Vinnie Strings, Joey Russo, Sonny the Chin, and Bobo Bigelow. They greeted me as if I were Neil Armstrong returning from a walk on the moon, which wasn't far from the way I felt. Seeing Bigelow's Mr. Potato Head grin made me think I'd made a wrong turn on my way back to Earth.

Darlene handed me a cup of coffee, and they started right in.

"Freddie Cash lost his toe to a runaway lawn mower. He was eleven years old," Darlene said. "His father rushed him to the hospital and then rushed back home to fire the gardener."

"According to Max Snail, who runs the poker games at Fort Mason, Freddie is a regular player and sat to the left of Vic Vigoda more than a few times," Vinnie chimed in. "Max can't say if the two had anything going outside the game, but they definitely knew one another."

"There was a second safe at Chancellor's house, in the downstairs study behind a portrait of Ronald Reagan. No brown manila envelopes," said Sonny.

Bobo Bigelow cleared his throat.

I looked at him for as long as I could stand it and turned to Joey Russo.

"You remember Spuds, don't you Jake?"

Bobo Bigelow, aka Spuds Lonegan, was an ex–car thief and present air travel consultant. There had to be a really good reason for Joey to have brought him in.

"How are you, Jake?" Bobo asked.

"What do you know, Bobo?" I said, meaning it literally.

"I saw Vic Vigoda the night before he took the swim. Came to me for plane tickets, San Francisco to New York, New York to Rio de Janeiro."

"Aren't there more direct routes to Brazil from here?"

"Sure. But he had me send the Rio tickets on to New York. Said he didn't want to carry them around with him. No skin off my nose, it was a lot more profitable for me and he paid in cash, nice crisp fifties and twenties. He also had me working on a passport for him. Too bad he never got to use it. I took a really flattering photograph of the guy."

Bobo was a real sentimentalist.

"Where did he ask the ticket be sent?"

"Tickets. There were two for Rio. Had me send them to some dame at the Plaza in Manhattan."

Bobo Bigelow was the only guy I'd ever met who could use the word *dame* and make it sound politically correct.

"The lady have a name?"

Joey took over from there.

"Her name is Brenda Bionda. Vigoda's sweetheart. She flew to New York the night that Lefty went into the Chancellor place. She checked into the Plaza and was waiting for Vic to follow. She paid for the room in cash. Twenties and fifties."

"How do you know?"

"I sent my cousin Sal over. He grilled the desk clerk before he went up to see Brenda," said Sonny. "She was expecting Vigoda. Sal had to break the news."

"How did she react?"

"She pulled a gun on Sal. He had to take it away from her. She had ten grand in her suitcase; she offered him five thousand to take her to the airport. So Sal put her on the phone with me," Joey said. "I told her that she wasn't going anywhere until she talked about the money and what she knew about Vigoda and the Chancellor murder. She said that I might as well have Sal kill her then and there because she wasn't talking about anything until she spoke with Tony Carlucci."

"Carlucci?"

"Yeah, said she couldn't trust anyone else. Poor misguided kid. So I told Sal to let her call Tony and call me back. After speaking to Tony, Brenda said she would talk but only to you."

"Why me?"

"Brenda said that you came highly recommended."

"An endorsement that I could have lived without. Can we get her back here?"

"She said no way. She's one scared girl—won't even talk on the phone. You may have to go to New York. Sal can tuck her away somewhere safe until you get there."

"Great," I said.

"I can get you a cheap flight."

"Shut up, Bobo, I'm trying to think," I said.

"And tickets to see the Mets and St. Louis when they get to Shea."

"Really?"

"Stay focused, Jake," said Joey.

"How long can Sal sit on her?"

"She's not going anywhere until you say so."

"Okay. I need a few days here. Maybe I can get there Wednesday or Thursday."

"Leiter is pitching on Saturday."

"Bobo, thanks for your help. Good-bye."

Joey helped get Bigelow out the door.

"What now, Jake?" asked Vinnie Strings.

I could use help from the others, but I really had nothing for Vinnie to do.

But if I didn't give him something he would drive me insane.

"The name Alfred Sisley mean anything to you, Vin?" I asked.

"No."

"Hit the streets, ask around. We need to find the guy."

Strings gleefully bounded out of the office to do his part. I asked Darlene to try to locate Freddie Cash, asked Joey if he could do anything to save me a trip to New York to see Brenda Bionda, and asked Sonny to get as much background on Lowell Ryder as he could find. I told them I was headed over to Vallejo Street Station to talk with Lopez. It was only then that I noticed the dog's head peeking out from under Darlene's desk. I'd forgotten all about him.

"Speaking of names, Jake. Does this animal have one?" Darlene asked.

"Tug McGraw," I said as I moved to the door. It was the first name that came to mind.

"He must be a southpaw," said Sonny.

"The dog is named after Faith Hill's father-in-law?" asked Darlene.

Joey Russo was laughing as I walked out.

I found Lopez in her office.

"Before I say anything, let's hear the department line on what went down Friday afternoon," I said.

"Lefty Wright tried to get hold of Katt's service revolver, and the officer shot him in a struggle in the police parking lot. Katt was briefly interviewed by IA and sent home."

I knew that if Lopez weren't skeptical, she wouldn't even be talking with me.

"Lefty was on his way to be freed on bail, why would he try to escape?"

"Maybe Wright wasn't so sure about the outcome of the bail hearing. Maybe he realized that even if he were cleared of Chancellor's murder, he was still facing parole violation and a third B and E conviction," Lopez suggested.

"I feel as if I'm missing something. Am I missing something? How is the death of Officer Katt being explained? A random incident of urban violence?"

"Look, Diamond. Let the police department handle it. There's nothing more you can do for Lefty Wright."

"Don't get me wrong, Lieutenant. I trust you. On the other hand, I have little faith in the department. No one seemed very concerned about who really killed Chancellor as long as they had

Lefty behind bars. Fewer will care that Lefty was iced. And one of your own officers was directly involved in what happened to Judge Chancellor, Vigoda, and Lefty. I'm far past having any doubt about that."

"You're talking about Officer Katt?"

Lopez knew exactly who I was talking about, but she wasn't talking about the cash I had seen at Katt's apartment.

Lopez was fishing. Hoping to find out if I knew more than the police did about Katt's involvement.

I ignored the question.

"I didn't have much interest in Chancellor myself, I never liked the guy," I said, "but now I know that Vigoda and Katt were killed to keep them from talking about what happened to the judge, and that interests me a great deal. You're wrong when you say that there's nothing more I can do for Lefty Wright."

"You're flirting with danger, Diamond," Lopez said.

"Well, I never got very far flirting with you, Lieutenant. Maybe I'll have the same luck with danger," I said, on my way through the door. "Thanks for your time."

I called Darlene to ask if she had located Freddie Cash. She said I could find him at the health club, the one he had allegedly been kidnapped outside of.

I pointed the Toyota toward Marina Boulevard.

When I walked through the door of the Bodies in Wonderland health club, I found myself in a narrow mirrored tunnel. There was a sign hanging overhead halfway down that read You'll Like the View a Whole Lot Better on the Way Out. It inspired me to test the theory without hesitation, but I bravely forged on.

At the end of the long corridor was a counter, which blocked further forward movement, and another sign that read Members and Guests Only Beyond This Point. As if this in itself wasn't discouraging enough, the person at the counter greeted me as if I were a postal worker with a grudge and a concealed Uzi.

She had a flat, round featureless face that mocked the expression "as cute as a button," a male or female weightlifter's body, take your pick, and a large plastic name tag that read Tammy or Tommy. The only thing that might have clued me in to gender was the copy of *Martha Stewart Living* lying open on the counter. But I could have been very mistaken.

I was banking that the voice would tip the scale.

No such luck.

"Can I help you?"

Tammy or Tommy had a voice like Alec Baldwin.

"I was hoping to find Freddie Cash," I said.

"What is your name, sir? I'll check Mr. Cash's guest list."

"What's your name?" I asked.

"Tammy," she said, looking first at her name badge and back up at me as if I was a moron.

"Tammy, please locate Mr. Cash and tell him that Jake Diamond is here to see him. Tell him that it's urgent and that if he doesn't appear within ten minutes I will break every mirror in the hallway."

"Wait right here," she said, jumping up to reveal legs that would have looked better on Richard Simmons.

"I'll be outside," I said, "if I can make it back to the door without falling down the Rabbit Hole. Tell Freddie to get into his street clothes."

Tammy moved quickly into the impregnable interior and I carefully made my way to the exit, looking straight ahead to avoid being immobilized my own infinitely reflected image.

I was pretty certain that I didn't look any better than when I had come in.

I certainly wasn't about to break any mirrors. It's not that I'm superstitious. I simply choose to stay away from broken glass whenever possible.

And I probably would have waited at least twenty minutes, but Freddie was at my side in nine.

"You caused quite a commotion inside, Mr. Diamond," he said.

"Maybe they can replay it for the aerobics class. Let's take a walk."

I settled for a bench at the Marina across from the gym and

invited Freddie to join me. I offered him a Camel, which he nervously refused. I looked out to Alcatraz Island, this time from another side. So far, I was still on dry land.

"Okay, Freddie," I began, "you can talk to me or you can talk to the police."

As inane as it sounded, I somehow knew that with Freddie Cash it would work.

"You were never really kidnapped and your father knows it. So where did the money go?" I asked. "If you can work Vic Vigoda into the narrative, so much the better."

"You don't understand, Mr. Diamond," he said.

"That's an understatement, Freddie, and that's why we're sitting here."

"My father didn't know a thing about it, at least until you broke your word and told him about the kidnappers taking a toe," Freddie said. "You told me you wouldn't mention it to him."

"Sue me. Keep talking."

"I needed money to pay off gambling debts. I was afraid to go to my father, so I dreamed up the kidnap idea. It almost worked, but somehow he suspected."

I almost felt sorry for the kid. He was so clueless.

"Nothing came close to almost working, Freddie. Your father was worried about you, he cares about you. Even now, after you deceived him and put him into a huge jam while you were at it. Whether he knew or not, he's guilty after the fact. You could both wind up in jail if this came out."

"Will it?"

"I don't know, Freddie. Are you still gambling?"

"Dad has me in a recovery program. I don't want to fuck up again."

"Keep telling yourself, Freddie. I don't care all that much. Tell me about Vigoda."

"I played cards with him a few times, that's all."

"How well do you know Lowell Ryder?"

"Not all that well. I'm just working for his campaign. It's more a school project than anything else."

"Don't let me find out that you're holding out on me, Freddie."

"I'm telling the truth, Mr. Diamond. What's going to happen to my father?"

"I'm not sure. I'll watch and think about it."

I left him sitting at the bench and headed back to my office.

Sixteen

"SONNY CALLED," DARLENE SAID when I walked in. "He wants you to call him. The number is on your desk. I'm going to take Tug out for a walk."

She went out with the dog and I went back to my desk.

"Sonny?"

"Jake, I'm working up a history on Ryder. Thought I'd tell you where I am. He grew up on an avocado farm in Folsom, a small town east of the state capital. Left for college after high school and never went back. I didn't get the details, but it seems he has a brother who served some time in prison, in his late teens or early twenties. An incident in a bar parking lot left another teenage boy dead. Might have to go to Folsom to get the whole story. I'm working on Ryder's law school years in the meanwhile."

"Good work, Sonny. Keep going forward. I'll check out the brother. Keep in touch," I said, "and thanks."

I called Lowell Ryder's office. I was in a flirting mood.

"Mr. Diamond, I'm sorry about what happened to your client," he said.

"I'm not sure I know what exactly happened, Mr. Ryder. But I'm determined to find out."

I gave him a chance to respond. He passed.

"In any event, I was wondering if you could tell me why you

think Officer Katt killed Lefty Wright in cold blood."

"I have no idea what you're talking about," Ryder said, "and I'm not sure that I appreciate your tone, Mr. Diamond."

Ryder was obviously not tone deaf.

I decided to put his hearing to the big test.

"Then you're really not going to like me asking about your brother."

"Mr. Diamond, I'm very tied up with work at the moment. Perhaps we should talk face-to-face, and I could clear some things up for you."

"That would be wonderful," I said, wondering about his definition of clearing things up.

"How about eight this evening? I could meet you at your office."

"Fine," I said, and hung up.

Minutes later I got a call from Jeremy Cash.

"I understand you had a talk with my son, Mr. Diamond," he said.

"That I did, Mr. Cash."

"Before I say what I'm about to say I want to assure you that I am not thinking of myself, only of Freddie. I'm rich enough and tough enough to take care of myself, but Freddie is young and soft and something like this could ruin his life. He made a great mistake, he realizes that he did, and it really didn't hurt anyone. I was hoping that it could be forgotten, that you could trust me to see that Freddie gets the help he needs."

"Mr. Cash—"

"Please, let me finish. I believe that you are an honorable man, and I would understand if you felt that you had no choice. And I certainly wouldn't insult you by offering to buy your silence. I can only promise that if you ever needed my help, in any way, I would be at your service."

"That isn't necessary, Mr. Cash."

"I would feel better if you would keep it in mind," he said.

"I'll keep it in mind, Mr. Cash. Good luck."

Jeremy Cash thanked me and ended the call.

When Darlene returned with Tug McGraw I called Sally. I felt like I had been wallowing in grime for days and that perhaps she could help. I found her at home and she invited me to drop over.

Sally French was my first client when I opened shop in San Francisco. I helped locate the mother who had put her up for adoption at birth. Sally moved up from department store clerk to entrepreneur, taking on more and more responsibility in running Bytemp, her newfound mother's successful sporting equipment wholesale enterprise.

And along the way she married me.

The turbulence of our marriage was due in part to Sally's insistence that I give up the private investigation business. And a lot due to my stubbornness.

When I look back I realize that I hadn't been doing my investigative work long enough or even well enough at the time to be so unwaveringly committed, and I certainly wasn't making a living at it. But it was my job, and at thirty-five a man likes to believe that a profession has been at least approximated. I was too vocationally insecure after my failed attempts at movie stardom to submit to Sally's constant pleas that I take employment in the sporting goods company. Going to work for my wife and her mother didn't seem the best route to a sense of personal self-worth and accomplishment.

I have since convinced myself that the stubborn decision to stay with Diamond Investigation was the right one. Unfortunately, I wasn't as confident during our marriage and had a difficult time justifying my position.

The truth be told, I didn't try for very long. I intuitively knew what I wanted to do and what I didn't want to do, but I couldn't make Sally understand what was not all that clear to me.

And in short time I gave up the attempt entirely, and it left both Sally and me frustrated and vulnerable.

So here we were, five years later. Sitting in the kitchen of the large house near the Presidio that we shared when we were married, slowly getting to know each other for the first time. And now I could explain, to anyone who cared to listen, why I felt that my work was valuable and haphazardly admirable.

There were times, however, the past week being a good example, when I felt as if I were swimming in a pool of thick mud. When the ugliness I saw around me had me wishing that I sold Korean baseball gloves and Taiwanese basketballs for a living. And the irony was that lately, when I had those occasional doubts about my career choice, I turned to Sally for a shoulder to lean on.

"That's terrible Jake," she said, after I gave her a quick recap of what I thought had happened to Lefty Wright, "I don't know what to say."

"I guess you could say it goes with the territory," I said.

"No, I couldn't. Listen, Jake, I was a nagging brat when we were first married. I was thinking more of myself when I pressed you to give up your work and jump into mine. I wanted you to give something up for me, but at the same time I really did believe that giving up private investigation wasn't all that much a sacrifice. I was convinced that in the long run you would be better off getting out before it sucked you in too deep."

"And here I am proving your case."

"No. I think differently now. I'm no longer afraid of how the job might affect you morally. I know that you're strong enough to rise above the murk and that you do help people who need someone and you won't sink down into it with them."

"But?"

"But I am afraid of the physical threat. I can't help feeling that there are less dangerous ways that you can make a living helping people. The last thing I want is to sound preachy, unsympathetic, or discouraging. I just worry about your safety."

"I'm bulletproof, Sally."

"Don't mock me, Jake. I'm serious and it isn't easy to say these things to you. Please trust that my intentions are unselfish."

"I absolutely do. And what's more, I appreciate the concern. But for now, it's too late for Lefty Wright to turn to someone else."

"Okay. Then do what you have to do and stop whining about it. And be very careful," she said. "We have time for dinner before you get back to work. Let's go to Little Mike's. It's near your office, and I'm in the mood for fried food and cheap wine."

When it was nearly eight we rose to leave the restaurant.

"Are you going to be in town this week?" I asked.

"Yes. Call me and do me a favor until then."

"What's that?"

"Keep dodging those bullets," she said, kissing me lightly on the cheek.

I put Sally in a cab on Columbus Avenue and walked over to the office to meet Lowell Ryder. I didn't notice the silver Mercedes at the curb until a voice called to me from its interior.

"Mr. Diamond."

I walked over to the vehicle and stooped to peer into the open passenger window. Lowell Ryder sat behind the steering wheel.

"I would like to speak frankly with you, Mr. Diamond, if you would be kind enough to grant me the privilege."

"I suppose you'll want me to get into the car."

"If you wouldn't mind."

"What the heck," I said, and climbed in.

"I'd like to tell you a story," he said when I was settled in.

"Like once upon a time?"

"No. I think that you are too intelligent to believe in fairy tales."

"Don't overestimate me. Care if I smoke?"

"Go right ahead."

I lit a Camel and turned to face him.

"Okay, the floor is all yours," I said.

"I don't know if you're aware that I'm a Stanford graduate, graduated with honors in fact, third in my class."

"I heard about the diploma, haven't seen the GPA."

"I was raised on an avocado farm, and my father wanted me to be an avocado farmer when I grew up. All that I ever wanted to be was a lawyer. My childhood heroes were Clarence Darrow and Atticus Finch. While other boys my age were reading Superman comics, I was reading about the great trials."

"Don't knock Superman. He had some great trials of his own," I said, hoping to move him off the soapbox, "and by the way, I was reading Voltaire."

"I have no desire to offend you or to be judgmental, I simply want you to understand how important a career in legal practice was to me."

"I think I got it."

"Would it be all right if I drive?" he asked.

"Sure. Taking me for a ride?"

He pulled away from the curb.

I tried to relax.

"I graduated valedictorian from high school and was accepted to Stanford for the fall. On graduation night, some friends and I went out to celebrate. My brother Chance came along with us. We did some serious drinking. Chance wasn't very accustomed to alcohol and before long decided that he'd had enough and left on his own."

Ryder headed out Broadway and turned on Van Ness toward Market Street.

"Fifteen minutes later I walked out into the parking area for some fresh air. I noticed that my brother's truck was still in the lot. I walked over and found him behind the steering wheel, he was white as a ghost. Chance told me that he thought he had killed another boy."

Ryder went silent for a while.

"Where are we headed?" I asked, not quite knowing what else to say.

Ryder ignored the question and kept driving. He remained quiet for a few more minutes and then continued on Market.

"In the parking lot, walking to his car, my brother heard what he said sounded like a muffled scream. He moved toward the sound and saw a boy, our age, on top of a girl on the ground. She was struggling to free herself; the boy was tearing at her clothing with one hand while holding the other over her mouth. She let out another yell and he reared back and punched her in the face. She went quiet."

Ryder turned onto Burnett and then onto Crestline Drive.

"Why are you telling me this, Mr. Ryder?" I asked.

"You brought up my brother, Mr. Diamond. I would rather you heard it from me."

Ryder pulled into a parking area and stopped the car.

"Is this where we get out and walk?" I asked.

We got out of the car and I followed him on the footpath up the hill.

The hill was steep and we walked in silence for a while. When he spoke again his voice was clear and calm. I, on the other hand, was breathing hard.

"My brother grabbed the attacker from behind and managed to tear him away from the girl. The assailant was immediately up on his feet and at my brother's throat. Then they were both down on the ground, the other boy had his hands around Chance's neck, and my brother felt as if he were about to pass out."

"What's at the top of the hill?" I said, wheezing.

"You've never been up here?"

"No."

"You're in for a treat," he said. "Where was I?"

"Your brother was about to pass out," I said, feeling close to it myself.

"My brother walked me over to a dark area behind some bushes off the parking lot. There was a body lying there. I checked to see if the boy was alive."

"And?"

"The boy was dead. His head was crushed."

"What happened?"

"As I said, Chance was feeling faint, flailing his arms wildly, trying to get free, and his hand hit a hard object. He reached for it, picked it up and smashed it into the boy's head. The boy went limp; his weight pinned Chance to the ground. My brother said that he could feel blood dripping on his neck and chest. He let go of the rock and pushed the boy off of him. The boy didn't move. My brother got up to see about the girl. She was gone. Chance dragged the body behind a large hedge," said Ryder, looking out from the summit. "Beautiful isn't it?"

We had reached the top of one of the hills at Twin Peaks.

From the heights we viewed a three-hundred-sixty-degree panorama of the city and the bay.

"I took my brother home. My father called the chief of police, Bill Gunderson. They had grown up together in that same small town. My father took Chance back to the scene, and my brother turned himself in to the chief. September came and I went off to college. That was more than fifteen years ago. Less than a year ago I prosecuted a businessman who had violated security exchange laws. The man was a friend of Judge Chancellor. The judge pleaded with me to go easy. I couldn't do it."

"I heard that the man committed suicide."

"I felt no joy in that at all, Mr. Diamond, but the man was guilty. In any event, Chancellor became my sworn enemy. The judge somehow learned about my brother's trouble and he warned me to drop out of the DA race or he would bring it out into the open."

"Why would something your brother did years ago, apparently in self-defense, undermine your bid for office?" I asked.

"It shouldn't have, but I couldn't be sure. The media are vultures, people are funny about family secrets, skeletons are skeletons."

"So you had to kill him."

"No, Mr. Diamond. I didn't kill Judge Chancellor and I didn't have him killed. But I wasn't about to submit to blackmail. I told Chancellor to do what he thought he had to do. I decided to make a complete disclosure and let the chips fall where they may. I was about to call a press conference for that very purpose when I picked up a morning paper and read that the judge had been murdered."

"And then you lived happily ever after."

"Mr. Diamond, I can't make you believe me. I can only ask that you suspend disbelief for the time being. Give me the benefit of the doubt. And if Lefty Wright was not directly involved in the judge's death, I will do all I can to clear his name. Isn't that what you really want?"

"What I really want is something you may not be able to offer," I said. "We'll have to wait and see. For right now, I could use a ride back to my office."

Ryder dropped me off in front of my building. I climbed into the Toyota and drove home.

I walked up to my apartment and let myself in. I went straight for the Dickel but caught myself just in time and put up some espresso instead. I settled in to do some reading. I was curious to find out what Edmond Dantès was up to as a free man.

I kept drifting back to Lowell Ryder's tale. It was almost too strange to be fiction, but there was a lot about the story that bothered me. Not the least of which was Ryder's concern that I might hear it from someone else. Who the hell was I to have earned a firsthand account?

Not to mention that giving Ryder the benefit of the doubt would push the progress of the investigation back to the getting-nowhere-fast stage.

On the other side of the coin, I was finding it very hard to believe that the mysterious missing envelope, which may have caused the deaths of four people, had nothing more to offer than fifteen-year-old news. News that was in the public record some-where. News that even Vinnie Strings could have managed to dig up given enough time.

Either Chancellor had something on Ryder that was far more threatening, or Ryder had nothing to do with any of it.

I put my mind on pause and traveled with Dantès to the Island of Monte Cristo.

S e v e n t e e n

THE NEXT MORNING I WAS up and out at dawn. I drove the Toyota over to Joey Russo's place to exchange it for my Chevy. Joey was already awake, sitting out on the front porch with a mug of coffee and the *Examiner.*

"Do you know how early it is?" he asked when I was out of the car.

"I'm taking a ride out to Folsom Reservoir."

"To do some fly-fishing?"

"A little research."

"Want company?"

"Why not."

We stayed long enough for me to catch up on the caffeine consumption and for Joey to sweet-talk his way out of whatever plans his wife had lined up for him that day. Thirty minutes later I backed the '63 Impala out of the driveway. Joey hopped in, and we headed for the Bay Bridge. As we crossed the bridge I looked at the sign for Treasure Island and Joey asked me what the stupid grin was all about.

"Just something I read last night," I said.

Folsom was a small village seventeen miles northeast of the state capital. The town sat on the American River, which ran between the Sacramento River and the reservoir. It was the small town where Lowell Ryder grew up wanting nothing less than to trade avocados for trial briefs. In less than two hours we were bent over pancakes in a small coffee shop directly across from the Folsom Town Library.

The diner was nearly empty but nonetheless held more people than were out on the main street. You could count the cars driving past the window on the fingers of a mitten.

"Strange place to come for research," said Joey, "unless you're interested in how long it takes a leaf to hit the ground."

"Actually we're here to look into a Reagan-era homicide. With any luck this burg has a local newspaper that they're so proud of, the library has it on film going all the way back to '85."

"They probably have the hard copies," Joey said, without sarcasm.

The librarian who assisted us reminded me a lot of my kindergarten teacher; inasmuch as they both resembled Casey Stengel. The major difference being that Mrs. Warren also had a voice like Casey Stengel. Mrs. Dewey, the librarian, on the other hand, had a voice that convinced me she had never been west of Sacramento or east of Lake Tahoe.

After explaining that I was interested in newspapers from nineteen eighty-five, not eighteen eighty-five, she set us in front of the hand-cranked viewing machine and brought over film from June and July of Ryder's high school graduation year.

"Do you need help threading it, young man?" she asked.

"No thank you, ma'am," I answered, unintentionally hurting her feelings.

We found it on the front page of the *Folsom Gazette* dated the last Saturday in June. An eighteen-year-old boy, celebrating high school's end at a teen hangout the night before, was found beaten to death outside the club. Folsom police chief William Gunderson was called to the scene by local farmer Calvin Ryder, and was met there by Ryder and Ryder's oldest son. The boy, Chance, nineteen, had come to turn himself in to the police. Ryder and his son accompanied Gunderson to the police station to be interviewed.

According to the boy, the dead teen had been attacking a

young woman and Chance Ryder intervened. A struggled ensued, and Chance hit the other boy with a stone in self-defense.

We followed the story into July and August. Chance Ryder was tried and convicted of voluntary manslaughter and sentenced to four years in prison.

Ryder's plea of self-defense depended on the girl in the parking lot coming forward. She never did.

"Find what you were looking for?" asked Mrs. Dewey, sneaking up behind us.

"Sort of," I said.

"Is Chief Gunderson still around these parts?" Joey asked.

"About a half block from here at his office, I suppose."

We thanked Mrs. Dewey for her help and headed for the police station.

When we walked in, the station was deserted except for a woman at the switchboard and a man at a large desk, reading. When we walked over to the desk, he looked up from the book and gave us a broad smirk. He looked like Luciano Pavarotti in a very tight cowboy costume.

"I love this guy," he said, holding out the book to display its cover.

It was *A Charge to Keep* by George W. Bush.

I swallowed hard and asked if he was Chief Gunderson.

Of course he was.

"Chief Gunderson, we were hoping you would talk to us about Chance Ryder," I said tentatively. "We were curious about the incident on graduation night back in 1985."

"You know what they say about curiosity, young feller," he said, "and why would I want to talk to you about anything?"

"Because Doc Brady told us that you might be willing to help," said Joey.

"Well, why didn't you say so. C'mon in boys, grab a chair. Just give me a minute here to drain the beast and I'll be right with you."

Gunderson rose and headed through a door out back.

"Drain the beast?" I said.

"It's a euphemism," said Joey.

"I'll bet. Who the hell is Doc Brady?"

"I'll tell you later. Think about what you want to ask him. I doubt you'll get more than five or six questions in before he starts itching to get back to that page-turner."

"That's a great thing to say to a guy who can't find out the time of day with less than three questions."

"How about I give it a shot?" Joey said.

"I can live with that."

Gunderson walked back into the room, wiping his huge hands on a paper towel. It was a good omen.

"So, what can I help you with?" he said, squeezing back into his seat.

"The Chance Ryder case."

"Ah, yes. So you said. It was a very big deal around here, as you might imagine. Both boys, Chance Ryder and Davey King, the boy who was killed, were real well liked by everyone. Never gave anyone any trouble. It was difficult to imagine Davey pulling something like that, forcing himself on a young woman. Jesus, the kid was the team quarterback; he was batting the girls off like flies. But at the same time, no one could imagine Chance hurting a soul unless there was a damn good reason. It's as puzzling today as it was the night it happened."

Gunderson went quiet and seemed to drift away. I had that uncomfortable feeling I sometimes got in the pit of my stomach, and it wasn't the pancakes.

For a moment I thought that the chief had fallen asleep. Suddenly his eyes popped open. Gunderson looked at us both and started up again as if he'd never stopped talking.

"No one wanted Chance to go to jail—it only compounded the tragedy—but there was no way around it. There were no witnesses, no one could explain or understand how or why it happened. The court gave him a fairly light sentence, and we all moved on."

"And the girl never surfaced?"

"Nope. Everyone wanted to believe that there was a girl involved, so we always figured it wasn't a local kid. A local kid would have come forward to set things straight."

"What happened to Chance Ryder?" asked Joey.

"He got out in three years; model prisoner we were told. We all expected him to come back here, to help his father on the farm. He never did. Chance finally went out to the coast. His younger brother was in law school down at Stanford, but Chance went south to L.A. He works in movies now. We haven't seen him around here since he left to serve his jail term, except on the big screen at the Globe Movie Theater up the street once in a while. He goes by the name Chance Folsom. Took the name of the town."

"Sort of like Vito Andolini," I said.

"Don't think I know him. What's he been in?"

"It's not important," I said. "Do you mind if I smoke?"

"Knock yourself out," said Gunderson.

We were running out of time.

"Is the father alive?" asked Joey.

"Still farming, but his health isn't too good."

"And you say that Chance Ryder never came back?"

"Lowell comes to see his father. I've bumped into him a few times. He's a big-shot assistant DA in San Francisco now. That kid wanted to be a lawyer since he was a tadpole. Chance never came back to visit Calvin. It surprises me, but so do a lot of things. Lowell says he hasn't seen his brother since prison."

"Thanks for your help, Chief," said Joey. "We'll let you get back to your book."

"If you see Doc Brady, tell him that I said hey," said Gunderson, not bothering to get up to see us off.

"Sure will," said Joey.

Then we were back on the street.

"Well, where does that leave us?" I asked, as we climbed into the Impala.

"On a rustic if desolate Main Street in a small American hamlet," said Joey. "Hopefully not for long."

"Who the hell is Doc Brady?"

"Thomas Brady is a medical examiner in Oakland. I've run into him once or twice around town," said Joey. "When we were in the library, I spotted him in a photograph, standing next to

Chief Gunderson and some others in a news photo from the crime scene."

"Why would Lowell Ryder tell me the story?"

"Because Chancellor somehow knew, and whoever clued the judge knew, and you threw the brother in Ryder's face. Then again, he didn't have to say anything, and experience tells me that unsolicited personal revelations are often attempts to keep the bulk of the iceberg underwater."

"I feel like I'm going around in circles," I said as we merged into the westbound traffic on Route 50.

It was a common complaint of mine.

"Did you ever hear the story of the guy who was having trouble pleasing his wife in bed?" asked Joey.

"Is this a joke?"

"Have you ever known me to tell a joke, Jake?" Joey said. "So this guy goes to the doctor and the sawbones takes one look at the guy and knows exactly what the problem is. You're in terrible shape says the doctor. I can see that you have no physical stamina. How can you expect to provide pleasure to your wife when you look as if you can hardly stay awake? You need regimented exercise. I want you to walk ten miles a day for two weeks. I absolutely guarantee that it will do the trick. Call me and let me know how it goes."

Joey stopped long enough for me to light up a Camel.

"Two weeks later the doctor answers his phone and it's his patient. So, how do you feel the doctor asks? Like a million bucks, never better, the guy says. And how's your sex life? How should I know, the guy says, I'm a hundred forty miles from home. Don't worry about going in circles Jake, just keep moving and closing in."

I dropped Joey Russo and the Chevy back at his place.

I moved toward the Toyota to head over to my office.

"You know where I am if you need me," called Joey, opening his front door.

"Thanks."

104

"Ever wonder what I do to make ends meet, Jake?"

"I've thought about it."

"Think about why you've never asked," he said, disappearing into the house.

Eighteen

D ARLENE," I SAID, WALKING INTO the office, not giving her a chance to ask where I'd been all day, "do you know what Joey Russo really does for a living?"

"Sure," she said, filling Tug McGraw's food bowl. I'd forgotten all about the dog again.

"Are you going to tell me or what?"

"No. If you're so interested, why won't you ask him?"

"I'll have to think about that. What did I miss?"

"Your cousin Bobby called. He's up from L.A. visiting his mother and wanted to know if you were free for dinner."

"Great, dinner with Mom and Aunt Rosalie. Lately they've been getting along like Tyson and Holyfield."

"Bobby said not to sweat it; he said he wants to take you out for steak. He knows your poison."

"Yeah right, like his mother is going to let him eat somewhere else."

"She has a date," Darlene said.

McGraw had ignored the food and lay curled at her feet under the desk.

I grabbed a cup of coffee and walked back to my office to call my cousin.

Of course my mother answered the phone.

"Jacob, I've been worried sick. I tried calling you all weekend."

"I had the phone unplugged, Mom. Why didn't you call last night?"

"I have my pride, Jacob. Are you all right?"

"Fine, Mom. Is Bobby there?"

"Yes. The poor boy comes all the way up here to see his mother and my thankless sister has other plans."

"He'll survive, Mom. Could you put him on the phone?"

"Are you coming for dinner tonight?"

"I don't think so, Mom."

"Very well," she said, and called Bobby to the telephone.

"Hey, Bobby, how's it going?"

"Great, I just landed a part in *Jurassic III*."

"Do you get eaten by a dinosaur?"

"I don't know yet. Anyway, how about celebrating over a couple of T-bones?"

"I thought you were on the Bugs Bunny diet. Do you happen to know an actor named Chance Folsom?"

"Sure, I know him. Did you see *Gladiator*? Folsom had a pretty good part in it. Remember the big fight about halfway into the film?"

"I didn't see it, Bobby. You think you can get me a picture of the guy?"

"I'm sure I can find one on the Internet."

"Could you do that for me, have a copy for me when I see you tonight?"

"I'll do better. I can probably download a photo and e-mail it to you. You can print it out there."

"You can do that?"

"A six-year-old could do it. You do have a computer and printer, don't you?"

"What do you think, Bobby? Hold on—I have another call."

I buzzed Darlene.

"Do we have e-mail and a printer for that computer out there?"

"Yes, Mr. Flintstone. Would you like the e-mail address?"

I wrote it down.

"Sorry, Bobby. Sure, send it," I said, reading him the address.

"How about I pick you up at eight? If I don't stop in to see Mom, I'll never hear the end of it."

"See you then," he said, and rang off.

I called Sonny to find out how Vic Vigoda's girl was holding up in New York.

"Brenda's getting real itchy, Jake," Sonny said, and gave me the phone number.

Sonny's cousin Sal answered the telephone.

"Sal, Jake Diamond. Let me speak to Brenda."

"How do I know you're who you say you are?" Brenda Bionda asked after I told her who I was.

"Brenda, you want to get out of there, don't you?"

"Yesterday."

"Then trust me. If we wanted to hurt you, it would've been done already. Answer a few questions, and I'll have Sal cut you loose. I'll even ask him to take you to the airport."

"What?"

"Was Vic involved in the Chancellor murder?"

"All he did was accept an offer of thirty grand to get into Chancellor's safe. Vic couldn't open a box of Cracker Jacks, so he brought Lefty Wright in for half. He had no idea about what was going to happen to the judge."

"And you don't know who hired him?"

"I don't know who was paying the bills. Victor wouldn't tell me. But he told me after Lefty was arrested that the cop was in on the deal."

"Katt?"

"Yeah. Tom Katt. What a fucking creep. Katt was holding a burglary rap over Vic's head, and making Vic dance all over town like a puppet. Lefty was supposed to get an envelope from the judge's safe and leave it out for Katt to collect the balance of the payment. Which, apparently, was all bullshit. When Vic heard that Katt had busted Lefty at the scene, that the judge was dead, and that the envelope hadn't turned up, Vic sent me here to wait. He said he was going to try to squeeze a little more cash out of Katt, and then we'd better take the money and run."

"Did Vic know what the envelope was?"

"If he did, he didn't say. But Vic knew something; it wasn't a recreational swim he was taking in McCovey Cove. And that's all I know, Diamond. What do I have to do, swear on my mother's grave?"

"No thanks, I believe you."

"That's great, especially since my mother is alive and kicking. The trouble is, maybe someone else thinks I know more and wants to see me do the dog paddle. I gotta get out of the country," she said.

Another dead end.

"Are you done with me, Diamond?"

"Yes. Put Sal back on. Have fun in Brazil," I said.

"I'd like to hire you to find out who killed Vic," she said. It was almost funny.

"Sure, Brenda, I'll let you know and send you a bill."

I asked Sal to deposit Brenda at the airport and went back out front.

Darlene had printed a headshot of Chance Ryder from the e-mail attachment.

"Nice-looking guy," said Darlene. "Looks like a movie star."

"Sure does," I said. "What time is it?"

"Almost four."

"I'm going home to convalesce for a while. Then I'll be at my mom's at eight if anyone needs me. I'll let her know where Bobby and I are going for dinner."

"You're not taking your mom?"

"She won't go out. She'll wait home all night to make sure that her baby sister gets back safe from her date."

I left the dog with Darlene. She didn't protest.

On my way home I stopped at Mara's Italian Pastry. I could at least tell Mom that we'd be back for dessert after dinner.

When I reached my apartment building I found Lieutenant Lopez waiting for me out front.

"I called your office, and your assistant told me that you were on your way home. Do you have a few minutes to talk?"

"Sure."

"Are those cannoli?" she asked, spotting the pastry box from Mara's.

"Come on up. I'll make coffee."

"Place hasn't changed much," she said when we walked into the flat.

"Why mess with perfection," I said, walking back to the kitchen to put up a pot of espresso. "Have a seat, and I'll be right with you."

When I carried the pastry out to the living room, Lopez was turning the pages of the Dumas novel.

"Good book?"

"Entertaining. It's about a guy who goes to prison for something he didn't do. Funny how some things never change."

"Look, Diamond. I'm here because of a promise I made to you. I said that if you could give me anything solid to go on I would follow it up. You still haven't given me anything. I'm here to clear my conscience."

"I've never held you responsible for Lefty, Lieutenant."

"That's beside the point. I'm here to give you a chance to tell me what you know or think you know. Everything."

"Okay. Let me get the coffee. Need a fork for the cannoli?"

"No thanks, I think I can handle it without."

I placed two cups of espresso on the small table between the sofa and my reading chair. I sat on the couch, since the chair was occupied.

"What do you know about the Cash kidnapping case, Diamond?" Lopez said.

"What I read in the papers."

"Weren't you working for Jeremy Cash?"

"You know client information is confidential, Lieutenant."

I wanted to know where she was headed before I accidentally jumped into her path.

"You play games, Diamond, and people wind up dead."

"How's the cannoli?" I asked.

"We found money," she said, shaking her head, "in Katt's apartment. A load of cash, in tens and twenties. The money that Al

110

Wright picked up outside Chancellor's house was also in tens and twenties, and so was the cash that floated up in Vigoda's wallet. If that isn't coincidence enough, the ransom for Freddie Cash was paid in the same denominations. So please excuse me if my curiosity compromises your credo of client confidentiality."

"If you're looking for a connection between the Chancellor murder and the Cash kidnapping, I honestly can't help you," I said, wishing that I wasn't being honest, "but you have to believe now that Katt was involved somehow in the judge's death and that Lefty could have been set up."

Lopez took a large bite of the pastry, washed it down with a sip of espresso, and waited at least a minute before she spoke. Lopez had a talent that I had never been able to master. Thinking a thing through before opening her mouth.

"It doesn't matter what I believe, Diamond. If I've said that to you once, I've said it a thousand times and I'm tired of saying it. I'm not an idiot. I believe that Vigoda and Katt were involved in something, but I don't know what. They were both walking around with a lot of unaccounted-for cash. And I do believe that Lefty was set up. But it's not enough to connect the dots for me. You haven't told me a thing that you haven't told me before. So, if there's nothing else, I'll take the rest of the cannoli to go," Lopez said.

"No need to rush off, Lieutenant. Finish your espresso," I said.

"I'm in a bit of a hurry; we're working on a big case. Trying to locate a German shepherd that disappeared from Katt's apartment. Do you have a paper towel," she said, rising, "I don't want to take your plate."

Lopez departed, letting me know in not so many words that the only worthwhile item I'd sent her off with was the cannoli. If she had come to clear her conscience about following all viable leads, I suppose the visit had done the job. If she had come to remind me of how little I had in the way of hard evidence, she had succeeded admirably. Lopez said I should feel free to call anytime I had more to tell her, using the word *more* very generously.

I had a hard time conjuring up a connection between Chancellor's death and Freddie Cash's phony abduction, telling myself that twenty- and fifty-dollar bills were pretty common. Still, I found myself suddenly very interested in who Freddie was in to for the gambling debts he kidnapped himself to pay off. I tried calling Freddie at his apartment and at his father's house at the beach. There was no answer at either place.

I had intended to take a short siesta before heading out to Pleasant Hill, but the coffee had me wired. I tried reading, but I couldn't concentrate. I was planning to pick up the Chevy for the drive over to meet Bobby, but I knew that the Russos would be having dinner and Joey would insist that I join them. I had little appetite for one meal, never mind two.

So after a quick shower, shave, and change of clothes I found myself in the Toyota, heading for the Bay Bridge.

Nineteen

I DROVE THROUGH PLEASANT HILL, heading for Hogie's Roadhouse in nearby Concord where I had shared a drink with my father years ago. I'd also been there a few times since Mom moved out from New York to live with her sister Rosalie after my father died.

On my way over, I thought about Bernie Diamond.

Bernie Diamond was a Jew from the Bronx. Bernie met Mary Falco, an Italian from Brooklyn, at a "Save the Rosenbergs" rally in Manhattan. They married after college graduation. Mary began teaching third grade at the local public school; Bernie landed a job reporting for the *Herald-Tribune* and worked for the newspaper until it folded.

Between weekly visits to the unemployment office, Dad wrote a book. The novel was about the younger brother of a slain president who decides to run for the same office. In the novel, *Promises Kept,* the former attorney general wins a close election, pulls our soldiers out of Vietnam during his first year in office, serves two highly respected terms, and is ultimately appointed to the Supreme Court. The book died on the shelves; a prominent book reviewer called it "science fiction." Undaunted, Bernie went on to earn a doctorate and a professorship in political science at Columbia University.

I hadn't spent much time with my father during the last five years of his life, after I relocated from New York to Los Angeles to pursue my film-acting fantasies. We shared an afternoon together when my parents came out to California for the funeral of Aunt Rosalie's husband. Bernie talked more than usual that day, mostly politics. It was as if he knew that his time was short.

When I complained about my waning hopes of becoming the next Harrison Ford, he put his hands on my shoulders, turning me to face him as you would a small boy. He must have considered it important, since he rarely crossed the line between the intellectual and the personal, particularly with his children.

"Son," he said, "before you aspire to making your name a household word, be sure that you know what the word means."

Then he jumped back over the line and went on at length about Dan Quayle.

Hogie's Roadhouse became extremely raucous at night; but it would be fairly quiet during dinnertime. I thought I'd kill an hour and then head over to Mom's.

I hopped up onto a bar stool, pulled out my Camels, fired one up, and waved the bartender over.

"Still drinking Dickel?" he asked.

I couldn't comprehend how the bartender not only remembered me but also remembered the bourbon I drank, almost three years after the last time I'd been in the place. I certainly didn't recognize him.

I could hardly remember who I'd seen that morning.

I wondered which of us was better off.

"Make it a double," I said.

"Are you sure you won't stay here for dinner, Jacob? I made a nice roast," Mom said when she greeted me at the door an hour later, "here, let me put the pastries in the icebox."

I had a good idea that it would go that way. I was so confident in fact, that I had picked up a couple of bottles of Chianti on my way over from Hogie's.

"Okay, Mom," I said, "give me a few minutes alone with Bobby before we eat."

"Of course," she said, taking the bakery box and beaming like a schoolgirl.

I followed her to the kitchen, opened one of the wine bottles, poured three glasses, handed one to her at the stove, and took the other two to look for Bobby.

I was trying to find out who wanted Lefty Wright dead and why. I thought that finding out who snuffed Chancellor was the key. Jimmy Pigeon had told me that the first three words in investigating a crime were motive, motive, motive. The only thing that had the faintest resemblance to a motive had to do with Chancellor and Ryder and the parking lot in Folsom, circa 1985.

I found Bobby in front of the television.

"What are you watching?"

"I rented *The Lost World*. I'm brushing up on the milieu."

"Any idea how I can find Chance Folsom?" I asked, handing him a glass of wine.

"I happen to know exactly where you can find him. He begins shooting a film in and around Denver next week. I found out he was doing it when I dug up his photo for you. Funny thing is, I was offered a role in the film but I decided to do the dinosaur flick, instead. I've always wanted to work with Laura Dern."

"What's the film Folsom is doing?"

"*The Cincinnati Kid*. Seems like all Hollywood can come up with these days are sequels or remakes of Steve McQueen pictures. Could've been fun, though. Hackman is playing the Edward G. Robinson part."

"Think you can get me on it?"

"In the movie?"

"A small part, or even as an extra? Anything that wraps early in the shoot."

"Do you have an active SAG card?"

"Sure. I send them fifty-two bucks every six months, and they send me another piece of flimsy plastic in another unidentifiable pastel color."

"I guess I could call my agent."

"Great."

"You'd have to get through an audition with the casting director."

"What've I got to lose?"

"And this is for what? To get close to Folsom?"

"Between you and me, yes. It's part of an investigation I'm working on."

"Like going in undercover? A private eye pretending to be an actor, I like it. I'll see what I can do, Jake."

It wasn't difficult to appeal to Bobby's love of irony.

"Thanks. Soup's on in fifteen minutes."

"Need any help?"

"No. Watch your movie, I'll yell when it's ready," I said. "Bet you're excited about working with Spielberg."

"Steven's not directing *III*. But I loved working with him on *Private Ryan*."

Bobby had lasted about two minutes on Omaha Beach.

"Why are they filming *The Cincinnati Kid* in Denver, couldn't the location people find southwestern Ohio?"

"Actually, the original took place in New Orleans. They were planning to shoot in Canada, but I heard they got a sweet deal with the Brown Palace Hotel for the big poker game, and there's a better catering service in Denver. And the way to an actor's heart is through his stomach."

T w e n t y

EDMOND DANTÈS HAD BEEN tossed into the sea from the cliffs of an island prison in a canvas body bag and was pulled out of the sea by the crew of a smuggling ship. Dantès had been fourteen years in prison. Now thirty-three, he could hardly identify his reflected image as the boy who had been locked up at nineteen. The priest, Faria, who had been Edmond's only human contact on the Château d'If, had died, giving Dantès the chance to escape. Faria had also made Edmond aware of the great treasure concealed on the Island of Monte Cristo, hidden by the Cardinal Spada to protect the riches from the clutches of the pope and the Borgias. Spada had died leaving the knowledge to the priest. Edmond lived for one thing only: to avenge those who had imprisoned him. To that end he sought to reach the island, retrieve the treasure, and approach his false accusers. And in order to do so without suspicion, Edmond Dantès would assume a new identity. He would go undercover, so to speak. Dantès would become the Count of Monte Cristo.

I hoped I could pull off passing as an actor.

The following morning I received a call at the office.

"Mr. Diamond, this is Cyrus Lentspring."

"What can I do for you, Mr. Lentspring?"

"Call me Cy. My therapist does. I'm Bobby Sanders's agent; he gave me a call. I think I can get you on the Denver picture. Two or three days' work next week, if you're still interested."

"Do I have to read for it?"

"No. The casting director trusts me, and they're desperate."

"It's that good a part?"

"It's not bad. Someone dropped out at the last minute. Ever see the movie?"

"It's been a while."

"Well, not much to your part. A long card game and a short scene following. Lancey Howard, the Hackman character, is the king of poker. The Kid plays against him. It's like *The Hustler* without the pool balls. What the Kid doesn't know is that the game is being rigged in his favor by a guy named Slade, the Rip Torn character in the original, who lost a bundle to Howard in the past and wants payback. You follow so far?"

"I think so."

"So the director wants to set it up by starting with the earlier game, where Lancey Howard wipes out Slade. Tells you something about the confidence Hollywood has in the ability of today's audiences to make intellectual leaps. Anyhow, you'd be one of the players in that early poker match, a small bit afterward, and then you'd be done."

"Sounds perfect. Thanks. I appreciate your help."

"Ten percent is all the thanks I require. I'll send a script over this afternoon. You'll need to find your way to the Brown Palace Hotel in downtown Denver by seven Monday morning."

"I'll be there. Who else is in the scene?"

"Hackman, of course, and the guy who plays Slade. Chance Folsom, he's not bad. I doubt you'd know the others."

"Okay. Thanks again, Mr. Lentspring."

"Call me Cy. My barber does."

I thought about calling to thank Bobby, but I wasn't sure yet how thankful I was.

I tried reaching Freddie Cash again. He wasn't at home, and his father wasn't sure where to find him.

I was thumbing through my copy of Stanislavsky's *Creating the*

Role, more or less to avoid having to face the dog issue with Darlene, how I'd dumped him in her lap and ignored him since, when she buzzed me with word that Joey Russo was on the line.

"Jake, I just spoke with Doc Brady. He remembers the incident in Folsom very well. Brady said that Chance Ryder showed up at the scene with bruises that would suggest a struggle, but that somehow his injuries didn't seem consistent with what he would have expected by looking at the dead kid's body."

"Did he speculate?"

"No."

"I may be able to find something out. I'm doing a scene in a movie with Folsom."

"You're kidding. What's the movie?"

"*The Cincinnati Kid.* My part shoots in Denver for two or three days starting Monday. A poker game."

"Not surprising. Who's playing the Kid?"

"I don't even know, to tell you the truth. I'll be done before he comes into it."

"They just love remaking those old McQueen pictures, don't they?"

"Let's just hope they steer clear of *The Towering Inferno.*"

"Anything I can do for you while you're gone?"

"Haven't thought that far ahead. I'll let you know."

"Jake. Do me a favor."

"Sure, Joey. Anything."

"Go out and talk to Darlene about the dog."

I'd known it was coming.

"Did she say something?"

"Just go talk with her," he said, "and make sure you come to see me before you leave for Colorado. And call Bobo Bigelow for plane tickets. I know he's a royal pain in the ass, but he knows how to cut corners."

I went out to face Darlene.

"Darlene, about the dog."

"Wait, Jake, let me speak. I don't ask too much of you, right? I don't complain much. I don't bug you for a raise every five years. I throw out the half-and-half when it turns to cottage cheese. I even tell your mother that you're not here when you are here, and that breaks my heart."

"Darlene—"

"Wait, please. I just want to ask one favor. I love this dog. He runs with me in the morning. He barks when someone comes too near the house. He warms my feet while I'm slaving at this desk. And he even likes the soy dog chow I get at the health food store. Can I keep him, Jake?"

I could have asked Darlene to give me some time to think about it, but I'm not that big a jerk.

"He's all yours, Darlene."

"Thanks, Jake."

McGraw peeked out from under the desk.

"You're one lucky pooch," I said to the mutt.

Darlene was almost as excited about my landing a movie role as she was about inheriting Tug McGraw. Darlene is probably the only human alive who has seen all the films I have ever done. She has gone to great lengths to hunt down videos of every one.

Darlene is hands down my biggest fan and has gone as far as to include me in the same sentence as Connery and Hackman on more than one occasion.

"No matter how bad the flick," she would say, "if Sean, Gene, or Jake are in it, it's worth checking out."

The fact that I would be doing a scene with Hackman contributed profoundly to her enthusiasm.

Later that afternoon the script was delivered to the office.

Since pinochle was my game, I decided that brushing up on the nuances of poker might not be a bad idea. I gave Vinnie Strings a call.

"Sure, Jake. In fact there's a small stakes game tonight at the Finnish Line in the Mission. Very friendly. We can watch the Yankees and Mariners on the big-screen TV while we play."

I knew the place; a subterranean betting parlor for irrepressible pony players like Vinnie. It might remind you of the joint in *The Sting*, but only if you had an extremely vivid imagination. It was San Francisco's answer to OTB, three mammoth TV screens pulling in live racing from Belmont to Pimlico to Santa Anita. Of course, wagering wasn't limited to the sport of kings. You could find someone there to cover football, basketball, hockey, baseball, and soccer; pro, college, even high school. You could also put down money on most of the local and national election outcomes.

"What are the odds on Ryder these days?" I asked Vinnie.

"Shorter than Mickey Rooney, Jake. He's running two to five. You'd get a much bigger bang for your buck betting on Hillary for President."

I told Vinnie I'd buy him dinner before the game.

I asked Darlene to get in touch with Bobo Bigelow for a round-trip plane ticket to Denver. She was so excited about the dog and the movie, she didn't complain.

The notion that I could learn something from Chance Ryder about what had happened to Judge Chancellor, Tom Katt, Vic Vigoda, or Lefty Wright was vague. There was really no reason to think that he'd ever heard of any of them. It was simply an idea. But for the moment it happened to be my only idea. I went back to my desk to study my lines.

Darlene entered my inner sanctum at noon and unceremoniously dropped a paper bag on my desk.

"Veal and peppers from downstairs. Eat up. I'm out of here in thirty minutes."

Darlene had told me at least a week before that she was leaving early that day to take her nieces to the zoo. Of course, I'd forgotten.

"Anything I need to do?" I asked.

"Just sit up front in the unlikely event someone shows up, and answer the phone if the spirit moves you. I'll take McGraw with us, I think he'd like the monkeys."

I tried to reach Freddie Cash again. Unsuccessfully.

An hour later I had put the script aside, realizing that I would get nowhere unless I had someone run lines with me. I figured that Vinnie would get a kick out of it. I had the Dumas novel in my coat pocket, so I pulled it out and started reading. I barely got my feet up on Darlene's desk when there was a knock at the door.

"It's open," I called, and assumed the looking-busy posture.

The man who walked in was in street clothes, but he was a cop if I'd ever seen one. I rose to walk around the desk and put out my hand.

"Jake Diamond," I said, "how can I help you?"

He took my outstretched hand tentatively and looked around the room. I invited him to sit and asked if he would care for coffee, hoping he would pass on the coffee, since there was none made. He finally settled into the chair across Darlene's desk, looking all the while like he was going to bolt. I sat and waited for him to speak. After a minute of silence I didn't know whether to try greeting him again or pick up the novel.

"Mr. Diamond, I'd like to remain anonymous."

"You're succeeding admirably. How can I help you?" I repeated, hoping for closure.

"I knew Thomas Katt," he said.

I made him for Katt's partner and did my best to be unthreateningly attentive.

"What can I call you?" I asked. "Pick something out of a hat, it doesn't matter what. It will make it a lot easier for me to form sentences."

I sat waiting again.

"You can call me Phil," he said, after pretending to think about it long enough for me to feel pretty sure that his name was Phil.

"Okay. Good. Now, Phil, before we go on let me assure you that nothing you say will leave this room."

Of course that wasn't true, and I doubted he would buy it, but I've said it so many times it's become a habit.

"I shouldn't have come," he said.

Jimmy Pigeon had taught me that fishing for information was just that, and there were more ways than one to land your catch. You could toy around and bring it in slowly with skill and finesse, or you could give a strong pull the moment you felt a nibble and hope to sink the hook. The way Phil was squirming in his seat I knew he was very close to being the one that got away. I yanked as hard as I could.

"But you did come, Officer Moss. And you care about what

happened to Katt because he was your partner. And you can't go to your lieutenant because you're worried about your job. And I'm kind of busy. So I'll ask you one more time for the hell of it. How can I help you?"

I held my breath. He got up, turned toward the door, turned back, and sat down.

"I think that Tom got himself involved in some real bad shit," he said.

"Do you want to tell me about it?"

"Do you have any coffee?"

"How do you take it?"

"Light and sweet."

I called down to Molinari's and asked Angelo's son to run up a couple of cups.

"Tom had been acting funny for weeks. I kept asking him what was up, but he wasn't talking."

"Funny how?"

"Showing up late, stopping while we were out on patrol to make phone calls, going off alone when we broke for lunch, saying he had to meet someone. A lot of behavior that was unusual for him. It just wasn't like Tom."

"And you can't think of anything that may have happened to provoke it?"

"I've been trying, but I can't."

There was a knock on the door, and Phil Moss jumped. I told him it was only the coffee and went to pick it up.

I placed a cup in front of him and took my seat behind the desk.

I gave him a minute or so to mix in the sugar and I pondered whether to try to move him along or let him proceed at his own pace.

I didn't have to be in Denver until Monday morning, so I decided to go easy.

"Take your time," I said.

"He was jumpy, anxious. And then the thing happened at the Chancellor scene."

"What thing was that?"

"When we came into Chancellor's bedroom we had our weapons drawn. We found the perp on the floor with his hands behind his head, and the judge under the bed."

"How did you happen to be the first on the scene at Chancellor's?"

"We were in the neighborhood. Tom was driving. A dispatch came over the radio reporting a disturbance. We were closest to the place, so we went in. The front door was unlocked," he said. "I took a quick look around the room and I saw a gold Rolex on the floor. I holstered my gun and knelt down to handcuff the suspect. Tom went into the wall safe, ignoring my complaints. Tom came back, kept the perp's head down in the rug and searched him, thoroughly, as if he was looking for something. Then the other officers ran in. I stepped aside to let the sergeant read the prisoner his rights. I glanced back to where I had seen the watch, and it was gone."

Lefty never mentioned that Katt had gone to the dresser and the wall safe and then searched him. Why? Maybe saying something could have saved him. Maybe not.

"Did you confront Katt about the Rolex?"

"Yes. Later that night when we were alone. Tom denied taking the watch, and I laid into him. I told him that he was jeopardizing both of us by lifting evidence, and that it was grand theft to boot. I said if he didn't find a way to turn it in, with a satisfactory explanation, I was going to the lieutenant. That's when he told me he couldn't give up the watch and that it was worth five thousand dollars to me if I kept it quiet. I told him that I wasn't interested in the money, so for good measure he threw in the fact that his life depended on it."

"Did he explain?"

"No. But he promised that he would if I could just give him a few days. Tom swore that if I claimed I never saw a watch he would never say differently. There's this thing about backing up your partner that gets programmed into every cop from day one. It's horseshit, but by the time the issue comes up, you're already hip deep in it. So I gave him some time. Enough time for him to end up with a bullet in his head. And now I don't know what to do."

"I can't tell you what to do, Phil," I said.

"Thing is, if I keep quiet to cover my sorry ass, then no one looks to find out who put the squeeze on Tom and who snuffed him. Unless you do."

"Don't count on it, Moss. I have my own agenda, and it doesn't include getting you off the hook and I don't share your sympathy for Officer Katt. My interest is in who's responsible for Lefty Wright. Odds are that if I stumble onto that, it will answer a lot of questions about Katt. Your partner was working for someone. He coerced Vigoda into complicity, and Vigoda enlisted Lefty. Vigoda and Lefty didn't know that the judge was going to be hit, but Katt damn well must have known. Who was he working for?"

"I don't know."

"I'm sorry to hear that," I said.

"Is there anything I can do to help?"

"I doubt it, considering your track record. I'll forget that I saw you today for the time being. I'm warning you, Moss, if I find out that you know more about it than you're telling me, I'll take you down."

I thought I'd better get him out of there before I fell into too many more clichés.

Officer Moss had confirmed a few things that I had been pretty certain about. But what did I really know?

It looked as if Katt didn't knife Chancellor, nor did Vigoda. They both had alibis. Vic was at Carlucci's and Katt was cruising with Moss, conveniently close to the murder scene. And killing the judge wasn't enough. Someone wanted the envelope badly, thought it was in the safe, and needed a way to get at it. That's where Lefty came in.

The killer waits for Chancellor to enter the bedroom and surprises him with a knife. In a struggle the Rolex falls to the floor. Katt shows up on cue to pick up the envelope where Lefty was told to leave it.

The envelope is nowhere to be found.

Katt is forced to keep Lefty breathing until he can find out where the envelope is.

And Katt grabs the Rolex.

Did Ryder figure in? What could I possibly learn from his brother? Did a rash of fifty- and twenty-dollar bills tie the Cash ransom money to the Chancellor murder, and where was Freddie Cash? Who was Alfred Sisley? What and where was the missing envelope, and where was the Rolex? I was shooting in the dark. And Jimmy Pigeon had taught me that it wasn't such a great idea unless you knew exactly who was there in the room with you when you opened fire.

I was going around and around in my head trying to fit the pieces together.

So I decided to give myself a break.

I called Vinnie to ask if he could help me run some lines. As I had expected, he was thrilled. I told him that I would pick him up at six-thirty, buy him dinner, and then we could work here at the office until it was time to leave for the Finnish Line.

With a few hours to kill before meeting Vinnie, no particular place to go, and a mild feeling of responsibility to man the phone, I put up my feet and returned to Monte Cristo.

The telephone woke me at seven-thirty. It took a while to re-member how to answer it.

"Diamond Investigation," I finally stammered.

"Jake, I'm getting hungry," Vinnie said.

Since I was running late, I called in an order of Chinese take-out and grabbed the food and a six-pack of Sam Adams on my way to Vinnie's place. I asked the restaurant to throw in a few pairs of chopsticks and two plastic forks, in case Strings didn't have any clean silverware.

Walking into Vinnie Strings's apartment was like stepping into a sixties black-and-white French New Wave film.

I placed the boxes of food and the beer on the only flat sur-face I could find in Vinnie's front room, one of those large wooden spools that were popular as furniture around the time Cat Stevens first released *Tea for the Tillerman*. What made this one more than simply anachronistic was that it still had cable wrapped around it. To my amazement, Vinnie produced two heavy white ceramic bowls. They looked as if they had been excavated from an archaeological dig at the site of a mid–depression era diner, but they served well as receptacles for cold noodles with sesame sauce.

We ate the other dishes, my spicy eggplant in garlic sauce and Vinnie's roast pork in roast pork sauce without vegetables, out of the paper containers.

I had brought along two copies of the end of my scene in *The Cincinnati Kid*, a dialogue between my character and Chance Folsom's character that takes place just after the poker game breaks up.

Between bites, Vinnie and I read the lines aloud.

It didn't take long to admit that the exercise wasn't going to help me much. It was no fault of Vinnie's. If you could say one thing about Vinnie Strings, it was that he tried hard. Vinnie had even affected a Southern accent while he read, having noticed somewhere in the script that the Slade character was from New Orleans. It was like having a conversation with Jimmy Carter on tranquilizers.

But that wasn't it, either. I was simply preoccupied.

"What's wrong, Jake? You look preoccupied."

I really didn't want to get into it with Vinnie.

"Nothing, Vin, I'm fine."

"Listen, we don't have to go to the card game if you're not feeling up to it."

"It's okay. I could use the schooling."

"There's nothing hard about pretending you're in a poker game. Especially when the cards you get dealt and how you play them are in the script, and you know when the camera is on you and when it's not."

"Maybe it'll take my mind off this case we're working on."

It had slipped out. And it was all Vinnie needed to hear.

"You know, Jake, there's something that's been bothering me about the case, but I've been reluctant to mention it because sometimes I feel that you really don't want to hear what I think."

There was no retreat.

"Sure I do, Vinnie. What's bothering you?" I said as sincerely as I could manage, while nervously breaking open a fortune cookie.

"You're pretty hung up about what happened to Lefty, right?"

"Yeah, I guess I am."

"Have you thought about why Lefty was killed?" Vinnie asked.

It was a good question.

And the answer was that I really hadn't.

"To close the Chancellor case?" I said, trying to sound intelligent.

"It doesn't wash," said Vinnie. "If Lefty was tried and found guilty, it closes the case. If he's found innocent, the case stays open, but by then the trail is cold as ice."

I'd said that very thing to Lefty.

"To avoid the possibility of something coming out if Lefty went to trial?" I said.

"From where? Everyone who might have known something is dead. The judge. Vigoda. And finally Katt. Whoever is behind this sealed up all the cracks. Who could possibly have been a threat in court?"

I suddenly noticed the small piece of paper that I had been unconsciously playing with while Vinnie had been surprising the hell out of me. It had come from the fortune cookie, which I had since mutilated. I glanced down and read the small text.

"You can expect to find enlightenment in the most unlikely of places."

It was an understatement.

"Lefty himself," I said, "Lefty knew something."

"That would be my guess," said Vinnie.

"What could he know? And if he knew something why wouldn't he have told Kay Turner or me about it?"

"I don't know, Jake," Vinnie said, "but you know he'd been holding out on you."

"I'll admit he was a bit reticent about mentioning the envelope he was sent into Judge Chancellor's place to get out of the safe," I said.

"Why?"

"I don't know. But Lefty told me that he didn't know what it was about, that he never found the envelope."

"So, why not mention it from the get-go? It could only have

helped his case, suggested a motive for the murder that went beyond a burglar caught in the act."

"I don't know, Strings, why did he hold it back? You tell me."

All of a sudden Vinnie had me hanging on his every word and treating him as if he had the answers to everything.

"Maybe Lefty did find this envelope," Vinnie said. "Maybe he was still hoping that it was worth ten thousand dollars to him."

"Jesus, Vinnie, I don't know."

"Just a thought, Jake," said Vinnie. "By the way, I've been asking all over town about this Alfred Sisley you asked about, and no one I spoke to ever heard of the guy."

My head was pounding so loudly I didn't hear the phone ring.

"Darlene," Vinnie said, handing me the telephone.

It was one of those old black jobs with a rotary dial and a handset you could have used for bench presses.

"Call Lopez. Right away," she said.

Darlene gave me the phone number.

I called the number. I could hear the commotion on the other end of the line when the call was picked up.

I waited while Lopez was summoned to the phone.

"If you've been trying to get hold of Freddie Cash, Diamond, stop wasting your time," Lieutenant Lopez said.

"What are you talking about?"

"I'm over at his apartment on Frederick Street at this very moment. I'm looking down at his body as we speak. I'm looking directly at the large bullet hole in his chest."

Twenty-one

THE TELEPHONE RANG, THANKFULLY waking me from a horrible nightmare.

I was sitting at a round poker table. I was looking down at the cards in my hand, a full house, aces, and eights. I instinctively checked my back. Finding no one behind me I looked up at the other players around the table. Freddie Cash, Vic Vigoda, Tom Katt, and Lefty Wright.

"I'll see your toe and raise you one," said Vigoda.

"I'll call," said Katt, picking up a cell phone and dialing the DA's office.

"I'll fold," said Lefty, bending an envelope in two and stuffing it into his pocket.

The table was covered with twenties and fifties.

A heard a phone ring. I couldn't find the phone. I heard a voice.

"It's Judge Chancellor, Diamond, answer the damned door."

There was a knock on the door, I called out.

"Who is it?"

"Alfred Sisley. Answer the damned phone," a voice said.

I found the phone.

"Jake, it's Darlene. Wake up and get down here quick."

"What is it?" I asked.

"Jeremy Cash is sitting in your office. I found him at the door on Columbus when I got here. I told him that I wasn't sure when you would be in. He said he would wait."

I jumped out of bed, and was at Darlene's desk in less than twenty minutes.

I walked through the door into my office. Jeremy Cash sat in the client chair, staring out the window with his hands folded across his lap. Cash looked as out of place there as Sir Laurence Olivier would have looked in an episode of *The Honeymooners*.

"Mr. Cash," I said, coming around my desk to face him.

"Mr. Diamond, I'm here on business," he said without ceremony, "I want to hire you. I want to know who killed my boy."

"Do you know who your son was in debt to, Mr. Cash? Who Freddie needed the ransom money to pay off?" I asked, in as businesslike a way as I could manage.

"No."

"Listen, Mr. Cash. I'm doing the best I can to try to find out who killed a former client of mine, and why. It's possible that it may somehow be related to what happened to your son. If that's the case, then I'm already working on it, and I'll be happy to tell you what I find out, no charge."

"What have you discovered thus far?" he asked.

"To be honest, not very much. And I'd rather not get into the details with you until I can establish a connection, if I can at all. I'm quickly running out of leads."

"Mr. Diamond. I feel the need to confess that I was not totally truthful at the time of our first meeting."

"Oh?"

"Freddie had come to me for money. A hundred thousand dollars. I asked him why he needed it, he asked me to trust that it would be used for a good cause. I told him that his answer wasn't satisfactory, and then he stormed off. That's why I suspected my son when the ransom demand was also one hundred thousand. I have never trusted coincidence. I can't help thinking that if I had given him the money, with no questions asked, Freddie might still be alive."

"Mr. Cash, my feeling is that simply handing Freddie the

money wouldn't have changed things. You were right to ask what he wanted it for, I only wish he had given you an answer. I think that where the money went, not how Freddie managed to get it, holds the key to what happened to your son."

"Who is paying for your services, Mr. Diamond?" he asked. "You say your client was killed."

"No one."

"Then please allow me to help you. It would help me a great deal, make me feel as if I was doing something for Freddie," said Cash. "I suspect from your efforts that we may agree that late is better than never."

"All right," I said.

What the hell. I couldn't work very much longer for free. I would be lucky if my wages for the film role would cover travel to Denver, getting a hotel, and maybe picking up a car to get around in. I accepted a three-thousand-dollar retainer from Cash for expenses, insisting that I would return what I didn't use and promising to keep him informed of my progress.

Cash handed me a personal check, thanked me, then turned and left the office.

I waited until I heard Jeremy Cash go through the outer door, then I went out to the front room.

Though I hadn't noticed on my way in, Darlene's dog was conspicuous in his absence.

"Where's McGraw," I asked, "leave him at the zoo?"

"Very funny, Jake, but you're not far off," Darlene said. "My boyfriend spent the night. I left the two of them standing side by side this morning eyeballing a two-pound slab of Canadian bacon."

"Think I have time to make it over there before it's all gone?" I asked.

"Cut it out, Jake. What happened in there?"

"We were just hired to find Freddie's killer," I said. "Jimmy Pigeon would have loved this one."

"Why so?" Darlene asked.

"We're probably looking for one murderer, but you'd think we were working four cases. Brenda wanted to pay me to find

Vigoda's killer, Officer Moss came to me to find Katt's executioner, Jeremy Cash wants to find out who murdered his son, and I'm all tied in knots about who killed Lefty."

"And you think that Jimmy would have appreciated the irony?"

"The part that would have tickled Jimmy is that this whole thing began with the assassination of Judge Chancellor and that I'm standing here wondering how long it will be before someone approaches us about solving *that* riddle."

"You can stop holding your breath," Darlene said, handing me a slip of paper. "He called while you were in with Cash. He would like to see you at noon for lunch at the Sir Francis Drake Hotel. He's buying."

There were three words on the slip of paper.

Governor Charles Krupp.

I rode the Powell Street cable car down to the hotel.

I was led to the governor's table by a kid in his early twenties who might have reminded me of Freddie Cash, if not for the white dinner jacket and wide-open eyes.

"Jake," Krupp said, rising from the table to offer his hand, "thank you for coming. You don't mind if I call you Jake?"

"Not at all, Governor," I said, accepting the handshake.

"Have a seat," he said, sitting. "What would you like for lunch?"

"I'm not really hungry, Governor. Coffee would be good."

I was actually starving.

"I think that you are aware that Andy Chancellor was a close personal friend of mine, Jake."

"So I understand," I said. Chuck.

"I'm very relieved that his killers have met with retribution, and that we can now try to put this terrible tragedy behind us."

A waiter brought coffee. I almost asked him to throw it in my face to wipe off the idiotic expression.

"Which killers would that be, Governor?" I asked, when the waiter was safely away from my coffee cup.

"I met with the district attorney earlier. It was suggested that three men conspired to burglarize Judge Chancellor's home. I learned how the robbery went terribly wrong when Andrew surprised the inside man. I was told how Officer Katt murdered his coconspirators to keep them quiet, and how Katt was later killed by a house burglar outside of his apartment. Quite ironic."

"Quite ironic, and quite an educational meeting with the DA, Governor, sir," I said, "and you're quite a fast learner."

Krupp looked at me with surprise. It was apparent that he wasn't accustomed to being talked to quite that way. I really didn't care.

"Pardon me?" he managed.

"Governor Krupp, I have no desire to offend you, but you have to be joking. Lefty Wright did not kill your friend Judge Chancellor, and it wasn't a stranger who murdered that horrible excuse for a police officer."

"And you have proof to back up these opinions, Mr. Diamond?"

"Of course not, Governor. If I had proof we wouldn't be sitting here having this ridiculous conversation."

"In that case don't you believe that it would be better to let it rest, close the book and move on. For the good of the city and the state, the peace of mind of our citizens, and the memory of a great champion of jurisprudence?"

"*Jurisprudence.* Nice word, what does it mean?"

"Mr. Diamond, you are coming very close to being insolent," Krupp said.

"Let's see if I can come closer," I said. "There is no peace of mind and there are no champions of jurisprudence when justice is ignored, and no one knew that better than Chancellor himself. I was hired by Lefty Wright to find out who killed the judge and like it or not I'm still working on it. You can close the book that was handed to you, but I'm reading a different translation. I have my own peace of mind to contend with."

"Mr. Diamond, you should be more concerned about the enemies you could make," said Krupp.

"Governor, I've been too busy lately trying to make friends to worry about making enemies. I don't need for you to like me if it's for the wrong reasons."

"I don't dislike you, Mr. Diamond. I'm only trying to do what I think is best."

"And you really believe that closing the Chancellor case is the best thing to do?"

"Yes."

"Then we simply disagree, Governor. I can live with that. How about you?"

"Will you keep me informed of your progress, Mr. Diamond?" Krupp asked.

"I truly don't know, Governor. I would have to be more certain that you were really interested and for what reason. Don't get me wrong, I don't distrust you, I'm just not sure yet that we share the same goals," I said, "and if you'll excuse me I have some work to do."

I left him sitting there and I walked back to the office.

"What happened?" Darlene asked the instant I stepped through the door.

"The district attorney's office wrapped up the Chancellor case in a neat if porous package," I said, "and handed it to Governor Krupp with a red, white, and blue ribbon tied around it."

"And he bought it?"

"That's the funny part. I'm not sure he bought a word of it. I started to get the feeling that all of his discouragement was meant to encourage me."

"I don't follow."

"I think that the governor wants to get the truth about Judge Chancellor's murder the safe way, without a high-profile investigation that might fail to achieve results. I think that he just dumped it right into my lap to sink or swim with. I think that I just had coffee with a very smart politician."

"Was the coffee any good?" asked Darlene.

Twenty-two

ONCE EVERY TWO WEEKS, on Thursday night, I played pinochle with Tom Romano and Ira Fennessy. Tom ran the Tomrom Detective Agency out of an office on Ninth and Market. Ira and his younger brother, Ed, ran FBI, Fennessy Brothers Investigations, out of an office on Montgomery. We took turns hosting the game, which on that Thursday was set for Tom's house in Pacific Heights.

We all loved the game of pinochle, but the get-together had additional benefits. It was a chance to catch up with each other's trials and tribulations, noncompetitively. We limited the throat cutting to the playing of the cards. We had even been known to help each other out from time to time.

It was not unlike group therapy.

We traditionally began the evening with what could best be described as small talk, albeit small talk with an often high level of enthusiasm. Movies, the latest classical CD releases, newly discovered breakfast joints, the cops to steer clear of. After a couple of hands, and a few drinks, we would eventually get down to cases.

Ira had just covered a six-fifty bid in spades. He bought two tens and the nine of spades in the kitty, buried thirty points, caught the other ace of trump hanging, and made the hand by five points. While I was shuffling the deck for the next deal, Tom brought up the murder of Judge Chancellor.

I filled them in on what I knew and what I thought I knew about the case.

"So, you think that the governor was actually egging you on?" asked Ira.

"I really do. I think that Krupp is cagey. He gave me a good push and then he scuttled out of the way."

"And your only suspect is Lowell Ryder?" asked Tom.

"Yeah," I said, "too bad, huh."

"It's weak, Jake," said Tom. "The guy is running for office, he has every reason to want the case set aside without having to actually be the guilty party. I doubt that what his brother did fifteen years ago would ultimately hurt the outcome of the election. Ryder is the biggest thing since sourdough bread right now. Put yourself in Ryder's shoes—well never mind that. But I'm sure you can see that if this case is the dead end it seems to be, it would behoove Ryder to let it rest. At least until after the votes are in."

"What about the Cash kid, Jake?" asked Ira. "Do you think there's a connection?"

"I don't know. Lopez put a bug in my head. I wish I knew who he was in debt to."

"You might ask Tony Carlucci," Ira suggested.

"I might."

"What is it, Jake?" asked Tom.

"What's what?"

"The thing that has you hanging onto Ryder. The thing that has you going off to Denver to play actor, to talk to a brother who hasn't seen Ryder in fifteen years."

"That's the thing, Tom. Why? Why did Ryder and his brother fall out of touch after what happened in that parking lot in '85?"

"Maybe Ryder is simply ashamed or embarrassed about having a brother who's an ex-con," said Ira.

"Maybe," I said, looking at my cards. "I'll bid four-fifty."

"Pass," said Tom.

"Seven hundred," said Ira.

"You've got to be kidding," said Tom.

"Pass," I said. I didn't have a single spade in my hand.

"I'm looking for an ace of spades," Ira said, turning over the three-card kitty.

Ten of diamonds. King of diamonds. Ace of spades.

"Those diamonds won't hurt," he said, smiling. "I think it's a lay down."

On Friday morning, I arranged breakfast with Joey Russo and Sonny. I asked them to put the word out through their pipeline that we were looking for whoever Freddie Cash was in to for heavy gambling debts and looking for Alfred Sisley. Before breaking up the card game the night before, Ira and Tom said they would do the same.

I called Troy Wasinger in Denver, to see if we could get together before the shoot began on Monday.

In the spring of 1989, I completed a run in an Off-Off-Broadway production of *The Desperate Hours*, in a basement theater on Third Street in the East Village.

I played the role of Glenn, the leader of a trio of prison escapees who hold a terrified Ohio family hostage in their suburban home. I pulled double duty as the set carpenter. My performance received a very good notice in the *Village Voice* and landed me a summer in Boulder with the Colorado Shakespeare Festival. My work in Boulder led to an offer to join the Denver Center Theatre Company for the 1989–90 season. It was an opportunity to earn an Actors' Equity card and four hundred twenty-five dollars a week. I leaped at it.

I met Troy doing *As You Like It* that summer, and he was preparing to begin his second season with the DCTC in the fall. Troy had a large loft apartment on Eighteenth Street, just north of the Sixteenth Street Mall and east of Union Station. He had two thousand square feet of floor space, twelve-foot ceilings, and he paid five hundred a month. The place was within walking distance of the Denver Center for the Performing Arts, on the edge of downtown, but was quiet and desolate after five in the evening and all weekend. Wasinger had a small room in the rear of the loft that he offered to rent for two hundred a month while I worked in town. I jumped at that, also. It was a wild and woolly year. We were two kids in our late twenties living as if we might never reach thirty.

At the end of the season I returned to New York and ultimately tried my luck in Los Angeles. Troy remained with the theater company and ultimately took a position teaching at the National Theatre Conservatory in Denver. The last time I had seen Troy was three years earlier, when he was in San Francisco interviewing prospective students. I hadn't seen Denver in more than ten years.

An unexpected business exigency was taking Sally out of town for the weekend, so I thought I might just as well get to Denver early and hang with Troy for a day or two before I began work on the movie. Troy said that he was free Saturday and Sunday and would love to run around like a twenty-eight-year-old for a few days. He promised me that I wouldn't recognize the city at all.

I decided to take advantage of the three-thousand-dollar advance from Jeremy Cash and take a room at the Brown Palace Hotel through Tuesday night. I passed on Troy's generous offer to put me up in his loft during my stay, but I gladly accepted his offer to pick me up at Denver International Airport on Saturday afternoon.

Darlene took care of the hotel reservations and was martyr enough to deal with Bobo Bigelow for the airline tickets and spare me the anguish.

Since we were both leaving town on Saturday, Sally and I arranged to meet for dinner on Friday night. She told me that she felt like cooking, so I said I would bring the wine. Sally hinted that she had some big news, but she wouldn't give me any clues. I left the office early, laid out what I would need for the trip the next morning, and spent a few hours looking over the film script.

At seven I hopped into the Toyota, stopped on Haight Street for a good bottle of Chianti, and headed over to the Presidio. Sally answered the door wearing my favorite perfume—balsamic vinegar and garlic. I followed her into the kitchen and uncorked the wine as she threw the salmon filets into a hot skillet. I could smell the stuffed artichokes baking in the oven. I could almost forget everything else.

"So," Sally said, as we polished off the meal, "how are you feeling about getting in front of the cameras again after all this time. Nervous?"

She was keeping me in suspense about whatever her big news was.

"Not really. Once they put you in a costume and makeup and turn on the lights, it's like riding a bike."

"Is it fun?"

"I never quite thought of it that way, but yes, it is. I mean it's work, but it's a bit like child's play. Make believe. Even with a small part, it feels good to be so fussed over. I'm thinking that I'll have a good time."

"Why did you get out of it?" Sally asked.

"It was too hard to be around the big stars. Don't get me wrong, a lot of these people are very generous. Even humble. But when you see the big private trailers, the chauffeured limousines, the personal staff, the fan attention, and you have an idea of the paycheck they're banking, it can make you envious. Covetous. It's not a great way to feel. I love the acting, in fact I was thinking about going back to the stage. The roar of the crowd, you know. Then Jimmy Pigeon came along, and something about what he did, or maybe how he did it, appealed to me. It's not so different when I think about it. When I'm doing the job well, which I occasionally do in spite of myself, it's like playing a role. The best and the worst part is that there's no script, no telling how it will come out."

"Do you think you'll learn anything in Denver?"

"I don't know. I'm trying to steer clear of expectations. I'm at the point where it's worth the time and effort, if only to be able to say I did all that I could and then let it go."

"So, it sounds as if you still think that Ryder might be tied up in the judge's death somehow. Or, at least, you're not convinced that he isn't," Sally said.

"Intellectually, rationally, it has nothing at all to do with Ryder.

But then there's that nagging voice in my head that has little to do with intellect or rationality. It whispers. It sounds like it's saying that the last straw is a straw nonetheless."

"How do you plan to get his brother to talk?"

"I have no plan at all, Sally. I'm working on pure predestination. If something truly needs to be revealed, it will be. Crazy?"

"Quaint maybe, not crazy."

"So, what's your news, or do I have to beg?" I said, hoping to guide the conversation toward something less metaphysical.

"I've been offered a position as public affairs director for the San Francisco Arts and Humanities Council."

"Wow," I said. It was a terse reaction but I meant every word of it.

"I think I can do a really good job," she said.

"There's no doubt, you'll be perfect. But what about Bytemp?"

"Bytemp can run very well without me. I've seen to that. I'll remain on the board of directors. It'll be a big cut in pay, though," Sally said. "I hope you don't just like me for my money."

"I'm not that shallow, Sal. It's never been about your money," I said. "It's always been about your looks."

"I'm only kidding, Jake. Of course I know it's only been about my looks," she said, looking really good saying it. "Would you do me a favor, Jake?"

"Name it."

"Would you take me out to a movie?"

"Sure, as long as it's not a Sandra Bullock movie. I don't know what it is, there's something about her smile that makes me want to shake her by the shoulders and snap her out of it. No one could possibly be that ecstatic."

"You can choose the movie. All I want is to sit in the dark, hold hands, and maybe ask if you would like to stay the night," Sally said.

I didn't need a mirror to know that I was wearing a Sandra Bullock smile.

Twenty-three

SALLY HAD ME UP and out of the house by seven the next morning. I went back to my apartment and threw the clothing I had laid out the night before into a canvas travel bag. I wasn't taking much; I'd be spending most of my time in costume. I had planned to take a cab to the airport, but Joey Russo called and said he had news that might be worth hearing before I left. Or not.

"Word is that Freddie Cash was into Charlie 'Bones' Mancuso for nearly a hundred grand in gambling debts," Joey said on our way out to the airport.

"Mancuso uses the payoff from Freddie to orchestrate a hit on Chancellor?"

"Possible," said Joey. "Trouble is, Charlie won't say and Freddie can't say."

"Any reason for Mancuso to want the judge dead?" I asked.

"I don't know," said Joey.

"Doesn't help us much."

"Unfortunately true," said Joey, "and here's the cute part. Charlie was arrested for murder a few months ago. Mancuso allegedly killed his brother-in-law, Mike Flanagan, but before the indictment the weapon mysteriously disappeared from the evidence room, no murder weapon, no case, and Charlie walked.

Whether or not Mancuso was directly involved in Chancellor's death, the ransom money could have had something to do with making the gun disappear."

"And it wouldn't be in Charlie's best interest to talk about it," I said.

"I would think not."

"And we really can't be sure that the ransom money is tied into the Chancellor murder," I said.

"We aren't sure," agreed Joey.

"But?"

"But, it's out there. Like the knowledge it took to invent the radio, once it was all out there it was only a matter of time before Marconi and three other guys figured it out at the same moment. Maybe something changes down the road, and what Bones knows or did becomes helpful. It's what you might call the positive view."

"Okay, I have nothing against that." I said.

"Have fun," Joey said, dropping me in front of the terminal. "Tell Gene he was great in *The French Connection.*"

"I'll tell him, but he probably knows already."

"Still, we all like to hear it once in a while. Break a leg. I'll talk to you when you get back."

Two hours later an announcement from the pilot woke me from a nap; I'd been going over my lines in the script before I dozed off. We were passing over the Rocky Mountains, making our approach to Denver. I'd never flown into Denver International—it didn't exist the last time I'd been around. From above, the airport looked to be about the size of Las Vegas. Troy Wasinger met me at the gate. His hair was on the long side; he sported a light cotton suit over a T-shirt, a pair of Birkenstock clogs, and rimless eyeglasses. He looked like a theater conservatory teacher.

"Well, here I am back in cow town," I said.

"Hold on to your hat, Jake. The cow jumped over the moon," Troy said. "How about the Satire Lounge for lunch and debriefing?"

"Sounds great," I said, and followed him outside.

The Satire Lounge on East Colfax hadn't changed. There were

no windows, and it took two or three minutes for my eyes to adjust to the dark. The Budweiser was in longneck bottles.

Food orders were still taken by young waitresses who were both gorgeous and unapproachable. The dishes were delivered by young men, authentically Mexican, who bowed when they set the plates on the table. The music roaring out of the jukebox was the same, except ten years older, all the selections from the fifties and sixties. The food was smothered in green chili so hot that it was impossible to determine if the meal had any taste of its own. I loved it.

After three beers and a chicken burrito covered with enough melted cheddar to shoot my cholesterol level through the roof, Troy dragged me back out into the light of day.

Troy dropped me off on Broadway in front of the Brown Palace Hotel. He said I should walk over to the loft after checking in, assuring me that he had a bottle of Dickel standing by.

"I made reservations for dinner at the Buckhorn Exchange, hope you've retained your taste for a good bison burger."

"And how. The hotel looks the same," I said, gazing up at the triangular facade. "Where's all this change you've been advertising?"

"Come up Sixteenth and over on Wazee Street. It'll give you the whole effect when you head over to Eighteenth," Troy suggested.

I walked into the hotel atrium, my eyes immediately drawn to the stained-glass canopy ceiling nine stories above. Live harp and piano music accompanied the traditional afternoon tea. I walked up to the check-in desk.

"Any chance for a room Wyatt Earp may have stayed in?" I asked.

I was given a room on the fourth floor. Although the desk clerk couldn't swear that Earp had occupied the room, he was positive that Spiro Agnew had.

I remembered the first time I had heard my father utter those two strange words, *Spiro Agnew*. It sounded like a dirty expression.

I later learned it was exactly how Dad had intended it to sound.

After checking in I walked over to Fifteenth Street and strolled the pedestrian mall toward Wazee as Troy had recommended. When I had left Denver years earlier, there was really nothing going on downtown aside from the shops on Sixteenth and the strip on Larimer between Speer Boulevard and Fifteenth known as Larimer Square. It was a different city.

The new businesses on Sixteenth were numerous. Espresso bars, bookshops, restaurants, wine stores, pastry shops. Bars, cafés, and retail stores crowded the cross streets, Lawrence, Larimer, Market, and Blake. When I turned onto Wazee Street I came face-to-face with Coors Field for the first time, and I passed art gallery after art gallery as I moved toward Eighteenth Street. The sidewalks bustled with pedestrians, where only a decade before few had dared to wander.

A large bookstore-slash-café occupied the entire street level of Troy's building on Eighteenth. The space had been vacant for years when Troy first moved in. I walked into the alley and rang the buzzer, remembering the day we had strung the wire along the outside of the building, and Troy threw a set of keys down from the window above.

The loft hadn't changed much. It was basically two huge rooms. The larger was the kitchen, dining area, and living room, with a washer and dryer thrown in. The ceiling was twelve feet high. The front room facing the street, partitioned by an eight-foot wall and French doors, was Troy's bedroom. A small room in the rear, walled with painted theater flats, had been my bedroom while I lived there.

Troy sat at the drop-leaf table we had hauled over from a garage sale, along with the four mismatched chairs. A liter bottle of George Dickel Original Tennessee Finest Quality Sippin' Whiskey No. 12 stood before him, unopened.

"I waited to let you do the honors," he said.

I broke the seal and poured two glasses.

"So," I asked, "what does a place like this rent for now that SoHo has come to lower downtown Denver?"

"The guy next door, who does public relations for the Rockies, pays eighteen hundred a month. An exec with the LoDo Development Association lives above him. He has a deck built out over the parking area and pays twenty-two. The woman above me owns the business below; she has stairs going up to a patio and garden on the roof and pops for twenty-four hundred. I'm still paying five bills. I was the very first resident here, when no one but a wino would even linger in front of the place. The landlord must be sentimental. Or using it as a tax write-off or both."

"Good deal"

"It would be great except I'm getting tired of the constant change. I liked it much better when the city wasn't crammed with people trying to make Denver into someplace else. It's loud, often pretentious. I'm thinking about subletting the place. I could get at least fifteen hundred, rent a small house west of town, and pocket the change."

We spent the rest of the afternoon sipping Dickel, reminiscing, and catching up. Troy gave me a few tips on playing the poker game scene.

"What's it like being a successful PI?" Troy asked.

"I'll let you know when I find out," I answered.

At seven we drove over to Tenth and Osage. The Buckhorn Exchange hadn't changed, either, since I'd last been there. Then again, the place hadn't changed very much since 1893.

We sat at the white-oak bar on the second floor while our table was set. The bar had been built in Essen, Germany, in 1857, and transported to Colorado for the opening of the restaurant.

The Buckhorn proudly displayed the state of Colorado liquor license number one on the wall behind the bar.

For appetizers we went with the rattlesnake marinated in red chili and the fried alligator tail. Who wouldn't? I had a difficult time deciding on an entrée, finally opting for the High Plains buffalo prime rib and sautéed pheasant combination. We topped it all off with Buckhorn's chocolate mousse, spelled "moose." I could hardly wait to get back to San Francisco to describe the meal in detail to a horrified Darlene.

The founder of the establishment, Henry H. Zietz, had scouted with Buffalo Bill, hunted with Teddy Roosevelt, and been given the nickname "Shorty Scout" by Sitting Bull. Legend has it that Sitting Bull's nephew later presented Zeitz with the military saber taken from General George Armstrong Custer at the Little Big Horn.

The remainder of Saturday night was a bar crawl from one live music haunt to another. Jazz, rock, folk, booze. Shots of Booker's Noe bourbon ran nine dollars, a shot of eighteen-year-old Macallan single-malt scotch was sixteen bucks, imported beers ran five to eight dollars a pop. With the way folks were spending money downtown, it was a good thing the Denver Mint was nearby.

Troy left me in front of the Brown Palace at two in the morning. He promised he would show me that there were enough of the old, reasonably priced, uniquely Denver attractions left in the city to make it a great place to live. That is if either of us could get out of bed on Sunday.

I clawed my way up to the fourth floor. I thought I spotted Hackman on my way in, but I was so loaded it could have been Woody Allen. I managed to get into the room without plummeting over the rail to the lobby below and somehow fought my way out of my clothing before I was dead asleep.

Troy woke me up with a phone call at eight and delivered as promised—a perfect Sunday from the annals of 1989.

We drove over to the Park Lane Restaurant for breakfast, with Warren Zevon crooning "Frank and Jesse James" from the cassette deck in Troy's 1974 Beetle.

We walked over to Washington Park and joined in a pickup touch football game and then strolled across to South High to watch the school team practice.

We had a late lunch at the Riviera Lounge on South Colorado Boulevard, then caught an afternoon performance of *The Seagull* at Germinal Stage Denver. It was the closing performance and we joined the cast for burgers and Denver's best fries at My Brother's Bar.

The entire day's activities cost slightly more than two shots of scotch the night before. And I could see why Troy Wasinger continued to love the Mile High City.

Troy left me outside the Brown Palace. I caught sight of a TV over the hotel bar, tuned to the League Championship Series game between the Mets and the Cardinals. It drew me over for a nightcap. Glancing around the room I spotted a group huddled around a table, and this time definitely identified Hackman among them. And Chance Folsom, whom I recognized from the photo my cousin Bobby had pulled off the Internet. I turned back to the ballgame and my shot of bourbon. A few minutes later a deep, melodic voice asked if I was here for the filming.

I'd chosen to take on the project under an old stage name.

"Yes I am," I said, "Jake Falco."

"Great handle," he said, holding out his hand. "How'd you come up with it?"

"My grandfather," I said, accepting the handshake. "How about yours?"

"Chance Folsom. Took the name of my town, a small place in central California," he said, smiling, "since Corleone was already taken."

I liked Chance Folsom immediately.

"Can I buy you a drink?" I asked.

"Absolutely," he said.

And I reluctantly began doing my job.

With all of the deception that went with it.

"Looks like we'll be doing a few scenes together," I said, as the bartender placed a glass of scotch in front of Chance Folsom. "It's been quite a while since I've worked to a camera, I have to admit I'm a little nervous."

"You'll do fine," he said, "what have you been doing instead?"

Sitting in a private detective's office waiting for the phone to ring.

"I've been in Chicago doing theater," I said. "Hollywood didn't quite pan out. I did *One Flew Over the Cuckoo's Nest* with Steppenwolf last season, and we'll be taking the production to New York for a three-month run this spring. I go into rehearsal next week for a new Mamet play at the Goodman. The author is directing. I'm not allowed to say too much about it."

I had done some homework to support my duplicity.

"I'm envious. I'd love to do stage work. I tried, but I was a terrible failure."

"And I want to do movies. Just goes to show you, actors are never satisfied."

"How did you get into this crazy business to begin with?" Chance asked.

Folsom had given me a wide opening; I had to step right in.

"I had some trouble with the law when I was younger, did some jail time. It sort of threw my loftier aspirations out the window."

I waited to hear about how much Chance and I had in common.

He changed the subject.

"Do you know Denver very well?" he asked.

"As a matter of fact, I did a year of theater here. It's changed a lot, but there are still a few unaffected spots. I can show you around if we get the time," I said. "That's if you're interested."

"Sure," Folsom said.

I decided that it was a good time to end my first interview with Folsom.

"There's an early read through in the morning," I said. "Guess I'll call it a night."

"How about the ballgame?"

It was the last thing on my mind.

"I'll wait to hear about it tomorrow. I'm a big Mets fan, and it seems that they always fare better when I don't watch."

"Good meeting you, Jake," Folsom said, offering another handshake. "I'm looking forward to working together."

"Ditto," I said, taking his hand guiltily.

I rode the elevator to the fourth floor and went into my hotel room. I decided to do some reading before turning in.

I picked up *The Count of Monte Cristo.*

Edmond Dantès had collected the island treasure and had begun forming his plans to avenge the wrongs perpetrated against him, using false identity and deception.

I thought about Chance Folsom.

I was deceiving him, and I wasn't feeling very good about it. I wrote it off it as a necessary evil. At the same time, I vowed that I would take care not to hurt an innocent man in the process.

I hoped it would be rationalization enough to allow me sleep.

Twenty-four

AT SEVEN THE FOLLOWING MORNING we gathered in a small meeting room in the hotel for a read through of the film's opening poker sequence. A round oak table, which would be used in the actual filming, sat in the center of the room. The scene had only eight speaking parts. Lancey Howard, known as the Man. Slade, played by Chance Folsom. Three other card players, Pig, Yeller, and Hoban. Shooter, the game's organizer and part-time dealer. Lady Fingers, another dealer. Felix, who fetched drinks to the table.

I was playing Hoban.

The director was very young, having graduated from directing music videos to TV commercials to this, his first feature film. The first thing he said after seating us around the table was a threat, a warning, or a statement of his eating preferences.

"I'm a strict disciplinarian," he said.

His called himself Jean-Pierre Montblanc. He was as French as Mel Brooks.

Montblanc quickly outlined his goals for the morning session. We would read through the script as written, without bringing any *acting* into the reading. After the initial reading we would read through the scene again. The second time around we would be supplied with props, including cigarettes, drinks, poker chips, and the cards themselves, and Montblanc would discuss blocking considerations, particularly for movement to and from the table.

"Most of the scene will be shot very tight," Jean-Pierre said, "and one of the cameras will be mounted directly above the table and will take in the individual card hands. With that in mind, think about leaning out from rather than in to the table."

We all muttered that we would keep it in mind.

A prop man sat in the corner setting up decks of cards that could be dealt out exactly according to the script.

The dialogue was fraught with cliché, the scene culminating with a large pile of chips in the center of the table. My character was third to fold his hand.

"It's getting a little too rich for my blood," I read, throwing down my cards. I had to choke it out.

The Man and Slade were left to butt heads. Lancey Howard won the match and cleaned Slade out.

"How the hell did you know I didn't have the king or the ace?" Slade says.

To which Lancey Howard replies, with a few lines that maybe only Edward G. could pull off, "I recollect a young man putting the same question to Eddie the Dude. 'Son, Eddie told him, all you paid was the looking price. Lessons are extra.' "

Slade throws in the towel, thanking the other players for the entertainment and Howard for the privilege of watching a great artist at work.

"Well now, you're quite welcome, son," Lancey replies. "A pleasure to meet someone who understands that for the true gambler, money is never an end in itself. It's simply a tool, as language is to thought."

Deep.

That brought an end to the scene; we were told that the opening credits would roll afterward over the arrival of Eric Stoner, the Cincinnati Kid, into Denver's Union Station. My scene with Chance would follow the credits. We were given a late morning break and told to report to the set for the rolling of the cameras at ten-thirty.

I waited to see if Chance would approach me. He didn't. I

went off on my own. I decided that I would hold off and ask later if he wanted to join me for dinner and perhaps go over our upcoming scene together, scheduled to shoot the following day. I walked to Market Street and had a late breakfast.

At ten forty-five we played out the scene, cameramen breathing down our necks and a large rig hovering ominously above our heads.

After a late lunch followed by a few more takes, I was done for the day. Since Chance had more work to do, I grabbed a quick word with him before I left. I invited him to give me a shout when he wrapped, if he cared to join me for dinner at the Imperial Chinese Restaurant.

I returned to my room and gave Darlene a quick call at the office. She didn't have much to report, but she did say that Lieutenant Lopez had phoned with what she said was a new finding in the Freddie Cash murder case. I resisted the urge to call Lopez. I was feeling distracted enough trying to stay in character as a fellow actor while trying to develop a friendship with an unknowing investigative subject.

I could have used a long walk, for exercise and fresh air after a whole day crowded around a small table in a smoke-filled room, but I was afraid of missing Chance Folsom if he called. Instead, I lay down on the bed and read some of the Dumas novel.

The phone rang at about eight-thirty, waking me from what was quickly becoming a customary early evening nap.

"Is it too late for dinner?" asked Chance.

"Not at all," I said, trying to sound awake. "I'll meet you in the lobby, give me about fifteen minutes."

At 9:15 we sat at the Imperial on South Broadway. The decor was too New Jersey suburban for my taste, but the food was top-notch, voted Best of Denver for thirteen years running. Seafood gumbo, spicy eggplant in garlic sauce, crisp sesame prawns, and steamed salmon in black bean sauce cluttered the table.

We were emptying bottles of Tsingtao beer at a fairly good pace.

Chance and I were both loosening up. We began revealing

information about ourselves. My revelations however, were to a great extent scripted.

Chance Folsom and I could hardly have come from more different cultural and geographical backgrounds.

At the same time we had more than I would have expected in common.

We left the restaurant and moved on to the Ship Tavern at the Brown Palace. We sat at the bar and continued our exposés.

Chance talked about growing up on an avocado farm. I spoke about growing up in Brooklyn with a fig tree in the backyard. Chance talked about the three-mile bus ride to his elementary school, I described the three-block walk to mine. We both loved baseball, had both played the game as preadolescents and in high school, and were both too young to remember when New York had the Dodgers and the Giants and California had no major league team at all.

We both had loving mothers who could cook up a storm. We both had fathers who were strong-minded and introspective, fathers whom we tried very hard to please. We both had brothers who were smarter than we were.

My brother Abe worked as an epidemiologist at the Centers for Disease Control in Atlanta. I told Chance that my older brother was a successful lawyer in New York. Chance seemed to accept the coincidence without suspicion. He told me that his brother was a California district attorney but never mentioned the name Lowell Ryder.

"When I graduated high school, I began working the farm full-time with Dad," Chance said. "It was expected of me. My brother, on the other hand, was destined for college education and a professional career in law and politics. It's all he talked about wanting from the time he was fourteen years old. And my father was going to see that he got the opportunity. At any cost."

"At any cost?" I asked.

"For my father, it was an opportunity to see his own thwarted dreams come true vicariously, through my brother. My old man grew up on the same avocado farm, and his old man wanted

153

Calvin to be an avocado farmer when he grew up. But my father had other ambitions, and he ran off to college against his father's wishes. He was doing very well, and had earned a full scholarship to law school when my grandfather died and my father had to come back to run the farm. He had no choice; my grandmother would never have survived without him. My father was always bitter about his sacrifice, and he often took it out on his family. Since he had the luxury of having fathered two sons, he could keep one on the farm and let the other go off and achieve what he never had the chance to have for himself. When my brother showed a strong desire to study law, my father was determined that nothing would get in my brother's way."

"Nothing?"

"What did your father have in mind for you?" Chance asked, shifting the spotlight back at me.

"My father wanted both of his sons to be scholars. I was on my way to NYU, with a full tuition scholarship to study journalism, and then I fucked up royally."

"What happened," Chance asked.

The answer was difficult to deliver.

"The summer after high school I stole a car and put it through the front window of a newsstand. I sent the man behind the counter to a hospital for five months. Instead of four years at NYU, I did three at Attica. When I got out I didn't know a thing except what my cellmate had taught me about acting."

I glanced up at the mirror behind the bar. The reflection of my face brought the word *louse* to mind. I realize that I had said too much. I realized that maybe I wanted to be caught in the lie. Chance Folsom wasn't stupid or gullible, only unsuspecting. He had no reason not to believe me. And yet, he didn't bite. Chance said nothing about his own prison experience. Instead he moved the talk back to baseball.

"Could be the Yankees and the Mets in the series," he said.

"Could be," I said.

And it was time to call it a night.

"We never did run lines," he said as we headed back to our rooms.

Except I'd been running lines all evening.

"I don't think we'll have much trouble," I said. "It's not exactly Harold Pinter."

"Thanks for dinner, Jake. I'll see you in the morning."

And with that we split up, Chance to the elevator and me to brave the stairs to the fourth floor. I had the feeling that it would take some prying to get Chance to talk about what transpired in the parking lot in 1985, and was beginning to feel that I didn't have it in me to drag it out of him.

I was thinking about letting it go, of admitting that the idea that Chance Folsom could throw any light on what happened to Judge Chancellor, Lefty, and the others had been a long shot to begin with.

The next day we worked on our scene together, and we wrapped it by late afternoon. Chance seemed aloof. I let him be.

I thought of calling Troy Wasinger for dinner, but realized that I was only looking for a convenient confessor. Instead, I moved up my flight to San Francisco. Without letting anyone back home know that I was returning early.

Chance Folsom caught me at the check-out desk for a quick good-bye, promising that he wouldn't miss getting to New York City for *Cuckoo's Nest*. I didn't know how to thank him.

I took a cab from the airport.

I picked up my mail and walked up to my apartment.

I took a shower and put up a pot of espresso.

I fell asleep in my reading chair, a Camel burning in the ashtray, the Dumas novel in my lap.

I had no dreams that I care to recall.

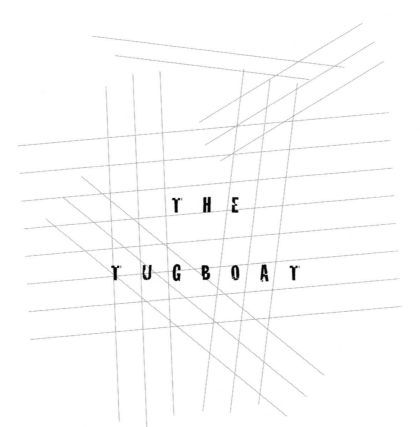

THE

TUGBOAT

There is neither happiness nor misfortune in this world, there is merely the comparison between one state and the other, nothing more.

—ALEXANDRE DUMAS

THE COUNT OF MONTE CRISTO

Twenty-five

THE FOLLOWING MORNING I summed it up for Darlene.

"So, you really didn't learn much," Darlene understated.

"Only that undercover work is not what it's made out to be."

"Lopez called again," Darlene said.

"I'm not sure that I care what she has to say."

"Why not reserve judgment until she gives you a clue," said Darlene, "unless you're too busy with something else."

It was the kindest way she could think to say "Get over it, Jake."

I called Lopez. I didn't feel up for a visit to the Vallejo Street Station so I agreed to meet the lieutenant halfway at Caffè Greco on Columbus. I could listen for as long as it took to swallow down a strong espresso.

It was an unusually mild day for late October. We took a table on the sidewalk in front of the coffeehouse. Lopez waited until the coffee was set on the table before she did what police detectives do. She began telling me why she wanted to meet by asking a question.

"Did Freddie Cash pull his own kidnapping?"

What the hell, Freddie was safe from prosecution now.

"Yes he did. His father never knew."

"Does the name *Charlie Mancuso* mean anything to you, Diamond?"

"Let me think," I said.

"I don't have time for games, Diamond."

"Charlie Bones?"

"The ballistics report on the bullet that killed Freddie Cash matched a weapon allegedly used by Mancuso in an earlier murder," said Lieutenant Lopez. "The gun was being held as trial evidence against Mancuso until it mysteriously disappeared from the police station."

"Okay," I said.

"Is that the best you can do?"

"I don't know what you want me to say, Lieutenant."

"Can you tell me what I'm thinking?"

Lopez was good. Trying to find out if I knew something she didn't know before she spilled her beans.

But I could be pretty cagey myself.

"No offense, Lieutenant, but you said you didn't have time for games and I left my crystal ball at home," I said, "I'd rather you just tell me what you're thinking, if you're so inclined."

Lopez took a five-dollar bill from her purse and laid it on the table.

"I just remembered that I forgot to water the plant in my office this morning, I'd better run," she said.

And with that she was up and heading toward Vallejo Street.

And I was left sitting to consider what a smart cookie I was.

"So, she just left you hanging?" asked Darlene, after hearing the synopsis of my meeting with Lopez.

"I hanged myself," I said.

"So, tell me what you think she was thinking," she said, "if you're so inclined."

"Don't be cute, Darlene."

"I can't help it. C'mon, give."

"Someone lifted the gun from police evidence holding. Either it made its way back to Mancuso, or someone else used it on Freddie. Making Katt as the cop who snatched the piece is a pretty safe bet. But Katt was already dead before Freddie was killed."

"Okay."

"I think Lopez is thinking there's a way to add it all up that pins the whole ball of wax on Charlie Bones."

"Mind if I try to do the math?" asked Darlene.

"Be my guest," I said.

"Mancuso puts the big squeeze on Freddie Cash for outstanding gambling debts. Freddie kidnaps himself, takes the ransom money and pays Charlie off. Mancuso uses the money to employ Katt, first to lift the gun from the police station and then to set up a fall guy for the Chancellor snuff. Katt enlists Vigoda, Vic enlists Lefty. Maybe Mancuso is afraid that Vigoda knows he's involved, so he dumps Vic into McCovey Cove, or has Katt take care of it. You rattle Katt's cage with talk about the Rolex and the envelope, he reports back to Mancuso, and Charlie decides that Lefty knows too much and pays Katt to shut the kid up. Then Mancuso knocks off Katt for good measure. Finally, Mancuso worries that Freddie could tie him to the twenties and fifties scattered around the dead bodies and puts one into Freddie's skull."

"And the judge?"

"Charlie Bones does the judge himself, just before Lefty shows up."

"I couldn't have said it better myself. I think that's exactly what Lieutenant Lopez may be thinking."

"So," said Darlene, "are you going to tell me what you're thinking, or are you going to drop five bucks on my desk and stroll out the door?"

"I'm thinking it's possible that Mancuso killed them all, but I'd be more convinced if the envelope that everyone seemed to be after had Charlie Bones's doom written all over it."

"Have they brought Mancuso in for questioning?" asked Darlene.

"I don't know. But I suppose I should give Lopez a heads up about the envelope if and when they do. And maybe I'll try to track down Katt's partner, Phil Moss, to see if he can connect the dots between Mancuso and Katt."

"And then?"

Tug McGraw peeked his head out from under Darlene's desk, as if he were waiting with her for my answer.

"And then we'd better hope that some paying job comes through that door pretty soon," I said.

"Be careful what you wish for, Jake. I bet you can't wait to see Lopez again after playing her so well at Caffè Greco."

"You love rubbing it in, don't you, Darlene."

"Of course not, Jake. How could you say such a thing? Anyhow, look at it this way. You get to visit Vallejo Street Station, after all."

Darlene kept a straight face.

I could have sworn the dog smiled.

I moved toward the door and then turned back with the thought of getting in the last word, but Darlene had her nose in a stack of past-due bills and McGraw had disappeared again under the desk.

At the police station, as luck would have it, I bumped into Officer Moss coming out as I walked up. I couldn't tell if he was happy to see me.

"Got a minute, Phil?" I asked.

"Sure," he said, "only, let's walk away from here."

I followed him across Broadway and over to Pacific Avenue.

"What's up?" he finally asked when we were out of sight of the station.

"I'm looking for anything that might tie your partner to Charlie Mancuso. Got something like that?"

"I saw them talking once or twice, couldn't tell you what about."

"Do you think Katt lifted Mancuso's rod from the evidence room?"

"Ask me that a month ago and I'd probably punch your lights out. Now, I don't know what to think. It crossed my mind, since Tom apparently had his price."

"But you couldn't verify it?" I asked.

"No."

"Katt ever talk about the Freddie Cash kidnapping?"

"No. When I heard that the Cash kid was killed with Mancuso's gun I tried to think of anything Tom might have said about the kidnapping. I couldn't."

"Is Mancuso in custody or been questioned?"

"Charlie Bones is MIA," said Moss. "Lieutenant Lopez has been scouring the earth for him."

"Call me if you hear anything," I said, and headed back to the station.

"Get to your plant in time?" I asked Lopez, through the open door from the hall outside her office.

"What is it, Diamond? Didn't I leave enough for the tab at Caffè Greco?"

"I came for a little give and take," I said.

"Well, as skeptical as I am, come on in. Take a seat. And give."

I accepted the invitation.

"The last time I saw Lefty Wright," I began, "he told me about an envelope. Vic Vigoda had promised him five grand down, which Lefty found under a rock, and ten more to pull an envelope out of Chancellor's safe. Lefty never found it in the safe. Katt searched Lefty before other police showed up, and also rifled the safe. I'd say he was looking for the envelope."

"What was Officer Moss doing while all of this searching was going on?"

"Trying to be a loyal partner," I said, "while picturing his entire career going down the drain."

"Lefty say what this envelope was?"

"Said he didn't know."

"And you're sure it wasn't Lefty's vivid imagination?"

"I've got it confirmed a number of ways. As you said yourself, Lefty Wright had to have a reason to go into the house if the money was outside. I don't believe he went in to kill the judge, so it had to be to hit the safe. Chancellor's law clerk saw an envelope matching the description that was given to Lefty, Katt searched the judge's cabin in Mill Valley, and someone turned Chancellor's office upside down. On top of that, Judge Chancellor mentioned something about a document that had come into his hands and he wanted it explored."

"Mentioned to whom? Explored by whom?"

"I can't say," I said, keeping Carlucci out of the conversation.

"Incriminating whom?"

"I don't know. Charlie Mancuso?"

"Not too helpful, Diamond," Lopez said.

"I'm trying my best, Lieutenant. Freddie Cash was in to Mancuso for some hefty gambling debts. That might explain the twenties and fifties going around."

"So, let me see if I follow. You think that Freddie Cash paid off Mancuso with the ransom money. Charlie paid Katt to lift the gun from evidence holding, get an envelope from the judge's safe, and frame Lefty. Then Bones killed everyone who could tie him to the judge's death, the ransom money, and the stolen gun."

"Isn't that what you think, Lieutenant?" I asked.

"I'm not entirely convinced."

"Mind telling me why?"

"There's nothing more you can tell me about the envelope?" she said.

"I think it had to do with someone that the judge was searching for. That's the best I can do."

"That's worthless information, Diamond. No offense."

"What is it about Mancuso as the lone assassin that you're having trouble with?"

"Tell me your doubts and I'll tell you mine, Diamond."

"What makes you think I have any?" I said.

"What happened to give and take, Jake?"

"I've told you all I know, Lieutenant. Scout's honor."

"You want to know what doesn't work for me, Diamond? I'll give you a hint. I can't decide if Charlie Bones is very smart or real stupid."

"What do you mean?"

"Think about it," she said, "and don't let the door hit you on your way out."

I left it open.

I walked back to my office. The note taped to the inside of the door informed me that L. L. Bruno had dropped by to take Darlene and McGraw out for lunch.

I went back to my desk. I determined that Angelo was deep-frying calamari for his lunch special. I turned on the pole fan and aimed it at my desk toward the window.

I lit a cigarette and I thought about it.

Charlie Bones was either very smart or very stupid.

He was either smart enough to work out an intricate plan. A plan to make the gun he used on his brother-in-law disappear, beat the murder rap, eliminate any threat Chancellor may have posed, silence everyone who could finger him, and all with cash that would be difficult if not impossible to trace back to him.

Or he was stupid enough to use the same gun he used on Mike Flanagan to kill Freddie Cash.

Either way, Mancuso was in the soup. If the weapon surfaced, even if he didn't use it to kill Freddie, it nailed him on the Flanagan murder. Mancuso had good reason to make himself scarce. There was really nothing he could say in his defense. He'd have to stay silent and invisible and take the credit for all five murders.

And I was at the point where all I could do was give him all the credit.

Twenty-six

Over the next two days, a few jobs actually came through the door of Diamond Investigation.

On Thursday, I helped the owner of a busy luncheonette on Market Street discover who was stealing him blind at the cash register. One of his cashiers had been under-ringing sales and walking out with fifty to seventy-five bucks in his pocket every afternoon. I watched the kid for a while from a table near the register. He was jotting numbers on a small slip of paper, keeping track of the money he was putting in but not ringing up. I told the owner to pull the register in the middle of the kid's shift and cash it out. The drawer held almost sixty dollars more than the register tape could account for. I sat down to a complimentary breakfast the next morning, watching the owner as he hung a Help Wanted sign in the window.

Later on Friday, I was looking down at an alternator from a 1999 Pontiac Grand Am that was sitting in the middle of my desk. The client suspected that his mechanic had charged him two hundred dollars for replacing a part that had never been replaced. He claimed that the greasy thing on my desk, which the mechanic claimed was the dead alternator he had removed, wasn't from his car. God only knows what could possibly have made him think such a thing. He had called the police and was told he would have to come up with something more than a hunch before they would investigate. I called Vinnie Strings. Vinnie was positive that the alternator on the desk came out of a 1995 Bonneville. Then he followed my client down to the street. Vinnie crawled underneath the Trans Am and asserted, without doubt, that the alternator on the vehicle was a factory-installed part. I assured the client that the cops could take it from there. He picked up the alternator and left for the police station.

Diamond Investigation was on a roll. A two-for-two streak.

Not much to beef up the memoirs, but it was always good to solve a few.

And it paid the bills.

Charlie Bones hadn't surfaced. He was now officially wanted by the SFPD for questioning in the murder of Freddie Cash. Mancuso apparently had nothing he cared to say about it.

On Saturday morning, an article in the *Examiner* attempted to tie together five killings that had raised the city's homicide statistics through the roof over the preceding three weeks.

Charlie Mancuso's Cadillac had been found in the long-term parking lot at San Francisco International Airport.

Sitting on the front seat was the gun that had killed both Mike Flanagan and Freddie Cash.

A gun registered to Charlie Mancuso, which for a short time had resided in the evidence holding room at Vallejo Street Station.

As the Governor may have put it, it was *quite* a stroke of luck that Charlie Bones had carelessly left such damning evidence behind before flying off into the sunset.

Bones could hardly have been more helpful, short of leaving a signed confession.

Or a nine-by-twelve manila envelope.

Or a street address on Alfred Sisley.

The hunt for Charlie Mancuso was in full swing and would continue.

Meanwhile, the state would be indicting Mancuso in absentia. The DA's office announced that they would proceed, sparing no resource and no expense, to present a criminal case that would guarantee the conviction of Charlie Mancuso for the murder of Judge J. Andrew Chancellor, and five others, whether Mancuso showed up for the trial or not.

It was all quite sensational.

The excitement surrounding the successful resolution of the multiple murder case didn't quite capture me. The news didn't make my day.

The word *anticlimactic* came to mind.

I entertained the possibility that it was disappointment, or jealousy, that I hadn't broken the case myself.

I decided that wasn't it.

And I have to admit I was more thrilled by the fact that the Mets and the Yankees would be starting the World Series in New York that evening.

I was having difficulty deciding where to watch the game. Life is full of tough choices.

Vinnie had invited me to watch game one at the Finnish Line on the big screen. He said he would buy the pizza, though he didn't say whose money he'd be using.

Joey asked me to join him and Sonny at the Russo house. His wife, Angela, was making stuffed manicotti, and there was a case of Sam Adams on ice.

Darlene said I was welcome to attend a World Series party with her boyfriend and some of his sports buddies. She said that Jerry Rice would definitely be there, and maybe Barry Bonds.

Of course my mother, one of the most vocal Met fans west of the Mississippi, begged me to drive out to Pleasant Hill for the broadcast. She enticed me with the promise of her famous homemade eggnog, which glided down the throat like silk and could take the paint off an automobile hood.

The most tempting invitation came from Sally. She told me that if we watched the game together at the house in the Presidio and the Mets lost, she would do anything she could do to make me feel better. The thought nearly had me wishing for a Yankee victory.

In the end, I accepted an offer that I couldn't refuse. Tony

168

Carlucci phoned and asked me to meet him at the restaurant at seven, as a personal favor to his brother John.

"Just say yes," Tony recommended, before I could get in a word about baseball. "My brother won't forget it."

I knew without having to check in with Joey Russo that if I said no, Johnny Boy Carlucci would *really* not forget it.

I told Tony to expect me at eight, he told me to bring my appetite.

When I arrived at Carlucci's, Tony greeted me at the bar with a menu in his hand.

"Whatever you want, Diamond, on the house. What are you drinking?"

"That's not necessary, Tony," I said.

"I insist, Diamond," he said. "My mother will box my ears if you don't eat."

Just then Mama Carlucci herself rushed up and gave me a bear hug. When I enthusiastically requested the linguini with mussels in marinara sauce, the woman was beaming. She rushed off to greet a new group of guests.

Tony had the bartender pour me a bourbon; he put it in my food order and asked me to follow him to the back of the restaurant.

"Sit, relax," he said, indicating the sofa in his office.

I sat. I looked around the room. There was a small TV on a wall shelf over Carlucci's desk. The game was scheduled to start in fifteen minutes. I wondered if it would be totally inappropriate to ask him to switch it on. Tony sat at the desk, looking up at me occasionally with a manufactured smile. Otherwise, he kept glancing back and forth between his wristwatch and the other door in the room, which I guessed connected to the side alley, as if he were waiting for Godot, or Santa Claus, or both. I couldn't have been less comfortable or more apprehensive if I had a daughter and she was just about to be married to a divorce lawyer. A light tapping on the alley door came just in time to keep both Carlucci and me from suffocating due to lack of exhalation.

Carlucci jumped up and over to the door, opened it quickly

and let in a tall well-dressed man. The man had thick, wavy jet-black hair. He was movie-star handsome. He greeted Tony with a slap on the back and then immediately turned his attention to me. He walked up to the sofa, unthreateningly, and extended his hand. I rose and accepted the handshake.

"Charlie Mancuso," he said. "Thank you for coming, Mr. Diamond."

"Sure," I said, wishing I were anywhere else.

"I'll go check on the food," said Carlucci, "and leave you two to talk."

"Why don't you put the linguini on hold for the moment, Tony," I said, "maybe send in another bourbon."

"No problem, Jake," he said. "Charlie?"

"Just some ice water, thanks, Tony," said Mancuso.

And then we were alone in the room.

"Mr. Diamond, what would you do if someone beat your sister so badly that she had to spend the rest of her life in a wheelchair?"

It was a challenging question, one that I would have had trouble with even if I had a sister.

"I'm not sure," I said.

"That's exactly what Mike Flanagan did to my sister. I confronted Flanagan, one thing led to another, and I shot the sick bastard. When the police stormed into my home to arrest me, terrifying my wife and my three children, they found the gun that killed him. And that was the last time I ever saw that weapon. Are you with me so far?"

"Yes," I said.

"A police officer named Katt approached me before my trial. He said he had the gun in his possession and would be willing to turn it over to me for a price. I told him that I wasn't interested," Charlie Bones said. "I wouldn't pay the price."

"Which was?"

"Katt wanted someone muscled for information and silence. He never said who."

"Did Katt say he wanted you to kill someone?"

"No, only that he wanted the *fear* of death clearly stated and understood. I'm not a hired gun, Mr. Diamond. I never killed anyone before or after Flanagan and then I couldn't help myself. My lawyers seemed confident that when they rolled my sister into the courtroom the jury might have understood my motivation somewhat. But then when the weapon went missing, the case against me was dropped. So I chalked it up to unbelievable luck and forgot about it. Until I learned that I was wanted for killing the Cash kid, Judge Chancellor, and I can't even remember who else."

"What about the money Freddie owed you, what about the ransom money?"

"I don't know about any ransom money, and I never collected from Freddie. I never really pressed him for it. I just told him that he couldn't bet anymore until he squared up. I'm no leg breaker, at least not over a couple of grand."

"Freddie Cash owed you two thousand dollars?" I said.

"I can't even remember, twenty-two, twenty-three hundred tops."

"Word on the street was that Freddie was in to you for a hundred thousand."

"Absolutely false," said Mancuso. "I would never let a kid like that get in so deep."

There was a knock on the office door. Tony Carlucci walked in, handed me a glass of bourbon and Mancuso a glass of ice water, and quickly vanished again.

"What about your car? They found the gun that killed Flanagan and Freddie Cash in your Cadillac."

"I don't know how the Caddy got to the airport. I certainly didn't leave it there. I had a few things to take care of before I disappeared."

"And you have no idea who set you up?" I asked.

"Aside from Katt, none. But whoever did, did a fine job."

"And you know nothing about a brown manila envelope?"

"No clue," said Charlie Mancuso.

"Wow," I said.

"That's one way of putting it."

"Why are you telling me all this?"

"Who else could I tell? I can't see that the police would be too interested in my sad tale. My wife believes me, thank God. I talked to John Carlucci on the phone from Quentin; I asked him if he knew of anyone who would care. He said that he thought you would."

"I don't know that there's anything I can do to help you," I said.

"But you would if you could. Johnny Boy told me about how you went to bat for the Wright kid, and how hot you were to find out who ran him over. I thought that you should know that it wasn't me. Maybe it's selfish of me. Maybe I'm thinking that with you back on the case there's an outside chance it might indirectly help my cause. In any event, there it is, now it's out there."

"Like the knowledge it took to invent the radio," I said.

"What was that?"

"Nothing," I said, "I wish I had the slightest idea where to begin."

"I'd better get going, I've got a ride out of town waiting. Way out of town. Good luck," Mancuso said, extending an open hand.

I took his hand and looked into his eyes.

I knew that everything he had told me was the truth.

"Good luck to you," I said.

"Isn't the series on tonight?" Mancuso said, switching on the television.

I watched him slip out the alley door and then looked up at the TV screen. The Yankees were ahead. I thought about Sally's offer. I used the office phone to call her.

I'd lost my appetite.

Fortunately, Mama Carlucci had left for the evening. I thanked Carlucci for the drinks, apologized for passing on the food, and begged him to tell his mother that I had thoroughly enjoyed my meal.

That night, Sally did help me get over the Mets' twelve-inning game one loss to the Yankees. More than that, she helped me put Lefty Wright and Charlie Mancuso temporarily out of mind.

The next morning, Sally and I slept late. We spent the morning with pancakes, French roast, and the Sunday *Examiner.* We took in a movie matinee. Chance Folsom had a short scene in the film, battling with sword and chain in the Roman Coliseum. I couldn't take my eyes off him while he was on-screen.

We had dinner at Thanh Long, a Vietnamese restaurant on Judah in the Sunset. We talked about Sally's new job, set to begin the next day. We talked about planning a trip down to San Diego one weekend, soon. We talked about ways to avoid anything to do with Halloween.

There was no talk of murder and deception.

After dinner we returned to Sally's house and watched the Mets lose game two. I somehow found the courage to leave and spend the night at home alone.

I read Dumas for a while before I turned in.

Dantès had located Caderousse, a former neighbor who had conspired to ruin Edmond for reasons of pure envy. Disguised as an Abbé, Dantès gives his enemy a priceless diamond. Caderousse's greed inspires him to kill a jeweler and then murder his own wife; so as to keep the treasure for himself. His actions lead to his own doom, which was exactly Edmond's intention.

Edmond Dantès had a knack for dealing out retribution to the guilty.

The advantage Dantès had over me was that he knew who the guilty were.

Twenty-seven

CALL IT FAITH, STUBBORNNESS, OR the lack of sense to say no. In any case, invest enough in what appears to be a hopeless cause, occasionally the long shot comes in.

When I walked in to the office Monday morning, I was greeted with a wet nudge from Tug McGraw. I opted to believe that it was an affectionate gesture, which surprised me, since the dog had barely acknowledged my existence since the day I rescued him from Katt's apartment more than a week earlier. I looked up at Darlene and could see by the expression on her face that there were bigger surprises to come.

"What is it?" I asked.

"Vinnie is waiting back in your office," she said.

"Vinnie? What time is it?"

I had the frightening thought that I had somehow lost track of half a day.

"Nine ten," Darlene said. "He's been waiting since eight."

"What is it?" I asked.

"I found him at the front door. I asked him what could possibly have him awake and down here before one in the afternoon. Vinnie gave me a wink, if you can believe it, and said, 'You'll see.' "

I walked over to the coffeemaker, poured a cup, and courageously headed to the back. When I came through the connecting door, Vinnie was pacing and fidgeting like a fifth grader waiting for an audience with the school principal. The difference was that he had a grin on his face so wide that I was afraid he might poke his eyes out.

"Wait till you see this, Jake," he said, bubbling.

Vinnie began waving his arm. I noticed that he was holding what I was finally able to identify as the classified section of the Sunday *Examiner*. For a brief moment, I fantasized that Vinnie had found a job.

"Sit down, Vin, you're making me dizzy," I said.

I moved around the desk and settled into my chair.

Vinnie unfolded the newspaper, sat in the seat across the desk, and handed it over with the back page facing me. The page was covered with auction notices.

"What am I looking for?" I asked.

"Bottom left," he said, almost giddily.

The display ad on the bottom left announced an auction of items from the estate of the late Judge J. Andrew Chancellor, to be held at Butterfield's Galleries that evening. The sale included antique furniture, collectable coins, stamps and books, Civil War and World War II memorabilia, fine china, silverware, and artwork.

The artwork included African masks, English porcelain, and French impressionist paintings. Among the paintings listed was *The Tugboat*. The artist was Alfred Sisley.

"What are the odds that this was the painting hung over Chancellor's bedroom safe?" I asked Vinnie.

"Even," he said.

"We need to get our hands on the thing."

"I called Butterfield's. The bidding on the Sisley will be starting at fifty thousand; they expect it to bring close to a hundred grand."

"It might as well be a million. Is there any other way to get close to it?"

"I suppose we could try stealing it," said Vinnie.

"Too bad that the only person I knew that could maybe pull

it off is dead," I said. "I wonder if Lefty had any idea of the cache he stumbled into when he slipped through Chancellor's kitchen window."

"He could have cleaned up if he had a little more time. We can wait to see who buys the Sisley and nicely ask to examine it in private for few minutes," said Vinnie.

Not a bad idea, really, if the right person bought the painting. An hour later I was in the Toyota, crossing the Golden Gate Bridge.

I had never asked anyone to put up a hundred thousand dollars before. Though I was about to ask someone who was accustomed to being asked, I'd decided to broach the question in person rather than on the telephone.

I considered taking Tug along for the ride, thinking McGraw might distract the ugly little ankle biter that had wowed me with his egg-juggling skills during my last visit. Darlene nixed the idea, suggesting that I would make a better impression if I could dig up a clean necktie. As far as bringing Vinnie Strings along, as much as he pleaded and as much as I appreciated his early-morning efforts, I never considered it for a second.

I parked in the circular driveway, walked to the front entrance, and pushed the doorbell. The chimes sounded a lot like "My Way."

"Mr. Diamond, come in," said Jeremy Cash.

I followed Cash to the kitchen. Kafka was thankfully nowhere in sight. Cash offered coffee, and I accepted. He asked what he could do for me. I told him.

That evening I sat beside Cash in the auction hall as he joined the bidding on the Sisley. Cash had assured me that he would not be outbid. He told me, after viewing the painting, that he actually liked it quite a bit. At the close of bidding, Jeremy Cash had purchased *The Tugboat* for ninety-seven thousand, four hundred dollars. He arranged to have it delivered to his San Francisco office the following morning, at which time I was welcome to examine the painting to my heart's content.

I thanked Cash, declined a dinner invitation, and went home to my apartment. I reheated one of my mother's frozen care packages, ziti Siciliano, washing it down with old Chianti that was just this side of becoming vinegar. I knew I had to find something to take my mind off the painting, and what it might tell me about the Chancellor case, or the suspense would wreck me.

The Count of Monte Cristo did the trick.

Jeremy Cash told me that he would phone as soon as the painting was delivered. Darlene took the call just past ten the next morning.

Cash had an office in the Transamerica Pyramid, near the top of the pyramid. There, he wrote, scheduled speaking engagements, and coordinated radio and television appearances. When I arrived at eleven, Cash's assistant greeted me with an apology. Cash had to attend a meeting with his publisher and would be gone until after lunch. She told me that I could use Cash's private office for as long as I needed. She escorted me to his office, opened the door for me, then went back out to her post. I closed the door behind me. The painting sat leaning against Cash's desk, wrapped in plain brown paper.

I placed the package on the desk and removed the wrapping, stealing a glance out the window as I worked. The view of the Golden Gate Bridge and the Sausalito Marina was spectacular. I moved the wrapping to the floor and looked down at the painting. I lifted the painting and turned it facedown. There was heavy paper backing stapled to the frame. It was the only place to look. I carefully removed the top row of staples, using a letter opener that I discovered on the desk. I lifted the painting again, held it at a forty-five-degree angle, and gently shook it from side to side. A nine-by-twelve-inch brown manila envelope slid out onto the desk. I replaced the staples, using Cash's brass paperweight. I patiently rewrapped the painting and leaned it against the foot of the desk. I walked around the desk and lowered myself into Cash's leather chair.

Finally, I picked up the manila envelope.

The envelope was addressed to Judge J. Andrew Chancellor at his courthouse chambers. There was a return address stamped in the upper-left corner. Officer Daniel Williams, Records Division, 46 Natoma Street, Folsom, California 95630.

I turned the envelope over and worked open the sealed flap. I noticed that my hands were shaking.

In the envelope, I found six sheets of paper. On top was a cover letter, addressed to Chancellor and signed by Officer Williams, acknowledging the judge's request for police records and compliance to the request by way of the photocopies attached.

The remaining pages were copied from the Folsom Police Department log for the twenty-eighth of June 1985, documenting every incident attended to by the police during the twenty-four-hour period. Traffic violations and accidents, robberies, disturbances of the peace, vandalism, assaults, all in chronological order. It looked to be a busy day for the Folsom police, and busier as the evening arrived with its graduation day events and celebrations.

The phone call from Calvin Ryder, reporting the incident in the parking lot, was logged in at nine-fifteen that night. Followed by the arrival of Ryder and his son Chance, accompanied by Chief Gunderson, at the police station at ten, the questioning and arrest of Chance Ryder, and Calvin Ryder's departure from the station at ten-forty. Chance remained in jail overnight.

The last entry of the night was made at eleven-ten. A young woman was picked up for vagrancy, taken to the police station, questioned by the chief of police, and then released by Gunderson at eleven forty-five. The woman's name was listed as Jenny Solomon, nineteen, of Sacramento.

I went through the five pages at least three times, trying to determine what Judge Chancellor had been looking for. Who was Chancellor willing to pay Tony Carlucci ten thousand dollars to find? Jenny Solomon was the only reasonable answer.

A teenage girl, alone, found wandering the streets a good distance from her home, and released with no mention of any attempt to contact parents or run a check with authorities in Sacramento.

I placed the pages back into the envelope and left Jeremy Cash's office. I thanked his assistant, asking that Cash call me as soon as he returned.

I rode the elevator down to the street and walked back to Columbus Avenue.

There was no longer any question about the subject of the envelope in the judge's safe. It had to do with a fifteen-year-old confrontation that ended in death. And if something in those five pages had Ryder scared enough to commit murder, somehow Ryder had to know that it had come into Judge Chancellor's hands.

I had a few phone calls to make.

Back at the office, I asked Darlene to try locating Officer Phil Moss and went to my desk to call Officer Daniel Williams at the Folsom Police Department.

Williams had met Judge Chancellor in mid-September. The judge had been down to talk with Chief Gunderson and had ultimately asked the chief if he could see certain police records. Gunderson had referred Chancellor to Officer Williams, who handled department archives. Williams told the judge that it would take a while to dig up the records, which were filed in cartons in the basement of the station. Williams promised to mail the information as soon as possible. He sent the package off to the judge the following week.

"Did Chief Gunderson know what was in the package to Chancellor?" I asked.

"Sure," said Williams, "he asked me, I told him. He's the chief, right?"

Right.

The chief who failed to mention Chancellor's visit when Joey and I had dropped in, the chief who may have mentioned the judge's visit and request for records to Lowell Ryder, the chief who would certainly hear about my chat with Officer Williams.

I quickly decided that Police Chief Gunderson should hear just what I wanted him to hear.

"Any idea what it was that the judge was looking for?" I asked.

"No, only what he asked to see. I'm just a paper pusher," he said, "you're the detective. How about I just send you copies of what I sent to the judge."

"Could you do that?"

"Sure, why not," said Williams. "It is public record, and it should be easier to find this time."

I gave Williams my address and phone number and thanked him for his help.

Darlene yelled from out front that Phil Moss was on the other line.

"Phil, it's time to pay your dues. Do you know anyone with the Sacramento PD?"

"Yeah, as a matter of fact I have an uncle out there, a captain."

Was I getting lucky, or what?

"I need anything he can find out about a Jenny Solomon. She would have been nineteen and living in Sacramento in eighty-five, and may have had some kind of run-in with the law."

"I'll get right on it," Moss said.

Darlene poked her head in.

"I'm going for lunch, Jake. Want to join me?"

"I'm waiting for a call or two."

"I'll bring something back for you, maybe you can sit out front and keep McGraw company."

I sat at Darlene's desk and fielded phone calls like a volunteer at a Jerry Lewis telethon.

Officer Dan Williams phoned. Williams said that it would take longer than he had thought to get the copies he'd promised. It seemed that the records had somehow been misplaced.

Why was I not surprised.

Jeremy Cash called.

"Did you find what you were looking for, Mr. Diamond?" he asked.

"Yes, I think so. But I can use some more help, Mr. Cash."

"Anything."

"The first time I met Freddie, he was attending a fund-raiser for Lowell Ryder. Can you tell me anything about their relation-ship?"

"I really don't know much about it. I know that Freddie was involved in Ryder's campaign, and that my son spoke highly of the man. Freddie seemed to think that he could earn a choice position at the DA's office after graduation, though I thought it very unlikely. I don't like to admit it, but Freddie was a poor student. I didn't really believe he would ever make it through law school."

Unless a highly respected and influential alumnus could pull a few strings, for a price. A campaign donation, perhaps. Something in the area of a hundred thousand dollars, possibly in twenty- and fifty-dollar bills.

And probably impossible to prove.

"This Mancuso, who they're saying killed my son, did he do it?" asked Cash.

"No."

"Can you say who did?"

"I really can't say," I said.

Which was the truth.

I could venture a good guess, but who could really say. Freddie Cash could say, if Freddie Cash was in any condition to say anything and if he ever saw it coming. And I was guessing that Lowell Ryder could say, but I doubted that he would.

Jeremy Cash didn't press me.

Tug McGraw was pushing his empty food dish around the floor. I realized how hungry I was myself as I poured soy chow into his bowl. Darlene walked in with a grilled-chicken Caesar salad just in the nick of time.

I retired to my inner sanctum and had swallowed my last mouthful when Phil Moss called.

Jenny Solomon had been wanted by the Sacramento police since the twenty-eighth of June 1985, for questioning in a robbery-homicide. The body of Ed Clarke, 42, had been found in Clarke's ice cream parlor at two in the morning. Clarke had been shot to death with a gun registered to him, which he kept at the shop. The cash register had been emptied. Jenny Solomon worked at the shop. A second employee, Susan Bryant, testified that Solomon and Clarke were alone cleaning the shop after closing when Bryant left shortly after eleven. A call to Solomon's mother, when Clarke's body was found, established that Jenny had never arrived home after work. An APB on Jenny Solomon went out over the wire to all surrounding cities and towns.

Out of the corner of my eye I spotted a flyer from the new sandwich shop up on Columbus Avenue. It sat pinned under a slab of plaster, the shape of Rhode Island. I yanked it out and flipped it over. It was the three-column inventory I had scribbled a week and a half earlier. I scanned the first column, things I thought I knew, concluding that I had batted a thousand. The questions in the center column, things I'd like to know, had all been answered.

The last column, things I'll never know, remained blank.

I decided to leave it that way for as long as I could.

An all-points bulletin on Jenny Solomon had gone out to all surrounding cities and towns.

Less than twenty-four hours later, the Folsom police had the fugitive in custody.

And Chief William Gunderson let her go.

Twenty-eight

THE NEXT MORNING, I WAS driving east, directly into the sunrise, thinking thoughts that should have been reserved for dark, menacing nights.

Like scary stories around a campfire.

I had picked up the Impala from Joey Russo's garage at daybreak, declining Joey's offer of company.

I was feeling like a coward but not wanting to act like one.

I had been feeling defiant, noble. Taking up the banner for Lefty Wright. Trying to empathize, to feel what Lefty had suffered at the hands of his betrayers.

I mistook it for bravery.

Until I learned about Jenny Solomon.

Then I began to see bravery differently. Charlie Mancuso, risking his freedom to defend a sister. And I caught a glimpse of incomprehensible courage, in a teenage girl who had lived through a twenty-four-hour nightmare fifteen years ago.

And for how many of the countless hours since.

I had ideas about what may have happened to Jenny Solomon that terrified me, had me wondering what could have put me in mind of such deceit, had me convinced that thoughts so black could be condoned only if they were true.

I had run to Sally, to hear her say it wasn't so.

183

Sally couldn't help me.

I couldn't sleep, I was up and out at dawn.

I was driving east, into the sunrise, to hear someone say it wasn't so.

I parked the Chevy in front of the Folsom Public Library and walked over to the police station to hear from Chief William Gunderson.

Gunderson sat at his desk, across the large room. I zeroed in on him. I must have looked a bit crazy. There were others in the room, though I couldn't say how many; they gave me a wide berth. Gunderson saw something, too, in my face or in the way I held my hands, that had him up and around the desk very quickly for so large a man. He caught up to me halfway.

"I came to tell you what I think," I said.

"Let me buy you a cup of coffee," he said, turning me around and leading me back out to the street.

I followed him to the small restaurant across from the library.

"Is that your Chevy convertible?" he asked.

"Yes."

"Very nice."

"It's my pride and joy," I said. "What's yours?"

"My job," he answered.

Gunderson led me toward the rear of the restaurant; stopping along the way to greet each of the handful of diners scattered at tables in front. Greeting all of them by name. We settled into a booth against the back wall.

A young girl quickly arrived, holding an order pad, pulling a pencil from behind her right ear. She was eighteen, maybe nineteen, years old. Her name tag read Rebecca.

"Good morning, Chief," she said, "what can I get for you, gentlemen?"

I felt very old.

"The strawberry rhubarb pie is the best in the state," Gunderson said.

It wouldn't surprise me.

"Just coffee, Rebecca," I said.

"So, Mr. Diamond," Gunderson said, after ordering the same and watching the girl start for the counter, "what exactly are you looking for?"

I was tempted to say that I was looking for the truth, but I doubted, after fifteen years, that anyone could possibly guarantee the truth. I waited, watching Rebecca place a stainless steel creamer and two heavy mugs on the table. She filled the two cups from a glass carafe and walked off.

"I told you all that I could about the Davey King murder case. Then I hear that you've been pestering Officer Williams. Now here you are again, coming all this way from the big city. What are you looking for?"

"I came to tell you what I think," I repeated.

"I'm a very busy man, Mr. Diamond. What makes you think that I'm interested?"

"I doubt you'd be buying me coffee if you weren't, Chief."

"Okay, Diamond, I'll bite. What do you think?"

"I think you picked up a girl named Jenny Solomon that night. A scared young girl, most likely disoriented and in shock, who had been attacked in a parking lot less than two hours before. And instead of helping the kid, you put her out on the street."

"That's far-fetched, Diamond. The girl had nothing to do with the King incident. She was legal age, said she was visiting a friend and just out walking. I had no reason to believe otherwise, and no cause to hold her."

"Except that she was wanted by the Sacramento police."

"How would I have known that?" he asked.

"You knew it, Chief. It was out on the wire, and I've confirmed that you received word long before you brought the girl in."

"And why would I cut her loose?"

I suddenly realized what I had suspected all along, and I said it with conviction.

"Because Jenny Solomon would have been able to testify that it was Lowell Ryder, and not his brother Chance, who killed Davey King."

"And who gave you that idea?"

"Chance Ryder," I said, "and you must have known that also, and you didn't want to have to explain why you went along with Calvin Ryder's version of events."

All of the air went out of Gunderson, like a punctured inner tube.

"Calvin was a lifelong friend, Chance was willing, where was the harm in that?"

"I'm in no position to judge the decisions of consenting adults. I'm aware of the gray areas. The harm came afterward, when the well-being of a teenage girl in great need of help was sacrificed for the cover-up."

"The girl robbed and murdered her boss," said Gunderson.

"We don't know that. We can't know what happened in Sacramento. But now, five men have been murdered in San Francisco and I'm convinced that it's connected to what happened to Davey King fifteen years ago. It's time for you to tell me all you know about that night."

"I'm sorry," he said, and quickly rose.

"I'll find out," I said, having no idea how I would.

"I wish you luck, Mr. Diamond" he said, already moving away. "You really should try the pie."

I watched him all the way to the front door. He stopped briefly at the counter.

"Ray, put the coffee on my tab, and anything else Mr. Diamond might like."

And he was gone.

"More?"

I looked up to find Rebecca holding a pot of coffee.

"Sure, thank you," I said, "and how about a slice of that strawberry rhubarb I've heard so much about. And Rebecca."

"Yes, sir."

"I'll take care of the check."

Twenty minutes later I walked across to the town library. I found Mrs. Dewey shelving books.

"Why, hello," she said, "you must have taken a liking to our quiet town."

I really couldn't say.

"I was wondering if you had a local phone book I could look at."

"What are you looking for?" she asked. "I think I know all there is to know about where everything is around here."

"I was hoping to locate Calvin Ryder," I said.

"Oh, Calvin. I'm afraid you won't find him here. The poor man is at the Mercy Hospice in Sacramento. Cancer. He doesn't have long, from what I understand."

I thanked Mrs. Dewey and walked back out to the Impala.

Phil Moss had acquired the address for me. Barbara Solomon on Ninth at Q Street in Sacramento. The night before I had talked about phoning the woman. Sally had a feeling that Mrs. Solomon wouldn't talk.

According to Moss, Mrs. Solomon had insisted, every time she was asked, that she had never seen or heard from her daughter Jenny since the night Ed Clarke was killed in the ice cream shop.

"I'm going to Folsom tomorrow morning," I said. "I'll stop to see Mrs. Solomon on my way back and explain why I need to find her daughter."

"She won't talk, Jake," Sally had repeated, "but I have an idea."

The letter was in my jacket pocket, addressed to Jenny Solomon.

I exited Route 50 at Sixteenth Street, drove over to Q Street and down to Ninth. The small house stood on a corner lot. I parked the Chevy, walked to the front door, and pressed the buzzer. The woman who answered looked as if she had been waiting for me to arrive, so that she could get finished asking me to leave. It took all of my charm to coax her out onto the front porch.

Sally had been absolutely correct. Barbara Solomon had nothing to say about the fate or whereabouts of her daughter, in spite of my insistence that I would do nothing to harm or jeopardize Jenny.

"Do you believe that Jenny was protecting herself in some way when Clarke was shot?" I asked.

"Mr. Diamond. Ed Clarke was a good friend of mine, a special friend. Jenny had always been a troubled girl, particularly in her teens, after her father passed away. Ed had been good enough to give her a chance working at his shop. I can't bring myself to believe that Ed would have done anything to harm my daughter."

"I understand," I said.

"You've come a long way. Can I offer you a cup of coffee before you start back?"

"That would be good," I said.

I followed her into the house and back to the kitchen. There was a photograph on the fireplace mantel, a pretty blue-eyed girl at her high school graduation. We drank coffee, silently, at the kitchen table. I kept forming questions in my mind, and fighting every impulse to ask them.

"Mrs. Solomon, do you know why Jenny may have gone to Folsom after she left the shop that night?"

"I didn't know she had gone there," she said. "The police never mentioned it."

"Let's say she had."

"There was a boy in Folsom that she had been seeing for a month or so. They had met at a concert here in town. I don't know of anyone else Jenny may have known out in Folsom."

"Do you remember his name?"

"It was an unusual name, Chance, I think it was. It was a long time ago."

I reached into my jacket for the letter I had written for Jenny the night before.

"Mrs. Solomon. Please. If you should happen to hear from your daughter, could you pass this along to her?"

I placed the envelope on the table. I didn't wait for an answer. I rose, thanked her for the coffee, and moved to leave. I could hear her rise and follow behind me. At the door I turned to her, saw the puzzled look in her eyes. She tried to say something but couldn't. When I pulled away from the house, she was still standing at the door.

On my way down from Folsom I had thought I would drop into Mercy Hospice to visit Calvin Ryder. I changed my mind. I couldn't bring myself to confront a dying man until I found the courage to confront his elder son, to confess to Chance Ryder, to tell Chance who I really was and why I had deceived him.

I wondered how long that might take.

And I wondered how long I could wait before having to admit that I would never hear from Jenny Solomon.

I pointed the Impala toward home.

I was crossing the Sacramento River into Rio Vista when I heard the radio news report. State police were investigating the apparent suicide of Chief William Gunderson, found dead from a gunshot wound in the men's room of the Folsom Police Station an hour earlier.

I drove, blind, all the way back to San Francisco.

I was thinking that I had the kiss of death.

I had instigated a hunt for Vic Vigoda and he had landed in McCovey Cove.

I had pressed Katt, and he and Lefty had been silenced.

I had uncovered Freddie Cash's self-manufactured kidnapping, and Freddie had turned up DOA.

I had pushed Chief Gunderson to the point where the only way to save his job, his pride and his joy, had been to take his own life.

I was ready to give it all up, before I condemned another soul, innocent or guilty.

Then I thought about what Jimmy Pigeon would have said to me.

Jimmy Pigeon, who had brought me into the business.

Jimmy Pigeon, who had promised from the start that the truth never came cheap.

Jimmy would have told me that I was giving myself far too much credit.

I walked into the office. The dog seemed genuinely glad to see me. Darlene happily reported that we had a few new cases to consider. I asked her, kindly, to hold the thought.

I made a quick phone call to the Brown Palace.

Chance Folsom had wrapped his work in Denver and would be back home in Los Angeles after the weekend.

And a letter to Jenny Solomon had made it at least as far as her mother's kitchen table.

I asked Darlene to fill me in on the prospective clients.

All I could do was to keep busy.

And wait.

Twenty-nine

THE WORLD SERIES WAS over.

With baseball in the record books, the spotlight turned to the gridiron. Sadly, the 49ers were playing in the dark. Darlene had flown to Charlotte to watch the Niners lose to Carolina, 34 to 16, their sixth loss in eight games. Darlene had decided to stay over until Tuesday morning; she had her hands full trying to cheer up a very melancholy defensive lineman.

I stopped into Molinari's for two cups of coffee, just as I had the last time Darlene took a post-game Monday off. Exactly four Mondays before. The day I got the call from Lefty Wright.

Angelo Verdi was going on about the murder trial. Charlie Mancuso was being tried for the murders of Freddie Cash and Mike Flanagan, notwithstanding that Mancuso was nowhere to be found. A conviction was imminent. Lowell Ryder was riding high, with the election only eight days off. Jeremy Cash was conspicuously absent from the proceedings, and Governor Krupp was keeping unusually silent about how far the trial at hand came toward solving the Chancellor homicide.

I had dog-sat Tug McGraw over the weekend, in Darlene's absence, and he waited patiently outside of Molinari's door for me to tear myself away from Angelo's commentary. He greeted me with a deep sigh when I finally emerged and followed me up the two flights of stairs to the office.

I stationed myself at Darlene's post. McGraw squeezed his way under the desk, causing us equal levels of cramped discomfort. With a good excuse for putting my feet up on the desktop, I dug the Dumas novel from my jacket pocket and did just that.

A small slip of notepaper marked where I had left off in Dantès story, marked the only real progress I could point to over the past four weeks—1,007 pages down and 71 pages to go. I glanced at the note. Chance Folsom's Los Angeles address and phone number, furnished by cousin Bobby, courtesy of his Screen Actors Guild directory.

I glanced at the note, looked at the telephone, and placed the note facedown on Darlene's desk.

Edmond Dantès had finally come around to dealing with the Crown Prosecutor, M. de Villefort. Three men, motivated by greed and envy, had falsely framed Edmond, implicating him in a Bonapartist plot against the crown. The case against Dantès would never have led to conviction and imprisonment, however, if it were not for the ambition of the public prosecutor, Villefort. Villefort's policy against the Bonapartists had to be extremely vigilant if he was to please the ruling Royalists and advance his career. Villefort's father is a known Bonapartist. Villefort feared that leniency in the case of the young Dantès, who he truly didn't believe guilty, might be seen as anti-Crown sentiment. Villefort prosecutes Edmond as a traitor and has him incarcerated as a dangerous criminal, insuring his own climb up the political and social ladder.

Edmond uncovers a secret from Villefort's past. Literally, a buried secret. Years before, Villefort had buried his newborn bastard child, alive. Bertuccio, a sworn enemy of Villefort, had dug up the child and saved the baby's life. Edmond, now the count of Monte Cristo, learns of the event when Bertuccio becomes the count's servant. The rescued child, Benedetto, is now a young man being brought to trial before Villefort for murder and prison escape. Dantès sees the trial as the means to disclose Benedetto's identity and ruin Villefort. If Edmond Dantès cannot prove that he was an innocent man, convicted and imprisoned with the help of Villefort's complicity, he will pull the Crown prosecutor down by whatever means available. When Benedetto testifies to the identity of his true father, and of the attempted burial, Edmond's retribution is complete.

Good old Alexandre Dumas could spin quite a yarn.

And Dumas had a huge advantage over Diamond.

He could write his own resolution.

Just before noon Joey Russo called, offering to drop by with some lunch.

Whenever Darlene was out of town, everyone who knew me well was afraid I would forget to eat.

Joey arrived at one with a covered plate lovingly prepared by his wife, Angela. Smoked mozzarella, fresh basil, Greek and Sicilian olives, and thinly sliced prosciutto. Perfectly supplemented by a warm loaf of seeded Italian bread and a cold six-pack of St. Pauli Girl.

"What's in the other bag?" I asked.

"A few of Angela's meatballs for the pooch," said Joey, "I thought we could slip him a treat while Darlene is away."

As if he understood English and welcomed the prospect of eating something not derived from soybeans, Tug McGraw popped his head out from under the desk.

"So, Joey, tell me," I said, as we cleared what remained in the platter of food, each working on our second beer, "how do you get to the truth?"

"Short of sodium pentothal and the rack?"

"Okay."

"Three ways I can think of. Scientific method, deductive reasoning, and finesse," said Joey. "The first requires plugging values into a known formula and seeing if both sides of the equal sign are actually equivalent. It doesn't work very well with the truth of human behavior, since there's no real formula."

"Deductive reasoning?"

"Better, but unless you're Sherlock Holmes and consider every single possibility you run the risk of throwing out the baby with the bathwater."

"Which leaves?"

"Finesse. Like in pinochle, when you try to finesse the ten of trump. You get someone to admit a truth in order to cover up a more damning truth. I knew a guy who confessed to robbing a liquor store because his only alibi was that he was at a motel at the time of the robbery, with his wife's sister."

"How did the investigation of a murder that went down a month ago turn into an investigation of crimes fifteen years past?" I asked.

"On the surface, it looks as if you're bucking for a guest spot on *Unsolved Mysteries*. If you want to get to the truth, you have to go where it takes you."

"I've come to a roadblock."

"Either you find a way around it," said Joey, "or you wait until the road reopens. If it's waited fifteen years, it can wait a while longer. And in the end, all scores will be settled, with or without our help."

"Do you really believe that?"

"Absolutely," said Joey. "Why don't you get out of this office for a while? The air is a lot better out there."

"I'll hang in a bit longer. In case Darlene checks up on me. Thanks for lunch. Thank Angela."

"You know how to reach me. Don't forget the meatballs for the mutt."

With that, Joey picked up the empty platter and headed out the door. I threw the meat into Tug McGraw's food dish, and he wandered out from under the desk to explore. Anticipating the dog's eventual return, I propped my feet back up on Darlene's desk and set to finish reading the Dumas novel. Shortly after closing the book at the end of the last page, I must have dozed off. A light knocking at the office door woke both the dog and me. I swung my legs down to the floor and went to open up to my late afternoon visitor.

The woman standing in the hall outside the door was in her early to mid-thirties. She wore her shoulder length dark blond hair in a ponytail. She had piercing blue eyes and a faultless complexion with no makeup. She wore a knee-length maroon rain-coat over a plain deep-blue A-line dress.

"Jake Diamond?" she asked.

"Yes."

"I'm Jennifer Hamilton. I used to be Jenny Solomon. And I'm here to find out if you are planning to turn my world upside down."

"Would you like to come in and have a seat?" I said, flustered.

She walked past me and settled into the customer chair. Mc-Graw peeked out briefly and disappeared again under the desk. I walked around to Darlene's side. I was grasping for an answer to her question. I couldn't find one. I opted for a question of my own, instead.

"Can I offer you something to drink? I can send down to the deli for coffee or a soft drink."

"Have any bourbon?"

"Give me a minute," I said.

I went back to my room and grabbed the pint bottle of George Dickel and the two small glasses from my desk drawer. I returned to the front, sat across from Jenny Solomon, and poured two drinks. She picked up her glass and took a sip.

"Well?" she said.

"I don't want to hurt you," I said.

"Then forget me," she said.

"I'd rather not do that, either."

"What do you want?" she asked.

"I'm looking for the truth," I said feebly.

"Ha," she said, "tell me what you're thinking."

"I'm thinking that you killed your mother's boyfriend because he assaulted you. I'm thinking that you ran, not wanting to face the consequences, or to face your mother. I'm thinking that you went to find Chance Ryder, because you had nowhere else to go."

"You're quite the detective," she said.

"I get a lot of help. What I would like to know is what exactly happened in the parking lot in Folsom and with Chief Gunderson afterward."

"And then?"

"And then I'll add up the score, tell you what I think the story is, and let you decide if you want me to forget you or not. It's up to you. I don't want to hurt you," I repeated.

She downed the rest of her bourbon and slid the empty glass toward me for a refill. I topped both of our glasses.

"I ran out of the shop and called Chance at home. His father told me where I could find him. I found the bar, but before I got in to look for Chance, I ran into his brother in the parking lot. He was very drunk. He made a pass at me. After what had happened at the ice cream shop, you can imagine that I wasn't in the mood for unwanted advances. I started for the bar, he grabbed my arm, and I broke away. Then I fell and he was on top of me. He must have knocked me out cold. Next, I remember the two boys struggling on the ground nearby. I jumped up and took off. I was wandering the streets in a daze. A patrol car picked me up. I was taken to the police station. I sat alone in a closed room for thirty minutes. I was released. End of story. Forget me."

"The boy who tried to rescue you was killed for his effort," I said.

"I didn't know that. I'm sorry to hear that."

"He was also accused of being the one who attacked you. Killed in self-defense. His name was Davey King."

"And Chance's brother got away clean?" she asked.

"Yes," I said, and decided to leave it at that. "How are you doing now?"

"I'm married to a good man. We run a small gift shop in Half Moon Bay. I have two beautiful young daughters. I manage a superficial relationship with my mother, who remains in denial after fifteen years. I have no interest in revisiting the past. I want to be forgotten. Jenny Solomon has left the building."

"Okay," I said.

"Okay?"

"Okay, thanks for dropping by."

I picked one of my business cards off Darlene's desk.

I spotted the Dumas novel. I turned to page 1,007 and put the card in to mark the place.

"Take this. My card is in here in case you ever need to reach me. If you like reading, I'm done with the book. I particularly enjoyed chapters 59 and 60. I'll forget I ever met you, Mrs. Hamilton," I said, handing her *The Count of Monte Cristo.*

She took the book, slowly rose, looked me once in the eyes, and was quickly out the door.

Then I was alone in the office, looking at the door that had just closed behind Jenny Solomon. At the deadbolt that you could unlock with a paper clip, the scratches Tug McGraw had contributed to the door's character, the coffee stain at the threshold, and the words *Diamond Investigation* in reverse on the opaque glass panel.

And I wondered what it would take to get to the other side.

Thirty

THE CALL CAME TWO DAYS later, on a Wednesday afternoon. I had just about given up on the Chancellor case. I felt like an inept Colombo, as if I knew who the killer was but couldn't spring the trap. And then Darlene buzzed me with word that a Mrs. Jennifer Hamilton was on the line.

"Diamond, I get the picture."

"Oh?"

"The Dumas book," she said. "You think that you can snare Ryder by getting me into court to spill the beans about that night."

"I guess I thought about it."

"Did you think about my being convicted for killing the ice cream man?"

"Sure, I've thought about that, too," I admitted. "But if we can get some kind of testimony, to suggest that Clarke had been hitting on you and conceivably threatened your life. I can get you the best defense lawyer that money can buy."

Well, that Jeremy Cash's money could buy.

"The other girl who worked with me, Sue Bryant, if she's still to be found. She saw some evidence of Clarke's lecherous intentions."

"How about your mother?"

"Jesus, Diamond, you're merciless."

"Jenny," I said, playing my last card, "Chance Ryder took the rap for his brother that night in the parking lot. Chance never knew who the girl was, he never knew about you. And he believed that Lowell had been the good guy. Lowell was on his way to Stanford Law School and the father asked the older brother to take the heat. Chance couldn't say no."

"That's a horrible story."

"Yes, it is. And Davey King is in the ground, for trying to do the right thing," I said. "Chance did the prison time for manslaughter and now he does movies."

"I've seen him in a few."

"And Lowell Ryder is about to be elected district attorney of San Francisco," I added. "Look, Jenny. This guy Ryder has killed five people to save his own skin. Not to mention letting his brother go to prison in his place. But this has to be about you. You have to want to get clear of the Clarke murder and settle the score with your mother. If you've really put it behind you, okay. But if not, this is the chance for you to throw it off once and for all, and I'll do everything I can to help. Regardless of whether we can nail Lowell Ryder."

"I'll have to see my mother before I can decide."

"Fair enough."

"And you'd better talk to Chance Folsom."

"Why is that?"

"Because if we go ahead with this, it's going to come out that his father was at the police station the night Gunderson had me there and that Ryder paid me off to walk out and disappear."

"Wow."

It was the best I could do.

"Good word for it," said Jenny. "Talk to Chance, I'll talk to my mother. I'll call you back."

And with that she was off the line.

And I was left to decide how to ask a son to help implicate his father in a criminal cover-up and perhaps expose his brother as an alleged multiple murderer.

Talk about a break in the case.

"So, let's see if I've got this straight," said Darlene the next after-noon at the airport, about to put me on a plane to Los Angeles, "Jenny Solomon turns herself in for the murder of her mother's boyfriend. Self-defense. She's found innocent, kisses and makes up with Mom and incidentally fingers Lowell Ryder for attempted rape and manslaughter after fifteen years. How is that going to strap Lowell with the rash of killings up here?"

"It probably doesn't, but it ends his career. And for Ryder that's probably worse than death."

"And what if no one believes her, about Ryder I mean?"

"His brother and his father can corroborate."

"You're dreaming, Jake," Darlene said, "but that's what makes you so endearing."

"I wondered what it was."

"Good luck," Darlene said as I walked through the boarding gate.

"Thanks," I answered.

As if I had any idea what kind of result could possibly be con-sidered lucky.

I had phoned Chance the night before. How are you, I'll be in LA for a day and a half. Maybe we can have dinner tomorrow night.

"Sure, sounds great, I'm looking forward to it," he said, com-pounding my feelings of guilt.

I was planning to stay at my cousin Bobby's place in Westwood. Bobby was on location for the dinosaur movie. I asked Chance to meet me there for a drink before we went for dinner.

I took a cab from LAX, having the driver stop and wait while I picked up a bottle of Dickel on the way. I broke the seal the moment I entered Bobby's apartment around seven. I found a clean glass and some ice and started preparing myself for Chance's arrival at eight-thirty.

By eight I was on my third drink, surfing Bobby's thirty-two-inch TV for distraction. As with almost everything else, there were too many choices. I ultimately landed on a Steven Seagal flick. I'd seen them all, but really couldn't say which one it was.

The doorbell rang at precisely half past eight. I killed the TV, picked up my glass, and opened for Chance Folsom. He followed me into the kitchen, where I poured him a bourbon and refilled my own.

"I hope you didn't open that bottle tonight," he said.

"Afraid so," I said.

"Cheers," he said, taking a long drink. "The Chicago theater community has never heard of Jake Falco. Before you get too drunk to speak, maybe you can tell me who you are and what you want from me."

Everyone's a detective. At least it gave me an opening.

So we sat at the kitchen table and he quietly listened as I related the events of the past month. Judge Chancellor, Vic Vigoda, Officer Katt, Lefty Wright, Freddie Cash, Charlie "Bones" Mancuso. And when I was done, Chance asked the obvious question, the question I really dreaded answering.

"So," he said, helping himself to another drink, "what has all of this have to do with me?"

"It has to do with your brother," I said. "I'm almost positive that your brother is responsible for the murders."

"Is that a joke?"

"No."

"My brother is some kind of big shot DA, why would he be running around killing people?"

"Precisely because he's a big shot DA who is about to be elected the chief San Francisco DA in a few days, with aspirations for political office that go at least as far as the governor's mansion. It's all he's wanted all of his life, you told me so yourself. And when Davey King came back to haunt him, threatening to destroy it all, your brother took steps and then totally lost control."

"Davey King was self-defense. I did the time for it and I'm the guilty party of record. Only Lowell, my father, Gunderson or I could say different; and not one of us will. Lowell has nothing to be afraid of. You're not making any sense."

"Davey King was as innocent as you were. It was Lowell who attacked the girl, it was Davey who tried to come to the rescue and he died for it."

Chance gripped his glass so tightly, I was afraid it would shatter in his hand. His eyes went blank, but for a split second before they did I saw something in his eyes that made me believe that the thought had crossed his mind more than once over the past fifteen years.

I waited.

It was going to be entirely up to him where it would go from there.

After a lifetime or two he finally spoke.

"Who could possibly tell you that?" he asked. "Who beside Lowell could possibly know that?"

Jennifer Hamilton had called me merciless. I had no choice. It was far too late for mercy. I felt as if I had plowed over Chance Ryder with an automobile, and that all I could do was to throw it into reverse and back up over the body.

"Gunderson could have told me, but he decided to kill himself instead. It was the girl who told me what happened in the parking lot that night."

"The girl?"

"The girl who Lowell attacked, the girl Davey King tried to protect, the girl that your brother was so afraid Judge Chancellor would find."

"Who was she?"

And so I said the name Jenny Solomon. And Chance came across the table and hit me so hard in the face that I was out cold for nearly ten minutes.

When I came to and slowly opened my eyes I was lying flat on the living room sofa.

Chance sat across from me on the armchair, with a half-empty bottle and a full glass of Dickel sitting on the table beside him.

As my eyes focused, he spoke.

"When I was a boy," Chance began, "I felt as if I owed my father everything, but I never imagined that I would be paying for the rest of my life. My kid brother was very intelligent. All my brother ever wanted was to become a lawyer. He graduated at the top of his high school class and earned a full scholarship to Stanford. On graduation night, I went with my brother to celebrate at a local saloon. After a few drinks, I decided to leave while I was sober enough to drive and could still hope to get some work done with my father on the farm the following day. I made it safely and I was sitting at the kitchen table drinking coffee with my father when my brother called. My father spoke with him briefly on the phone, I heard him tell my brother to come directly home. Then my father told me what I had to do to help my brother and to help him. My father had sacrificed for his family, and he expected me to do the same. I couldn't say no. My brother couldn't say no. My father was not a man you could say no to. He was a very determined and frightening man. The fierce discipline Calvin handed out as we were growing up left no doubts about the consequences of not obeying his wishes."

And so it was that Chance Ryder was given his first acting role, as a stand-in for his brother. A scandal could have ended his brother's dreams before they began, his father explained to Chance. Calvin Ryder asked his oldest son take the heat. Calvin called Gunderson and filled the chief in about the incident in the parking lot, substituting Chance for his brother as the son who killed Davey King in self-defense.

"To help sell the story, my father put his hands around my neck and choked me until red marks appeared," said Chance, "then he took me back to the parking lot to meet the chief and turn myself in."

It was a heartbreaking tale.

And now I had told Chance Folsom that his sacrifice was a cover-up for a crime committed against someone he had cared about. It would change everything Chance ever believed or felt about his family. And I wondered if I had any right to be the bearer of such ill tidings, since I had nothing to offer in the way of consolation and hearing his story had taken me no closer to solving a single thing. And then he asked the question that made me wish I were still out cold.

"Did my father know who the girl was?" he asked.

"Jenny claims he did," I said.

With that he emptied his glass with one long swallow, placed it on the table, rose from his seat, and walked over to and out the front door without another word.

With great difficulty I managed to rise, stagger over to the table, and grab the bourbon bottle.

I was still holding it when I woke up on the floor the following morning.

Thirty-one

I HADN'T HEARD A WORD from Chance Folsom after he had walked out of my cousin Bobby's apartment in LA that Thursday night. I had received a call from Jenny Solomon Hamilton on Saturday night. She had visited her mother and was calling to tell me that she had decided to let sleeping dogs lie.

"So, what did I do wrong?" I asked Sally after the call from Jenny.

Sally had come by on Saturday evening with Vietnamese take-out in hand.

"Nothing," she said, "it has nothing to do with you. It's about children protecting their parents when it should have been the other way around. Chance won't put his father through it, no matter that his father and brother hung him out to dry. You told me that Calvin Ryder is dying of cancer. What could you expect a son to do? And Mrs. Solomon. It's obvious that she couldn't handle the truth about what Ed Clarke did to her daughter, she's been denying it for fifteen years. And Jenny knows that it would tear the woman to pieces. No, Jake, you can't blame yourself. It was a no-win situation."

"So, that's it? Lowell Ryder skates?"

"Unless you can bluff the guy," said Sally.

Which is exactly what I tried to do the following afternoon.

I had made up my mind to drop in on Ryder unannounced. I had counted on finding him at home, relaxing alone after an arduous campaign on the Sunday before Election Day. I couldn't have been more wrong.

Ryder lived in a huge Victorian on Russian Hill, at Filbert and Jones, not far up the hill from my office. As I approached the house I could see the group of people milling about in front, male and female, ranging in age from college to thirty-something, holding drinks, exchanging talk and furtive glances and generally looking handsome.

I put on my party-crashing attitude.

It was obviously a pre-victory celebration; the participants were surely campaign contributors, staff and volunteers. The mood was festive; the prize trophy was in the bag. They all had the "I backed the right man" look on their beaming faces. When I strolled through the gate of the white picket fence they all seemed glad to see me. When I asked where I could find Lowell they looked at me as if I were important. As I walked around to the back of the house as directed, I could hear the whispered inquiries as to who in the world I might be.

I found Ryder holding court in the large yard behind the house, which overlooked the Bay and the Golden Gate Bridge. There were dozens of people; there was food and drink everywhere. I didn't recognize a soul other than Ryder himself; then again I didn't get around much. A bartender was splashing Jack Daniel's into a row of glasses. I was tempted to grab one, but decided I would wait to be offered.

"Mr. Ryder," I said, coming up through his audience, "I was wondering if I might have a word or two in private."

Ryder looked up at me and smiled broadly, not batting an eye. The group around him reacted very differently and shrunk away.

"Mr. Diamond," Ryder said, "nice of you to come. Can we offer you a drink?"

I wondered which we he was referring to. I must have been out of my mind.

I had come this far, so I went the distance.

"Sure, is there somewhere we could talk," I said, "I'll only take a few minutes of your time."

I suppose I convinced him that I meant business. He excused himself, took me by the arm, grabbed a couple of bourbons with his free hand, and led me into the house. The house was packed as well. I followed Ryder up the stairs to a small sitting room that must have been the only empty square footage on the property. He invited me to take one of the two chairs in the room and he took the other.

"You're on, Diamond. What's on your mind?" he asked.

I couldn't help feeling as if he had been expecting me. Sooner or later.

"I spoke with your brother about what happened back in eighty-five. And with Jenny Solomon."

"And you came to tell me you're upset that I lied to you at Twin Peaks."

"It's a little more than that, Ryder."

"Oh, yes. I almost forgot. Chance said something about me being suspected of committing half of the San Francisco homicides in the past month."

"You spoke with your brother?"

"After all these years he finally got in touch," said Ryder, "and all he wants to talk about was Davey King. You really are something, Diamond, and you picked a terrific afternoon for a surprise visit. But after Tuesday's election I doubt that I'll have time for you at all. So I'm going to tell you what I told my brother, and then I'll have to rejoin my guests. I killed King in self-defense. I was drunk, yes. I was rough with the girl. I tried to kiss her, she broke away, and we both fell to the ground. She began to scream and I belted her. It was a reflex action, I was suddenly cold sober and really scared and I needed to shut her up and get out of there. I was about to get up when the King kid grabbed me from behind. If I hadn't found the rock he would have choked me to death. I believed it then, I believe it now. It was a major fuck-up that would have ruined my life, except my father wouldn't allow it. He told Chance and me what to do and what to say and we

207

did and said it. There was no debate. Nobody was ever the same afterward, but I survived and Chance survived and it seems that Jenny Solomon survived. And no one wants to go back there. There's really no point."

"But Chancellor could have dragged you right back," I said.

"He threatened to and I told him to do what he had to do, in not so many words. And I'll tell you the same thing. But no one will back you up."

"So you still insist you had nothing to do with Chancellor's death?"

"Not a thing."

"Have any theories?"

"I'm obviously putting all my cards on Charlie Mancuso."

My drink was empty. And so was I. I wondered if I even cared anymore, since no one else did. Maybe everyone had gotten what they asked for, some just paid a little more. Or a little sooner. I didn't know whom to feel sorry for. I felt sorry for everyone. Lowell Ryder was right; no one was going to back me up. As Mark Twain so aptly put it, Everyone complains about the weather but no one does anything about it.

"Thanks for the drink," I said.

I rose, walked down the stairs and out of the house.

I walked down the hill to my office and picked up the Toyota.

I drove while trying to decide where to drive to.

I thought about going to see my mother, and then about checking to see if Sally was at home.

In the end I found myself back at my apartment, alone, a glass of Dickel in hand, cracking open a paperback I had picked up from a street vendor that morning.

Crime and Punishment by Dostoyevsky.

I'm a sucker for the classics.

Thirty-two

It WAS THE LAST MONDAY in November. I was still feeling the effects of the obscene amount of food my mother and Aunt Rosalie had forced me to consume on Thanksgiving.

I was sitting in the Toyota, parked on Bryant Street across from the Potrero Center Station Post Office. From where I sat I could see the wall of post office boxes, and with the use of binoculars I could identify each box by number. I was waiting for someone to show up for mail at box 6170.

The assignment had been referred to me through Sonny the Chin. A good friend of his wife was trying to track down her ex-husband. There were two small children who weren't getting their child support entitlement. Tracking down a deadbeat father through the courts was excruciatingly slow. On the other hand, if you could turn the culprit over to the police on a silver platter, results were promising.

I hadn't been able to nail down a residence for the subject, Ted Benson, but had been able to connect him to a small mail order business working out of a P.O. box. Just before eleven, I watched a young woman empty box 6170, put all the mail into a large envelope, and drop it into the mail slot. Cute.

I followed her on foot from the post office to a small diner on Seventeenth Street, at the opposite side of Franklin Square. I watched her enter and walk through a door behind the counter. I lit a cigarette and paced back and forth in front. Ten minutes later she reappeared in a green apron over her white shirt and black slacks, with a guest-check book in her hand. She walked over to a newly seated table of diners, pulled a pencil from behind her ear, and began jotting down food orders. From where I stood I could read the name tag on her shirtfront, Joan Hiller. I wondered what her relationship was to Ted Benson and if she knew what he was hiding from.

I decided to watch the P.O. box a while longer before confronting the woman, for fear of frightening her or giving her opportunity to warn Benson.

On Tuesday no one showed up at the box, at least according to Vinnie Strings who sat in for me and swore he had stood guard all day.

Now, Wednesday morning, I was back on the job myself. I had been sitting across from the post office since 6:00 A.M. It was the only way to assure a parking spot from where I could view the boxes, just in case someone other than Joan Hiller came to gather the mail from 6170 this time.

It was almost eleven and I was working on a hero sandwich that Angelo Verdi had thrown together for me at Molinari's at the break of dawn. I had been reading an article in a day-old *Examiner* on the jury conviction of Charlie Mancuso for the murders of Mike Flanagan and Freddie Cash. Lowell Ryder was the cat's meow. Ryder had won the DA's office in a landslide victory on Election Day three weeks earlier.

The rap on the passenger window caused an involuntary hand jerk, which shot a meatball out from the end of the sandwich like a clown out of a cannon. It bounced down my chest and landed neatly on the newspaper I had draped over my lap. I had tucked my pocket-handkerchief into my collar and spread it across the front of my shirt to protect against such a contingency. I looked down at my makeshift bib. The handkerchief resembled a Salvador Dali painting. I glanced up to the passenger window to find Vinnie grinning down at me. I wrapped the handkerchief, the errant meatball, and what was left of the sandwich into the newspaper, tossed it carefully into the backseat, and reluctantly un-locked the door.

"I brought you a cold drink, Jake," he said, opening the door and slipping into the passenger seat.

I was grateful, since the drink I had in the car was warmer than the sandwich had been.

"A little early in the day for you, isn't it Vin?"

"When something excites me I can't sleep. I love this stakeout thing. I'm envious, Jake. You have a great job."

"You call sitting in a car all day watching people pick up mail a great job?"

"It's the idea of it. Would you rather be slinging patties at Burger World?"

"Don't tempt me," I said.

"That's the trouble with the world, Jake. No one appreciates what they've got."

Just then I spied Joan Hiller walking into the post office with a large brown envelope under her arm.

"Hold that thought, Vinnie," I said, and jumped out of the Toyota to follow her in.

I stood back as she emptied the P.O. box and carried the mail over to a nearby counter. I casually strolled over beside her, pre-tended to fill out a certified-mail slip, and watched as she stuffed the mail into the large envelope. I quickly scribbled the Daly City address written under the name T. Benson on the front of the envelope. She looked at me for a moment without expression and then decided to smile. I returned the smile, resisted the urge to say something to her, and walked back out to the car.

"Get your man, Jake?" Vinnie asked.

"Maybe," I said, not feeling all that proud of myself.

I dropped Vinnie off in front of the Finnish Line and drove over to the Vallejo Street Station. I spotted Sergeant Johnson as soon as I stepped through the door. As usual, he wasted no time expressing his joy at seeing me.

"Diamond," he said, "great to see you, but I was just on my way out."

"Could you do me a quick favor before you run away," I asked, forgoing the snappy comeback.

I took his deep sigh for an affirmative.

"There's a Ted Benson being run through the court system on child support arrears. I don't really know the status of the case. I was hoping you could check if there's a bench warrant out on the guy."

"And if there is?"

"Then I think I could tell you where you can find him," I said.

"Give me a minute, Diamond," he said, and walked over to the PC terminal at the front desk.

He was back after five minutes.

"The answer is yes," he said.

I handed him the P.O. slip with Benson's address.

"I hope this isn't a wild goose chase like the missing Rolex you put me on to."

"What do you mean?"

"Chancellor wore a pocket watch on a gold chain. It was on his body when they found him. If he was wearing a wristwatch at the same time, the judge was a stranger bird than everyone says he was," said Johnson. "I never really understood what the Wright kid was trying to sell with the Rolex story, but it looks like it was a bill of goods."

"Unless Lefty did see a Rolex on the floor, only it wasn't Chancellor's watch."

"A Rolex was never found, Diamond."

"Jimmy Hoffa was never found, but it doesn't mean he didn't exist."

"You never know when to give up, do you Diamond," he said.

"You're right about that, Sergeant, and it usually results in my giving up too soon," I said.

I walked out of the station, jumped into the car, and headed back to the office. I walked past Darlene straight back to my desk. I called directory assistance for Mill Valley and was given a phone number for Bob Gentry.

"Mr. Gentry, I don't know if you remember me, Jake Diamond?"

"Sure I do, the San Francisco PI. I read about what happened to that Officer Katt. What in the world do you folks have going on down there?"

"I'm still working on it, I was hoping you could help me out."

"I'll try, son. Shoot."

"The last time you saw Judge Chancellor, that Sunday before he was killed."

"Yes."

"Was he wearing his Rolex?"

"Andy never wore a watch on his wrist. Claimed it gave him a rash. He carried a pocket watch, quite a beautiful piece really. I'd often tell him, half jokingly, how much I would love one like it. He would tease me by promising he'd leave it to me in his will, or by putting it up as a bet in the chess matches we played and he always won. In fact, we played chess that Sunday, and he wagered that if he didn't have me checkmated in three moves, he would hand the watch over to me right then and there. Of course, three moves later the game was over."

"Thank you, Mr. Gentry," I said, "you've been a great help."

"I'll take your word for it, Mr. Diamond," he said, and rang off.

I walked back out to Darlene's post. Tug McGraw peeked out from under her desk. I sat in the customer chair. Darlene broke the silence.

"Good to see you, too, Jake. Glad you could drop in."

"The Rolex belonged to Chancellor's killer," I said.

"Do you think Katt knew it?"

"I'm guessing it's what got him killed."

"But you didn't find it when you searched his place," she said.

"And unless he was toting it around and his murderer picked it off him outside the door that day, the watch is still out there somewhere."

"Any ideas?"

"I may have. Anything important happen this morning?"

"Have you seen today's *Examiner*?"

"I've only gotten as far as yesterday's."

"Lowell Ryder went out to Sacramento last night. His father

died in a hospital there. The wake is today and the funeral service and burial are tomorrow morning in Folsom."

"Do I have anything scheduled for tomorrow?"

"Are you still staking out the post office?"

"No."

"Then, though I hate to rub it in," Darlene said, "you're wide open. Thinking of going out to pay your respects?"

"Yeah, I am," I said, "and hopefully Chance Ryder will be there to accept them."

I sat at the back of the church during the funeral service. The church stood on Natoma Street, between the Folsom Public Library and the police station. Looking around I spotted familiar faces. Mrs. Dewey, the librarian. Ray, the counterman from the town diner. A few of the uniforms I had seen the last time I visited Chief Gunderson.

Lowell and Chance Ryder sat in front, only for decorum's sake it seemed. They hardly looked at each other, and they never exchanged a word.

When the service was complete I stepped out to the street and stood waiting for Chance. Lowell Ryder appeared first and was met with handshakes and shoulder pats by a number of attendees at the top of the church steps. He was receiving equal doses of condolence for his loss and congratulations for his recent victory. He finally broke away and was almost into the limousine when he saw me. He walked over to where I stood and extended his hand.

"Mr. Diamond, I'm surprised to see you here," he said. "Good of you to come."

He was away and into the limo before I could say a word. I turned back to the church entrance and saw Chance coming down the stairs.

"Business or pleasure, Jake?" he asked as he walked up to me.

"I just wanted to pay my respects."

"On such an occasion," he said, "I'll give you the benefit of the doubt. Coming to the cemetery?"

"No, I think I'll pass. Did you get to see your father before he died?"

"As a matter of fact I did, thanks to you. Just after you gave me your spin on what happened with Davey King and Jenny Solomon I had this idea that I needed to hear it from him. Of course, when the time came all I could do was to ask him how he was feeling. And his answer didn't sound all that sincere."

"I'm sorry," I said.

"My father was a simple man. As much as he supported Lowell's ambitions, as far as he was willing to go, I don't think that he ever really understood them. I believe that he considered farming, working with the land, more admirable. When I came out of prison my father offered me a gift, a job picking avocados and a partnership in the business. When my brother graduated Stanford, Dad gave him a gold Rolex. The funny thing is, I've finally come to realize that my father considered his gift to me more valuable."

"I noticed that your brother was wearing a silver Elgin today. I wonder why he didn't wear the Rolex your father gave him. Do you think he's come to feel the same way?"

"I don't know," he said, "want me to ask him for you?"

Intentionally or not, Chance was rubbing my nose in it.

But I'd come this far, and I'd left my pride in San Francisco.

"If you can give me a few days, we could ask him together," I said.

"You're thinking that now that my father is gone, I'll be more inclined to entertain your wild notions about my brother."

"Maybe I am."

Chance Ryder started toward a second limousine, which would take him to the burial. He stopped and turned back. He looked into my eyes for a good minute. He looked as if he were trying to melt me down into a wet spot on the sidewalk.

"I'll give you a few days," he finally said.

He entered the car and was gone.

I stood planted to the spot until I heard Mrs. Dewey's voice, which sounded a lot like Casey Stengel's, calling my name from the top of the church steps.

I was suddenly rushing to my Impala.

Minutes later I was heading out of town, back to the city by the Bay.

To search for a wristwatch.

Thirty-three

WHETHER OR NOT YOU ever actually find what you're looking for, the looking can take a very long time, and the odds can range from even to impossible.

Though there is one circumstance where you can hope to end a search quickly and efficiently, one way or the other, with a good fifty-fifty chance of success.

Ironically, that's the case when you can only think of one place to look.

And that's exactly what I had going for me.

It was Saturday, late morning. Two days after Calvin Ryder's funeral, twenty-three shopping days until Christmas. I thought it better to confront Officer Phil Moss when he was off duty, away from the police station. His house was in a small subdivision in south San Francisco, just below Hillside Boulevard close to Sign Hill Park. I ran into at least six cul-de-sacs before I finally found the place.

I pulled up in front of the house. Two boys, five and seven years old maybe, were making a valiant attempt at throwing a plastic ball back and forth. The kind of plastic ball that did nothing but curve. They paid no attention to me as I passed them and went on to the front door. I rang the doorbell. A minute later a woman wearing denim overalls came around from behind the house. She looked as if she had been wrestling a tossed salad.

"I'm working in the garden," she said, "in case you were wondering. Boys, if that ball goes into the street, forget you ever saw it. What can I do for you?"

"I was looking for Phil Moss," I said, slipping a word in edgewise.

"That would be my husband, aka the guy out back destroying very expensive machinery. I hope you're here to fix the lawn mower."

"Not exactly."

"Are you selling something?"

"No, just a visit."

"Go around the house, Phil's the one with the fan belt hanging from his left ear. Do you think if I duct taped the holes in that plastic ball it would go straight?"

"I do," I said, and started around back.

If Phil Moss was surprised to see me, he did a real good job of not showing it.

"Moss," I said, coming up to him, "it's time to fess up."

"How about a beer?" he asked, moving to a nearby cooler.

"Not before noon," I said, "but if you had some kind of bourbon I'm sure it's noon somewhere."

"C'mon inside," he said, grabbing a beer.

I followed him in.

I sat at the kitchen table while Moss fixed a bourbon on the rocks. From the window I could see his wife in back, tackling her vegetable garden.

"I didn't know about any of this until after the fact," he began, taking a seat at the table, "and the longer I kept it quiet the less chance I had of coming forward without seeing my life go down the toilet."

"Maybe we can still save your skin, Phil, for the sake of your family. But only if you level with me, one hundred percent."

"After we left Chancellor's place I laid into Tom about taking the Rolex. He was really terrified. He said he was being paid to get something from the judge's safe. Tom said that he simply had to go into the house on the pretense of investigating a reported disturbance, grab an envelope from the dresser top, and get out. He said that he never expected to find Lefty Wright at the scene, and certainly never expected to find Judge Chancellor under the bed. I believe him on that, I saw his reaction when we got up the stairs and into the bedroom."

"Okay."

"Tom said that not finding the envelope was really bad news, and that finding it was his only chance of survival. He pleaded with me like he was begging for his life. He even offered me money. He begged me for some time to work it out. And I stepped into the quicksand."

"Did he say anything about grabbing Mancuso's gun from evidence lockup and trying to enlist Charlie Bones to put a scare into the judge?"

"No. But it wouldn't surprise me. Especially after what happened to Vic Vigoda. Vic came to us, like I was in on the thing, and tried to put the squeeze on Tom for more dough. Tom told Vigoda he could count on it, and the next day they fished the kid out of McCovey Cove. By then, I was so deep in it I couldn't budge."

"And he never said who was paying him?"

"No."

"Did he have an idea about who killed the judge?"

"He said he had a very good idea. He said he had proof, and that it was the only thing that would keep him alive."

"The Rolex."

"Yes."

"And he gave it to you to hold."

"What's going to happen to me?" he asked.

"I'm not sure. You may have to testify that you spotted the Rolex in the judge's bedroom that night. What you say about what happened after that is up to you. I'll say that someone delivered it to me anonymously. You say differently and we can both go down."

"Why take the risk?" he asked.

"I couldn't explain it," I answered.

It may have been the truest thing I'd ever said.

Moss rose from the table and walked over to the sink. He opened a cabinet above it and rummaged in back. He came back with a gold Rolex in a plastic bag. He handed the bag to me, picked up my empty glass, and fixed me another drink.

"How was this handled?" I asked.

"Tom was wearing plastic evidence gloves. I'm sure he didn't touch the watch with his bare hands. The only prints on the Rolex are those that were there before we arrived. The bag is a different story, but it's easy enough to take care of."

Without much trouble I was able to read the inscription on the back of the watch face. I decided not to ask Moss if he knew who the Rolex belonged to. I knocked down the fresh drink in one shot and rose from my seat.

"Good luck," I said, moving toward the front door.

"I have a feeling you're the one who's going to need it," he said.

Somehow, miraculously, I made it out of the subdivision without hitting a single dead end.

I might have taken it for a good omen if I believed in them.

I pulled the Impala into the alley off Union Street and parked behind Molinari's. I looked down at the gold Rolex in the plastic bag beside me on the car seat.

There was only one way it would work. And it would require the trust of someone who had every reason in the world not to trust me.

I picked up the bag, placed it into my shirt pocket, and climbed out of the Chevy.

I walked around to Columbus Avenue and up the stairs to my office to call Chance Ryder.

Feeling a lot like the boy who cried wolf.

Thirty-four

Take away the people and Earth is a magnificent planet. A garden. An Eden.

Take away the people and Earth is a big rock, covered mostly in water, revolving thoughtlessly and involuntarily around a larger rock with no one to care.

And therein lies the advantage of having human beings aboard. There is always the outside chance that someone will care.

The office of the San Francisco District Attorney was spacious. It had to be to accommodate the massive oak desk that separated me from Lowell Ryder by at least four feet. The look on the DA's face told me with no uncertainty that Ryder would have preferred the distance to be more like four miles.

I had arrived without an appointment. You can get away with it more often than not in my business. After all, who would really take a PI seriously if he always warned you he was coming? Getting past a receptionist can be tricky or simple, depending on your approach. In this case, I confronted her with the news that Bruce Willis was out in the hall and when she ducked out for a look, I slipped into Ryder's antechamber.

Ryder could have reacted to my intrusion in many ways, and I thought that I had prepared myself for any of them. Instead, he surprised me by greeting me by name and inviting me to take a seat. I thought briefly about waiting for Ryder to ask me what in the world I wanted this time, but the look in his eyes told me that the stage was mine.

Usually an investigator is looking for the who and the why. This was one of the rare cases in my illustrious career where I thought I had those little details figured.

What I didn't know and really wanted to know was how the hell it all actually happened.

"I have something that you want, and you have something that I want," I said. "Let's make a deal."

"What could you possibly have, Mr. Diamond, that would interest me in the least?"

I couldn't blame him for trying.

"I have a gold Rolex with your name on it, corroboration that it belongs to you, a witness that puts it in Judge Chancellor's bedroom the night he was murdered."

I waited a beat. There was no reaction. I summed up.

"If that's not enough," I concluded, "I've got both your and Chancellor's fingerprints on the watch."

That was as far as I could go for the moment. If he didn't have something to say, we would be sitting in silence at that large oak desk for a very long time.

When he finally spoke, I have to admit I was disappointed.

"Are you wired?" he asked.

"It's not my style, but feel free to pat me down."

"How about I have no idea what you're talking about?" he suggested.

"Okay, now we're getting somewhere. I give you a phone number. You call. And you become a believer. Care to give it a try?"

"Sounds like a trap."

"Believe me Mr. Ryder, you're already trapped. Now it's only a matter of what you're willing to do to get sprung. Here, use my cellular. I'll dial. Use this to hold it," I said, pulling out the phone and a handkerchief. "Simply ask the person who answers whether or not what I've claimed is true. After he says yes, we can move on."

"Why should I believe it?"

"Trust me, you'll feel compelled."

I punched in the number. I handed Ryder the phone wrapped up in the handkerchief. He asked his question, he got his answer, and he handed the cellular back over to me.

"It was my brother," he said.

"You have a good ear," I said. "Are you ready to listen to what I want from you?"

"Why not," he said.

He was getting so listless I was afraid he might fall asleep.

"Lowell, snap out of it. This is no time to go simple on me. I need for you to pay attention."

"I'm listening, Goddamn it," he said, raising his voice slightly.

I would have preferred a shout, but at that point any reaction at all from the man was a great relief.

"I want whatever is left of the hundred grand you got from Freddie Cash. My math may be a little off but I figure it for at least fifty thousand."

"You're after money?"

"Sure, why not? I'm as greedy as the next guy, or should I say the last guy. But I'll have a little more insurance than Vic Vigoda, Lefty Wright, and Tom Katt did. I'll keep the watch in a safe place. Pay me off and you don't have to worry about me turning you in. I keep the Rolex simply to insure against my premature retirement."

"And that's it?" he asked.

"Well, not quite. It's going to take a little help to ease my guilty conscience. You'll have to resign from your office and give up politics forever. I hear there's an avocado farm down in Folsom that needs some attention."

"You're really enjoying this, aren't you?"

"Not particularly. It takes an awful lot to get me feeling so vindictive, Mr. Ryder, but you managed admirably."

"Let me think about it," he said.

"It's a onetime offer, and there's something else. I'm cursed with this morbid curiosity. I need to know everything about what happened, from start to finish."

"I'm not sure I know where to begin."

"Begin with the money. The ransom money. Since you're probably the only player who wasn't driven by it."

"Including you?"

"Let's leave me out of it for the time being," I said.

Ryder picked up his phone, buzzed his receptionist, and asked her to hold all calls. He swung his chair around toward the huge windows looking out over Van Ness Avenue, as if it were beyond his motor skills to speak and face me at the same time.

"It was last spring. One of my professors from Stanford invited me to speak to his class. I had just thrown my hat into the ring for the DA's office. Speaking in front of a hall full of first-year law students was the last thing I wanted to do, but it wasn't a good time to say no to someone who could do me a lot of good. At the end of the lecture this kid swooped down on me, telling me how much he admired me, how much he wanted to help in the campaign, how much he would love to work by my side in the future. I could tell he was trouble from minute one. But when he told me his name and who his father was, I forgot to be rational, thinking only of how a connection to a rich and famous writer might come in handy sometime. Call me an opportunist and you can consider yourself a good judge of character."

Ryder waited for me to interrupt. I passed. He continued.

"I had this naive idea that when a rich kid needs money; his rich old man just forks it over. So, when I suddenly needed some big money, I simply asked Freddie Cash. He was thrilled to help. I never thought that the crazy kid would have to kidnap himself to get it. And I never guessed that the money would cause so much havoc. I never saw any of that ransom money myself, never held a penny of it. So, if you're really after what's left of it, you came to the wrong place."

"You never touched the money? How did that work?"

"I wouldn't exactly say it worked. Katt walked into my office one afternoon and told me that the judge wanted to see me. I was a little surprised, since Chancellor hadn't given me so much as a glance since the time I convicted his friend and the poor bastard killed himself. So I met with the judge, as I told you that night we walked up to Twin Peaks. Chancellor told me he knew about my brother's jail time and invited me to drop out of the running. I told him to do what he had to do. And that was the last I heard of it until Katt dropped by again, this time on his own behalf."

"Katt approached you?"

"It gets better. Seems that Katt had been doing legwork for Chancellor, looking into my skeleton closet. It was Katt who tipped the judge to my brother's prison stint. Now, Katt decides there may be some currency in jumping ships. He tells me that the judge has a lead on Jenny Solomon and is looking to track her down. In the same breath Katt tells me he can get the judge off my back. All he needs is fifty thousand dollars for expenses."

"Did he lay out his plan?" I asked.

"No, I didn't want to hear it. All I wanted to hear from him is that no one would get hurt, physically hurt. I'd never heard of Vic Vigoda until Katt called me and said that the kid was squeezing him for more money. I told him I didn't have any more to invest; the entire fifty grand from Freddie had gone directly to Katt. I told Katt that the Vigoda kid was bluffing, that Vigoda wasn't going to talk to anyone if he wanted to stay out of jail. Then the kid winds up at the bottom of McCovey Cove. I can convince a jury of just about anything, but I couldn't convince that maniac Katt to chill out."

"What happened to the rest of the ransom money? Jeremy Cash forked over a hundred grand for his son."

"I couldn't tell you. I asked Freddie for fifty and that's what he gave Katt. If he scored more from his old man, he must have kept the change."

"How about Lefty Wright?"

"I'd never heard of him, either. Wright let Katt know that he had the envelope from Chancellor's safe, that he wanted to be sprung from jail and paid what was owed him before he would hand it over. I arranged to have Wright released on bail, just to keep him calm until we could work out the details. The Wright kid could have saved himself, but he was still after the money. He never came clean, not even to the sap who was trying to help him."

I resented being referred to as a sap, but it beat being played for one.

"Katt shut him up for good," I said.

"Either you believe that the kid was shot trying to escape, or you imagine Wright said something that Katt didn't like hearing and Katt pulled the plug. Who knows."

I felt fairly sure that we both knew.

I had figured Katt for Vigoda and Lefty. Ryder seemed to be taking the long way around getting to Chancellor. There was still Freddie Cash to talk about. And of course, Katt himself.

"So you decided it was time to take care of Katt," I said.

"Yes and no. I decided it was time to put an end to it. I should have done it as soon as Vigoda took the swim. By not doing it, I was as guilty of Wright's death as Katt was. I was ready to march right into Vallejo Street Station with my hands above my head."

"You didn't kill Katt?"

"No."

"Who did?"

"I have no idea," Ryder said, "and if you're going to ask me about Freddie Cash, I'm afraid I can't help you there, either. I can only say for certain that it wasn't Katt. The gun was the only thing I had to go on, and it pointed right to Charlie Mancuso."

"This isn't going quite the way I thought it would go," I said.

"Tell me about it," Ryder said, without irony. "You did pretty well. I put myself into this corner, but you managed to find me cowering here. You want me to give up politics and pick avocados? You got it. You want me to tell it all to Lieutenant Lopez? Lead the way. I was a drunk teenager in a nowhere town and I fucked up royally. I thought that I could run away from it, but it caught up to me. I made criminals of my father and my own brother and unleashed a monster when I made a deal with the devil Katt."

Ryder finally swung his chair back around and looked straight into my eyes.

"I never killed anyone who wouldn't have killed me first," he said, "but I'm a murderer nonetheless and I deserve to go down as one."

"Chancellor?"

"I really don't know, Diamond. Katt had something to do with it. I've been going on the assumption that Mancuso was involved."

"I don't think so," I said, "I believe he was set up."

"Who was left to set him up?"

"How did your Rolex get into Chancellor's bedroom?"

"It had to be Katt. Vigoda and Wright were squeezing him and he turned around and squeezed me. It was the day Vigoda was killed. Katt was down in the parking lot leaning on his car and called me over. He said he needed more money or things were going to fall apart. What an understatement. I was tapped out. He made reference to the Rolex. I took it off my wrist, laid it on the hood of his car, and walked away. I had no idea it wound up at the Chancellor place until you said so. Katt must have handled the watch very carefully if it only turned up my prints and the judge's. I guess he had plans for it that went beyond the local pawn shop."

"Unbelievable," I said.

But I found myself believing every word of it.

"Was there anyone with Katt when he stopped you in the parking lot?"

"There was someone in the car, another man, in the passenger seat. I saw him when I dropped the watch on the hood, but I couldn't see his face from where I stood. I later figured it was Charlie Mancuso. What happens now?" Ryder asked.

"I don't know," I said.

"What do you want me to do?"

"I don't know yet, I'm sort of in shock at the moment."

"You'll let me know?" he asked.

"You'll be the first to know," I said.

I rose slowly from the chair. My legs were rubbery. I had a headache that could have floored a hippopotamus. I had arrogantly walked in with all the cards and found myself stumbling to the exit door with a fistful of straws. All short straws.

"Diamond," Ryder called before I could slip out, "tell my brother that I'm sorry."

I had called Chance Folsom and told him that I had his brother's Rolex in my hands, and what I thought it meant. I had asked him to trust me, to sit at his phone and wait for a phone call that could confirm my suspicions. Chance was right there when I handed the cell phone to Lowell.

"Tell him yourself," I said.

It wasn't my intention to be cruel.

I was going to have enough on my hands telling Chance Folsom that Jake Diamond was sorry.

On my way through the outer office, Ryder's receptionist gave me a look that could freeze molten lava.

"Did you catch a glimpse of Willis?" I asked.

"Very funny," she said, and buried her face in a file folder.

I walked out into the hall.

There was a bank of telephone booths along the wall outside what had once been Judge Chancellor's office. I called the Vallejo Street Police Station and asked for Sergeant Johnson.

"What now, Diamond?" he said.

"I need a big favor, with no questions asked."

"You're some piece of work, Diamond. What do I look like to you, Santa Claus?"

Actually, Johnson looked more like Frosty the Snowman.

"No," I said.

"Lucky for you, because I know who's been naughty and nice."

"Please, Johnson, one time. I'm offering what could prove to be a big payoff for you. Satisfaction guaranteed, if you're not one hundred percent satisfied, I'll never ask again."

"Never?"

"Never."

"Knowing what a screw-up you are Diamond, I like the odds," he said. "What do you need?"

"I need to know the coroner's official estimate of the time of Chancellor's death."

"That's public information, Diamond, what do you need me for?"

"And I need to know what time Katt rolled out on duty that night."

"And you're not going to tell me what this is about?"

"That's the deal. I'll let you know if it pans out," I said.

"Call me back in a few hours."

"Thanks," I said.

"Don't thank me, Diamond, I'm betting against you."

On my way out the back exit of the Hall of Justice I ran into Hank Strode.

"How you been, Jake?"

"Up and down, Hank."

"That Chancellor thing turned into quite a complicated mess," he said. "Does anyone have any idea at all about what really happened?"

"I'm working on it, Hank. I'm working on it."

I was almost through the door when Hank stopped me.

"Jake."

"Yes?"

"You'll never guess who was in the building today. Came right through here and gave me a big hello."

I hated to spoil it for him, so I didn't.

"Who?"

"Guess."

"I can't, Hank. C'mon, the suspense is killing me."

"Bruce Willis," he said.

"How about that," I said, turning back to the exit and smiling in spite of my mood.

Sometimes I just can't help it.

Thirty-five

I SAT AT THE BAR in Little Mike's, working on my third bourbon, looking to kill a few hours before I called Sergeant Johnson, looking to kill the dull pain behind my eyes.

Mike must have thought I was looking ragged because just as I ordered a fourth, Joey Russo walked in.

"You all right, Jake?" he asked, taking the stool beside me.

"I'm trying real hard to get there, Joey."

"Maybe a little too hard, buddy," he said, waving off Mike before he placed the fresh drink in front of me. "What's going on?"

"I'm clutching at straws," I said, remembering something Lefty Wright had accused me of.

"There's an empty table in back," Joey said. "Let's talk about it. Mike, do me a favor and send over a pot of espresso."

Joey gently took me by the arm and led me to the table.

"So?" Joey said when we were seated.

"There's a couple of popular expressions I'm having real trouble with."

"Such as?"

"Degree of guilt," I said, "and just punishment."

"Good ones," Joey said. "Lowell Ryder?"

I filled Joey in on what I had learned and hadn't learned from my earlier meeting with the new district attorney.

"Guilt and punishment. That's a tall order, pal. And, no dis-respect, I'm pretty sure it's beyond your job description as an investigator," said Joey. "I would leave determinations like that to those at least more legally, if not more adequately, equipped. And in the end, to the big scorecard in the sky."

I knew he was right.

"In the meantime, it's not like you have nothing to hone your skills on, Jake. There remains the question of Judge Chancellor and Freddie Cash."

"That reminds me, I have a call to make," I said.

"Sergeant Johnson, it's Jake Diamond."

"Call me Santa, and Christmas is coming early this year. The M.E. says that the judge was no more than two hours dead when he was examined that night. Since his body was discovered at ten, anytime between eight and ten would be a very accurate time frame. Officers Katt and Moss checked out their cruiser at three that afternoon and checked it back in after their shift at eleven."

"Are you sure about those times?"

"Positive. I checked the log and asked Moss for extra mea-sure."

"You asked Moss?"

"Yes. I bumped into him at the end of his tour this afternoon and asked him. Any reason why I shouldn't have?"

"No," I said, "no reason at all."

"Remember our deal, Diamond. Unless you have something to tell me that I'm dying to hear, cross my name off your phone list," Johnson said, and hung up.

"I need to get down to Sign Hill Park," I said to Joey.

"My car is right out front. Tell me about it on the way."

Joey Russo sat in the car; I walked up to the front door and rang the doorbell. The door opened and she stood there, much more serious than she had looked when I first met her two days before, the two young boys peeking out from behind her.

"Mrs. Moss, Jake Diamond. Do you remember me?"

"Sure, the lawn mower repair man," she said, trying to sound calm.

She didn't do a very good job of it.

"I need to speak with your husband," I said.

"He left."

She said it as if she weren't sure he would ever come back.

"What happened?"

"I don't know what's happening. I'm frightened. Phil came home very agitated; he wouldn't even answer me when I asked him what was wrong. He went to the garage, grabbed the package, jumped into the car, and drove off."

"The package?"

"I stumbled across it yesterday. I was afraid to say anything to Phil about it. It was a lot of money. It had to be thousands and thousands of dollars."

"You have no idea where he may have gone?"

"No," she said. "I don't know what to do."

The fear in her voice had the two boys grasping tightly to her skirt.

"I can't tell you what to do. You may have to just sit tight. Maybe your husband will come back. If you get to a point where you can't wait any longer, you might want to call Lieutenant Lopez."

"Is Phil in a lot of trouble?"

"Yes, I'm afraid he is," I said. "I'm sorry."

"Can you help him, Mr. Diamond?"

"I don't think so. I think I finally realized that it's out of my hands."

"I have to feed my boys," she said. "they shouldn't miss dinner."

"No, they shouldn't," I said. "Good luck."

I turned and walked back to Joey's car. I slid heavily into the passenger seat.

"It's what happens when people coexist, Jake. When people depend on one another, someone makes a mess of it and others suffer. We're only humans."

"I wouldn't know where to look for him or what to do if I found him," I said.

"There's no reason for you to be part of it anymore, Jake. Just get out of it. When was the last time you had something to eat?"

"I can't remember."

"Let me take you home for dinner. Sonny and my daughter will be there with the baby, and Angela will be thrilled to feed you. We'll have a few beers and complain about the 49ers. Maybe we can watch that Tom Hanks movie, decide if we'd all be better off living alone with a volleyball."

"Sounds like the perfect thing to do," I said.

And it was.

Joey dropped me in front of my apartment building on Fillmore Street. I grabbed my mail from the box in the hall and climbed the one flight up to my place. I unlocked the door and had one foot in when I felt the gun against my ribs.

"Be careful with that thing," I said.

"Just get inside and be quiet," said Officer Phil Moss.

I guessed that when Joey said that there was no reason for me to be part of it anymore, he hadn't considered this one.

Thirty-six

He HAD ME SEATED IN my reading chair; he sat opposite me on the sofa.

"I wish you wouldn't point that thing at me, Phil," I said.

The guy was a bundle of nerves.

"Shut up and let me think."

I was tempted to say that some thinking on his part was long overdue.

I controlled myself and kept my big mouth shut.

"I need that watch back," he finally said.

"What good is that going to do, Phil?"

I have no willpower.

"Shut up, I told you. Give me the Rolex."

"Look, Phil, here's the deal. You tell me what happened with Chancellor—the *first* time you and Katt arrived—and I'll give you the watch. Or you can just shoot me."

Great line. Who the fuck ever thought that one up!

"Katt got the watch from Ryder," I said. "It was in the bedroom when Lefty Wright arrived. Katt had to have been there before Lefty. You were with Katt from three in the afternoon, so you had to have been there also. Just tell me what happened."

To my surprise he did just that.

"We were cruising our usual rounds, I was driving, Tom took

a call, said it was a reported disturbance at the Chancellor house. He told me to park down the street. We got out and walked to the house. Katt asked me to check the front door and he went around the side. I didn't know it then, but he expected that Lefty Wright had been there and gone by then. Wright was supposed to be in at seven and out before eight."

He stopped. I thought I would die waiting.

"Go on, Phil."

Please.

"I was standing at the front door and Tom opened it from inside, told me to come in. I froze. He had to pull me in. He said that he heard some commotion from upstairs. I couldn't hear a thing. He told me to wait while he went up to check it out. I watched him go up. I never felt so much like running out of a place. But I couldn't move. When I heard the front door being unlocked from outside I nearly blacked out."

"Chancellor?"

Moss looked at me as if he couldn't remember where he was.

"Chancellor, Phil?" I repeated.

I had to keep him going.

"Yeah. I ducked into the room off the entryway. I watched Chancellor move into the kitchen. He poured himself a drink of something. Then there was a loud sound from above, I almost screamed. Katt tells me later that he went up to grab some fucking envelope from the top of the bedroom dresser and it wasn't there. Chancellor comes out of the kitchen heading straight for the stairs. And he's got this big knife in his hand. And I feel like my feet are cemented to the floor. When he gets to the top I finally break loose and head up after him. I must have pulled my gun. When I got to the bedroom, the judge was down on the floor with the knife sticking up out of his chest. 'The crazy bastard tried to kill me,' Tom says. 'You were in his fucking bedroom,' I say. And then Tom pulls a bag out of his pocket, and spills this gold Rolex onto the floor next to the body. He picks up one of Chancellor's hands and presses the judge's prints onto the watch. Then he starts shoving the body under the bed. With the fucking knife still sticking out. Then Tom is literally pushing me ahead of him down the stairs and we're running back to the car. He yells at me to get behind the wheel and drive. I'm sitting there in shock. I can't even get the fucking car started. Tom yells at me again, and this time he's pointing a gun at me. It's not his service revolver. I'm sure he's going to shoot me if I don't get the car moving. Finally I manage to get the key to work and we're out of there. Katt's got me driving around the neighborhood in circles and he's holding that fucking gun on me the whole time. Almost two hours later he takes another call. 'There's a disturbance at Judge Chancellor's house,' he says. I thought I was dreaming. I nearly laughed. We're going back to the place. We pull up in front. He's got the siren going and the lights flashing. He tells me to follow him, says it's our only chance. I have no idea what the fuck he's talking about. I'm running up the stairs behind him. We get into the bedroom and the Wright kid is already down on the ground in the prone position. I already told you the rest."

"Katt talked you into believing that you were already in too deep to save yourself. He asked you to hold on to the watch. Told you that he could make everything okay and make you a little wealthier in the process."

"More or less. But I never really believed it for a minute."

"Why did you kill him?"

"When I heard that he had killed Lefty Wright, I was afraid he would turn the whole thing around on me somehow, since I had the Rolex. I went over to his place to stash the watch in his apartment. I had a key, because I sometimes took care of his dog when he was away. I ran into Tom at the door, and he immediately went for his service revolver. I had my weapon drawn already and I shot him without a moment's thought. I was about to drop the watch into his pocket when I heard someone inside the apartment and I ran. Was it you?"

"Yes."

"How's the dog?"

"The dog is fine, Phil. Focus. We're almost there. You're doing great. Tell me about the gun."

"The gun?"

"Yes, Phil. The gun. The gun Katt had pointed at you the night

Chancellor died. The gun Katt had lifted from evidence holding. Charlie Mancuso's gun. The gun he gave you to hold along with the Rolex."

"Oh, that gun," he said.

"Yes, that gun. The gun that killed Freddie Cash."

"It was an accident."

"Fine, Phil. Just tell me about it."

"I went to Freddie for the money. Tom had told me that there was another fifty grand coming and that we could split it. I wanted something for my family in case I went down. I told the Cash kid that if he gave up the money, then no one would ever know the truth about the kidnapping. The stupid kid tried to rush me and the gun went off."

"And you tried to frame Charlie Bones."

"Katt had told me enough about Ryder and the fucking envelope everyone was after. They were already looking for Mancuso. I stole his car, drove it to the airport, and left the gun on the seat."

"Did you ever think of blackmailing Ryder with the Rolex? I'm pretty sure Katt had that in mind."

"No. I know Ryder. I didn't think he would cave in. I figured I'd do better with the Cash kid. I had this ridiculous idea that at least one thing might go right."

"What now, Phil?" I asked.

"How the fuck should I know? You tell me?"

"I can't."

"I just want to see my wife and my boys," he said.

"We can do that, Phil. Just give me the gun."

It was as if he had forgotten about the gun in his hand, and good old Jake had been nice enough to remind him. He looked at the weapon, then back at me, and then pointed the thing directly at my head. His hand was shaking, and tightening at the same time. At the risk of being melodramatic, I really believed it was curtains. Then there was a rap at the door that made us both jump.

It's hard to believe that the gun didn't go off.

"Who is it?" I called, once I could breath again.

"Lopez."

I looked over at Moss. He placed the gun down on the coffee table and folded his arms across his lap. The expression on his face was very close to a smile. I may have been wearing the same one.

A shared look that seemed to say we were both glad that it might finally be over.

"Come right in, Lieutenant," I called, "I think we're just about done."

Thirty-seven

PHIL MOSS WAS ARRAIGNED THE following morning on charges of second-degree murder in the case of Officer Thomas Katt, SFPD, and for the involuntary manslaughter of Freddie Cash. Assistant District Attorney Stephen Kincaid, who had lost the election to Lowell Ryder, would be prosecuting.

On Wednesday, a day later, Lowell Ryder resigned his newly acquired office. He gave no reasons. He apparently decided to wait for the chips to fall. Steve Kincaid was appointed acting DA.

Charlie Mancuso was cleared of all charges in any of the deaths related to the Chancellor homicide, and was able to return to his family. No one, including the acting district attorney, was certain if Mancuso would ultimately face charges for the killing of his brother-in-law, Mike Flanagan. The case had been dropped when the murder weapon disappeared from evidence holding and would have to be reopened if Mancuso were to be tried. However, the weapon was also important evidence in the Moss trial. Mancuso would remain free until the DA's office ironed out the details, and Mancuso's lawyers continued to feel confident Charlie "Bones" would fare well in any eventual trial in the Flanagan case.

I had called Jeremy Cash after Moss's arrest and tried to explain to the best of my ability the circumstances of Freddie Cash's death. I related that the ransom money was partly involved, but that the police were unaware of its existence and it would be best if that remained the case. I told him I had no idea where the money had ended up, that I would be willing to look into it if he were interested. Cash assured me that the ransom money had been meant to save his son and had no other purpose for him.

Cash did ask if I would allow him to buy me a drink. On Wednesday evening I met him in a bar downtown.

I thought Cash wanted to thank me for bringing his son's killer to justice and I wasn't very sure about how I would accept that particular show of appreciation. As is often the case, I was way off the mark. What Jeremy Cash wanted from me was an entirely different matter.

"Why do you think Freddie rushed that officer? Why not just give up the money. It couldn't have been that important to him. He had to have known that I would always see that he was well taken care of."

Sometimes I really prefer mundane chatter.

"I can only guess that your son was protecting you, your reputation," I said. "I'm guessing Freddie was afraid that if it came out that the kidnapping was a hoax, you may have been suspected of complicity or at least knowledge after the fact. I think Freddie saw Moss as someone who might harm you. I think that the fear was misguided, but that the intention was unselfish."

I had told Jeremy Cash that Freddie had given up his life to protect his father.

I had no idea whether I had helped the man or made him feel worse.

"This officer, Moss, does he have a family?" Cash asked.

"Two young boys," I said.

"They will suffer because of the actions of their father."

"Yes, they will."

"If there is anything I can do to help."

"I'll keep that in mind," I said.

On Thursday, I received a call from Mrs. Moss. She had visited her husband in jail and he had asked to see me. I arranged, with some help from Lopez, to meet with Moss in a private interview room.

"What's on your mind, Phil?" I asked, passing him my pack of Camel straights.

"I'd like to make a deal," he said.

"Are you really in a position to do that?"

"You tell me," he answered. "I never mention the Rolex, the fact that you had material evidence in a murder case in your possession and never brought it to Lopez, and you do a little something for me."

I doubted that Moss could make anything of it, doubted that anyone would take him seriously. He had no proof that the Rolex was ever at the Chancellor house, and the mysterious wristwatch had become a legendary joke among the likes of Sergeant Johnson. And if the Rolex were to take anyone down, I had decided that it wouldn't be my decision.

And if it took me down as well, so be it.

As Vinnie Strings would say, "a gamble is a gamble, winning or losing is an afterthought."

And besides all that, I needed to hear Moss out.

"What did you have in mind?" I asked.

"I have the fifty grand I took from Freddie Cash's apartment. I've got it stashed away. I want to get it to my wife and kids. They're going to need it. I don't expect them to get much help from the department. I need you to get it to Mary, but only if it's safe. Only if it can't come back at her that she received it."

Mary. It was the first time I had heard his wife's name. It was a mother's name.

I told him I would do it.

He told me where I would find the money.

The next day I delivered it to his wife, telling her that it was a gift from Jeremy Cash. One that he would really like to remain anonymous.

That afternoon, going through the mail at my office, I found a short note from Jenny Solomon. It simply read: "I'll be fine. Do the same." It was followed by a passage from *The Count of Monte Cristo*:

> *Until the day when God deigns to unveil the future to mankind, all human wisdom is contained in these two words—wait and hope.*

On Friday I went down to Los Angeles to see Chance Folsom. I met him on a sound stage where he was working on a film. I had arranged to meet him for his noon lunch break. I told him I had a gift for him.

We walked around the studio lot to a spot where we could be alone.

"You can do what you like with it," I said, handing him the plastic bag that held Lowell Ryder's Rolex.

"Do I have to decide right away?" he asked, holding the bag as if it were contaminated with the Ebola virus.

"No."

"Are you going to lose sleep wondering what I decide?"

"I think I'm going to sleep a lot better now that it's out of my hands," I said.

"Nice gift," he said.

"Sorry about that."

"I've got one for you."

"Oh?"

Chance reached into the shoulder bag he had been carrying and pulled out a book. He handed it to me. It was *Promises Kept* by Bernard J. Diamond. I turned it over to look at the photograph of the author.

"You look a lot like him," Chance said.

I had never really seen the resemblance before.

"It's a fairly recent development," I said. "I've been searching for a copy for a long time; it's impossible to find."

"It's not *what* you know, Jake, it's *who* you know," Chance Folsom said. "And who knows you."

He reached over and opened the back of the book. Stamped

inside were the words "Purchased from the Folsom Public Library."

"Thank you, Chance," I said.

"Thank you, Jake," he said, holding up the watch, "for keeping it in the family."

He had removed it from the plastic bag and was turning it in his hand.

So much for evidentiary fingerprints.

"This inscription," Chance said, " 'Love, Dad.' How would anyone know this watch belonged to my brother?"

I didn't have an answer. He wasn't really asking for one.

"I wonder why he didn't have Lowell's name inscribed?"

"Maybe, at the time, he wasn't sure who he would give it to. You'd better get back to work," I said. "Maybe I'll see you around."

"How about we meet for the premiere? Or did you forget that we did a film in Denver together?"

I had forgotten.

"Count me in."

We shook hands, then he headed back toward the set and I went for the exit.

As I walked I opened the front of the book.

I read the dedication: "For my sons."

I closed the book and looked up.

I could see the giant HOLLYWOOD sign on the hill above me.

Dwarfed by the huge midday sun.

And beyond both, something more grand and more humbling.

The rest of the day.